Conscience
Interplanetary

By the same author:

THE LOAFERS OF REFUGE

AN AFFAIR WITH GENIUS

GOLD THE MAN

Conscience Interplanetary

Joseph Green

Doubleday & Company, Inc.,   Garden City, New York
1973

ISBN: 0-385-01086-9
Library of Congress Catalog Card Number 72–96240
All Rights Reserved
Printed in the United States of America
First Edition

Acknowledgments

The following stories, in a rewritten form, have been incorporated within this novel.

"The Decision Makers," Copyright © 1965 by Galaxy Publishing Corp.

"The Shamblers of Misery," Copyright © 1969 by Mercury Press Inc.

"The Butterflys of Beauty," Copyright © 1971 by Mercury Press Inc.

"The Cryer of Crystal," Copyright © 1971 by The Condé-Nast Publications Inc.

TO CHARLEY AND GERETHER, WITH LOVE

Conscience
Interplanetary

1

"I've put us in a polar orbit, Conscience Odegaard," said the planetary shuttle pilot, turning around to speak to his only passenger. "Ground Control says the blowstorm should clear up by the time we make a round. They don't average four a year, and it's just bad luck that we arrived in the middle of one. I'll depolarize the floor viewplate and let you look Sister over direct while we wait."

He touched a control, and the floor in the center aisle grew milky, then transparent. The harsh, xanthic light of Capella G flooded in. Below them, stretching endlessly to the horizons, was a vast expanse of deep blue water. The air was crystal clear and almost cloudless.

The pilot made a few final adjustments to the attitude controls, then relaxed and said, "The underwater continent they call Atlantis is on the other side, and we'll pass over the station in a few minutes."

Allan stared with interest at the featureless surface of Capella G VIII, the fifth planet on which he expected to set foot. Born on Earth, he had visited Mars with his family in 2042, at the age of fourteen. He had made the "milkrun" to the Centaurus trio, and landed on the Alpha binary's single minor planet, as part of his Conscience field work. As a commissioned operative in the Practical Philosopher Corps he had left Earth some five months earlier, and completed his first assignment on Castor IV before reporting here. From the appearance of Sister he would be lucky to find enough solid ground on which to step.

They were moving toward the planet's northern pole, and the edge of the North polar continent soon came in sight. Allan saw a narrow ledge of ice, hugging a low and rocky shore.

"The station is under those," said the pilot, pointing far ahead. Allan gazed where the finger indicated, but saw only the white-tinged clouds of the blowstorm. But at least the swirling stormwinds offered a more lively view than the placid sea below.

The Decision-Maker swam leisurely just beneath the surface, listening to the vast pulsebeat that was the life of his people. It had been some time since he had eaten and his eyes, obedient to that primal command, were alert for prey. But hunting did not interfere with the more mental functions which occupied the group part of his mind.

He angled to the surface for air, glancing briefly at the humans' Gathering-Place while his head was above water. The round gray buildings squatted on the ground like overlarge toadstools, well back from the rocky shore a hundred body-lengths away. He could dimly see them through the thin snow a driving wind had brought down off the mountains.

The-fish-which-flys comes, Decision-Maker, came a strong projection from the south. It was a composite voice made by many individuals, and accompanying it was a clear image of a small, sleekly streamlined winged ship.

He swam to the surface and turned his eyes to the sky. The ship was not visible through the flying snow. He called for strength from all people in his immediate area, received it, and projected. He found the ship immediately, now almost

2

overhead. And yes, the human Decision-Maker he had been expecting was inside.

As the shuttle moved inland the concealing clouds fell behind. Allan saw great mountains rearing craggy heads in an immense annular formation, the dominant feature of this continent. A thin sheet of ice covered most of the lower land between the peaks, sparkling and glittering in the sunlight. It made Allan think of a gigantic diamond in a Tiffany setting. Then they were over the great sea once more.

"There're the first peaks of Atlantis," said the pilot after a few minutes, pointing again. Allan saw three small islands floating like green jewels on the blue water, the last two curving sharply away to the left. Then the view was monotonous until they reached the southern polar continent, where the mountains seemed taller and the icecap even thinner.

Allan sat back and relaxed, knowing he had seen the planet's entire land area. Capella G VIII could become visually dull in short order. He wondered what it would be like to be stationed here.

In a little over an hour the shuttle was approaching the station again, and this time they were cleared to land. The pilot was good, the touchdown scarcely jarring the small craft when its four legs contacted the ground. The cleared area was far too small for a horizontal rolling landing, but the versatile shuttle could also come down vertically, riding a tail of flame.

Two people were waiting when Allan descended the outside ladder. A big, smiling man in cold-weather clothes helped him loosen his helmet. The fresh air was so cold he almost strangled on his first breath.

"I'm Station Manager Zip Murdock, Conscience Odegaard," said the big man in a hearty voice. "And this is Phyllis Roen, our biologist."

The tiny woman by the big man's side, small even in the bulky cold-weather gear, said, "I'm afraid I'm responsible for

3

getting you here, Conscience Odegaard. Zip and the others don't feel a question even exists."

Murdock glanced up at the cargo hatch, where the pilot was already rigging the small crane. "They don't need us for the unloading. Let's go inside and get you settled, and then Phyllis can bring you up to date on our problem—if we have one."

The sun had moved behind a high cirque in the west, and deep shadows were creeping across the field. Allan started with them toward the foamfab buildings, which huddled at the base of a rocky ridge two-hundred meters inland. From the rise to the sea the ground had been cleared of loose rock, the debris forming two rough walls of stone on each side. The half of the cleared area nearest the beach was used for the landing field.

They had taken only a few steps when there was a loud yell of warning behind them. Allan turned, to see that the scene had suddenly and dramatically changed. From behind the rock walls near the water, and from the sea itself, fist-sized rocks were appearing and flying toward the Earthmen. The unloading crew was scrambling for shelter, yelling wildly and drawing their laser pistols.

"It's the seals!" said Phyllis, and there was fear in her voice. Murdock had already drawn a laser, its dark red jewel glinting in the fading light. There were no attackers in sight, just the rocks appearing from nowhere and arcing toward them. After a moment Murdock, in apparent frustration, fired at a cluster of rocks near at hand. The hit boulder sparkled briefly, absorbing the heat but not all the light. Other beams began to flash as the unloading crew got into action. The little landing area became a weird tangle of multicolored lights, shifting shadows, and coruscating rocks. Most of the beams fired were not only wasted, they left the gun's owner dangerously exposed. The small crystal in a hand laser had to cool five seconds between pulses. In that length of time an armed oppo-

4

nent, even one throwing stones, could kill a defenseless man.

Allan saw his first seal clearly when it left the shelter of some rocks and ran for the water, dragging a wounded comrade. They were tiny creatures, only half his height, and they moved with an odd, stiff-jointed swing from one leg to the other that looked awkward but was quite fast. Murdock saw them also and lifted his gun, but the beam hissed through the air where they had been as they dived together into the sea. And abruptly the creatures were gone and it was quiet again, and now darkness was stealing swiftly over the narrow beach.

"The little devils are getting bolder," said Murdock, holstering his gun. "That's the first daylight attack on dry land."

Allan knelt and picked up one of the stones which had just been flung at them. It was apparently obsidian, and had been hand-chipped until it had several sharp edges, each capable of penetrating a spacesuit. Primitive, but deadly.

"How did they propel them so far?" Allan asked Phyllis. Before she could answer an excited voice called, "Miss Roen! Miss Roen, I've found a dead one in the rocks! Do you want the body?"

Allan saw the small woman visibly hesitate, and then call back, "Yes, please! Take it into the lab!"

"I'd better stay here a moment and assess the damage," said Murdock, moving toward a man who was lying on the ground holding a bloody arm. "If you'll go with Phyllis, Conscience Odegaard . . . ?"

As they approached the buildings Allan saw two sentries standing on rocky eminences, where they could observe the entire area. Large floodlights brightly illuminated the ground around them. Evidently these civilians had learned to take some rather military precautions.

There was no airlock, but the station personnel had built an anteroom where both spacesuits and cold-weather gear were hung. Allan shed his suit with thanksgiving, and turned to find Phyllis Roen already out of her heavy clothes and waiting for him.

The tiny woman was obviously an Eurasian. She had very black hair streaked with gray, and features which were delicate without being pretty. He estimated her age at around thirty-five. She still looked very good to him; the months in space between landings were long and usually lonely ones. There were only a few women in the Space Service at present, though the number was slowly growing.

"Do you like what you see, Conscience Odegaard?" Phyllis asked, and though she was smiling there was an edge in her voice. He realized he had been staring.

"I'm sorry," he said quickly. "And please call me Allan." He paused, not wanting to explain that "Conscience" was a popular term rather than an actual title, and he had already grown tired of hearing it. A doctorate in philosophy was the highest academic achievement on his record, but to qualify as a Practical Philosopher, master's degrees were required in political science, alien psychology, sociology, and biology. The Conservationist Party, with tremendous fanfare, had established the Corps of Practical Philosophers to fulfill a campaign promise, after taking power in the election of 2060. The new agency was manned by civilians, but every operator automatically became an officer in the Space Service Reserve. The public had swiftly christened the P.P.s the "Consciences of Mankind," and the name had stuck.

The mission of the P.P. Corps was to identify and save from exploitation those worlds containing intelligent species. It had been well-proven on Earth that when unequal cultures met, the higher inevitably eroded and eventually destroyed the lower. Guns, antibiotics, and powertools were far more easily absorbed than mechanized agriculture, birth control, and a nine-to-three job. The resulting strains on the delicate fabric of social organization always pulled a culture apart.

In the twenty-first century Mankind badly needed a professional conscience. Thousands of worlds in the Hyades group

6

containing Earth, and the neighboring clusters of Ursa Major and Scorpio-Centaurus, had already been explored. More were being discovered every day. Nowhere was there a sign of another space-traveling species. But millions of new lifeforms had been found, many of them in the early stages of intelligence. Despite the customary short lifespan, hardship and misery endured by the members of a species just entering the new world of the mind, they were better off developing at their own pace than being force-fed from a higher culture. With the possible exception of small scientific research stations, like this one on Sister, the World Council had decreed that planets containing such species were to remain uncolonized. If the situation justified it a Conscience could request a deviation from the World Council, but their primary mission was to nurture intelligence by arranging for it to flower in planetary isolation.

The exhaustive academic requirements facing a P.P. trainee deterred all but the most hardy, and only a dozen people had made it through that initial class with Allan. All had been commissioned colonels in the Space Service Reserve. Others would follow, but for the moment there were more cases awaiting decisions than the first small band could possibly handle.

Phyllis smiled, and this time it seemed more sincere. "Allan it is; and the guys call me 'Miss Roen' only during seal attacks. Now if you'll come with me I'll take you on the penny tour, and after dinner we'll have a look at the dead seal."

2

The Decision-Maker's body had relaxed into the state of lazy somnolence which was the nearest his kind approached sleep, but his group mind was still active. As he moved automatically toward the dark surface for air he thought over the matter of his opposite among the humans, and finally concluded there were too many unknowns at present. He was unable to perform his function.

He could, and did, reach one conclusion, and communicated it to those individuals whose added consciousness within his mind enabled him to be a Decision-Maker. It was that the people would make no further attacks at present. The next move would be left to the humans.

At dinner Allan met about half the station's complement of forty scientists, and discovered there was a general air of cheerful optimism prevalent. On some tiny stations on bitterly hostile worlds he had heard of isolation and confinement souring personal relations until the whole crew was ready to commit murder. He was surprised, as Phyllis kept rattling off names and professions, to find meteorologists, geologists, and glacialists dominating the group. Usually it was chemists, biologists, and the new generalists called "Environmental Adjustors."

Zip Murdock did not appear for dinner. Apparently he and the unloading crew were still busy outside.

The departing thunder of the planetary shuttle's rockets penetrated the aerated walls as Phyllis led Allan into the lab. The seal was lying on a table in the cold room, an area ventilated to the outside atmosphere. Phyllis produced light but warm clothing for them, and they went inside.

Allan looked down at the prone form on the table, the sleek skin marred by a deep-burned hole in the neck. It was the head that gave that first strong impression of seal. The face had a black, square-cut nose, long whiskers, a rounded ridge of forehead rising abruptly above the muzzle; but the body ruined the illusion. The lower abdomen split into two short legs, each ending in a large flat pad. The upper members, though equally short, had a jointed section, and the ends terminated in long ridged fingers of cartilage, with a thin membrane between.

Allan ran trained fingers over the musculature of a leg. The large muscles on the front and back were equal in size, a wonderful arrangement for swimming but somewhat awkward for walking. Yet he had seen two of them actually running when they retreated after that brief attack on the landing field.

He asked Phyllis how they did it. She grinned, an impish grimace on her small face. "They fool you, Allan. A bit more adaptable than they look. Watch."

She lifted one pad clear of the table, held the leg with her other hand, and slowly forced the pad to move. It revolved until it was perpendicular to the body, and he saw that it was set in a very flexible bone socket. She dropped the leg, rolled the creature on its side, and twisted the other pad in the opposite direction. It also moved to the perpendicular.

"One pad before, and one behind. A very stable arrangement," said Phyllis. "It gets around with relative ease on land, even though it looks awkward to us; and you saw how they threw stones with those arms."

"Not with the arms alone. Look what they brought in with this fellow." Allan stepped to another bench, picked up a long flat strip of hide she had not noticed, and folded the ends together. A wide section in the center formed a pouch.

"A sling! Of all weapons!" There was a touch of awe in Phyllis's voice. "Well, *this* should convince Zip, if he still needs convincing!"

"That the seals are intelligent? I doubt it. Animals have used tools before."

"Yes, but—they didn't have these earlier, you see. They live an almost entirely aquatic existence, and the only artifacts we've seen have been sharpened basalt spears. This is a dry land weapon. They just *invented* it, to use in fighting us."

"That's an interesting supposition, but how can you be certain it's a recent invention designed just to fight humans? This continent you're trying to raise has been dry land several times,

9

I understand. Quite possibly these creatures have used the sling in the past, and retained an instinct of how to build it."

"A far more sensible explanation than intelligence," said a new voice, and Allan turned to see Murdock entering the cold room from the outside. The big man stamped some clinging snow off his feet, and walked to the table. "H-m-m-m, a nice fat one. Let's have him for dinner tomorrow, Cissy."

"Zip! Please, I have a hard enough time living with the memory that we *did* eat a few!"

"And they were a little fishy tasting, but not bad," said Murdock cheerfully. "Better than the concentrates every time. Look, I've got to change and go eat. Don't let this dizzy female fill your head full of nonsense, Conscience Odegaard."

"I do not form premature conclusions," said Allan, his voice carefully neutral. Murdock, and most of the scientists here, were university employees, the result of a steadily increasing trend for large universities to contract colonization evaluations. They had almost edged out the competing private companies, and the government had long ago settled for supervision of the contracts. These people had a strong vested interest in seeing that his decision went against the seals.

"Fine. Cissy is unabashedly prejudiced on the question. I'll see you later in the evening, then."

As the big man closed the door behind him Allan turned to the short woman and asked, "Even in an unmilitary organization such as this, isn't that manner of speaking to you a little familiar?"

She gave him a cool glance. "Perhaps, but that's because he's my husband as well as station manager. We've entered into a trial marriage contract, and plan on full matrimony when we get back to Earth."

"Oh, I see. That's odd, I wouldn't have thought you compatible types."

She shrugged. "Who says we are? Perhaps it's just sex drive and propinquity, on both sides. I'm sure you know most women

10

here have trial marriage contracts with just the one man the law allows, but actually live in a polyandrous condition with several males. Zip and I share only with each other, and were perfectly happy until we started quarreling about the seals. I had to go over his head to get you in here, and he's going to be a long time forgiving me for that."

Allan found himself wishing heartily he had not ventured into such personal ground. It was presumptuous of him, and her answer had twisted the knife of bitterness again. Kay had quickly divorced him when he had announced he was giving up his teaching post to train for a difficult career in space; there would be no "widow's wait" for her. She had married again before he finished his final studies and left Earth, and when he visited his children his little daughter was already calling another man "father."

Allan beat a hasty retreat. "I'd like to see your notes, if you've already performed a dissection," he said, turning toward the door. "Tomorrow I'll run one on this chap; will you be available to help?"

"Of course," said Phyllis, reverting to business as easily as he. "I ran several, and I've never seen a body better adapted for both swimming and walking. But the brain is—very odd. You'll have to see it for yourself."

She escorted him to his cubicle, then left with word that she would see him later in the lounge. He found his luggage stacked on the bunk, and an hour later, showered, depilated, and dressed in clean clothes, he headed for the lounge. Most of the station's off-duty personnel were there, including Murdock.

"Come sit by me, Allan," the big man called. "I'll split my shaker with you."

Murdock was drinking *maquella,* a mildly intoxicating new beverage that had no aftereffects. Allan accepted a glass and sat down.

"What do you think of our operation so far?" asked Murdock pleasantly.

"I hardly know enough about it to think at all. Can you give me a general rundown on your plans? I was amazed to find Phyllis the only biologist here, and that you have a high percentage of glacialists."

"He could talk about it all night," said Phyllis, who was sitting on Murdock's other side. "But the basic fact is that Sister is so nearly Earth-like chemists and biologists aren't really needed. The only genuine problem is raising Atlantis, and the general opinion is that this can be accomplished by a slight change in the weather."

"Yes, all it requires is a new ice age," said Murdock with a chuckle. "But to give you some background—the median temperature on Sister is somewhat higher than humans prefer, and the open land area almost nonexistent, except for two polar continents covered by ice. Offhand it looks very unpromising. But this planet has a very fortunate peculiarity. All three major landmasses have the same distinguishing feature, a great circle of volcanic mountains surrounding a lower inland area. Atlantis is the largest and lowest of the three, and almost entirely under water. We propose, not to raise the continent, but to lower the ocean level.

"The means of accomplishing this is relatively simple. Sister, despite the high concentration of water vapor in the air, has a low precipitation rate. The atmosphere is exceptionally clean, due to the tiny exposed land surface and low volcanic activity, and there is very little dust to serve as sublimation nuclei for raindrops. Precip is almost entirely dependent on giant condensation nuclei, and that too is small because the oceans have a low salinity rate, and there is very little sodium chloride in the air. Briefly, we propose to stimulate the precip rate by blowing up the smallest of the four moons, in such a fashion most of the material turns to dust. We will slow it below orbital speed with the explosions, and create a rain of dust into the

12

upper atmosphere which will continue for many years. Precip will rise to several thousand per cent of normal. Over both polar regions this will come down as snow, and the rapid accumulation in the two enclosed continents will swell the existing icefields until a sizable percentage of the planet's water is locked up in ice. The world ocean level will fall, we estimate slightly over three-hundred feet, and that will bring all the ring of mountains and about half the interior of Atlantis above the surface. In addition, the present high temperature on that continent will drop to bearable limits. And then you can send in the colonists."

"It sounds almost too simple," said Allan wonderingly.

"That's an explanation in very broad terms. There are a few relevant details to be worked out, such as the large sun-mirrors we'll have to post above each pole, to artificially stimulate the firn fields and turn snow to ice by continuous melting and refreezing, the four mirrors we plan to place above what will be the largest lakes on the continent, both to help dry them up and stimulate the precip rate, the river shaping that will have to be done when the dropping ocean level starts them flowing, and a few thousand smaller details, some of which we can't even imagine yet. This will be the first attempt to terraform an entire planet by weather control. But if the plans work out, within a hundred years nine-tenths of Atlantis will be growing grass, and that's a land area of almost eight-million square miles. The farming and industrial activities of the colonists should keep the dust level high, and make the new precip rate self-perpetuating."

"It's a big undertaking, but everyone thinks it can be done," said Phyllis earnestly. "When you compare that much surface to those tiny areas on some of the new worlds, where every square foot of soil has to be treated and retreated before it will take Earth plants, you can see what a wonderful opportunity this is."

"Yes, we've taken at least two-thousand cores out of the

13

higher areas in Atlantis," resumed Murdock. "They show it's been raised and inundated three times within the past hundred-thousand years, obviously a result of volcanic activity causing a temporary increase in the dust level. Plant growth was extensive each time the water receded, and we have a fairly thick layer of humus-rich soil on which to plan an economy. The sea has both animal and plant life in great quantities, including many species, like the seals, which can live on either land or water. I think Sister, within two-hundred years, can support a hundred-million people."

"Weather control is still not an exact science, even on Earth. Can you really be this sure of how your dust and mirrors will affect this planet?"

"No, but we're certain enough to recommend going ahead with it, once we've finished our current job of assessing the ice-carrying capacity of this pole. After all, there's no intelligent life to be harmed if we blunder."

Phyllis glared angrily at Murdock, but chose not to answer the challenge. Most of the people in the lounge had been drifting out as they talked, suppressing yawns. The tiny Eurasian rose, said good night to Allan, and left also.

"I'm prepared to offer you any assistance within my power, Allan," said Murdock, rising. "Just let me know what you need."

"Thanks; I'll probably call on you. Phyllis and I are going to dissect that seal in the morning, and see what we can learn."

They learned very little Phyllis had not already known. Allan pushed back from the table after four hours of intense work, and turned off the recorder into which he had been making a running commentary. The seal was basically a variation of its distant cousins on Earth. There was nothing of unusual interest about its bodily processes, with the exception of that baffling brain. The pan was small, the cranium narrow, the actual size less than a quarter that of a human. But the outer cell layers were creased, folded, and corrugated until

14

he estimated the actual surface area must equal or exceed that of *Homo sapiens*. It was like nothing he had previously seen.

They washed and went to lunch. Phyllis had been a competent but not brilliant helper, and the notes she had taken on what little she had observed of the seals' behavior were of no help. Her belief that the creatures were intelligent was apparently based on intuition rather than accumulated data.

"I think we've learned as much as we can from a dead specimen," he said after the meal. "What we need is a *live* seal. How do we go about getting one?"

"That's a hard question; we've never captured one. They carry away their wounded after an attack, and it's almost impossible to catch them in the water. Several of the men tried, when we were"—she made a moue of distaste—"eating them."

"I'll discuss it with Murdock tonight," said Allan.

3

I should be the one! the Decision-Maker projected into the night, his individuality for once overriding the group consciousness and speaking clearly. *Mine is the risk, let mine be the body!* . . . but the soft, insistent voices of the individuals comprising the group memory cried *No! No! It may not be! No danger to the Decision-Maker! No danger! No danger . . .* and he yielded, letting the desire to offer himself for the trap the humans were setting fade from his mind. With its passing came the need for decisions.

The humans were establishing a work party near the edge of the water, the work to continue after dark in hopes of luring the seals into an attack. Men with stun guns were hidden throughout the rocks, and three large lights had been concealed at high points overlooking the area. The seals' movements must be planned to insure that the humans captured only the one individual the group selected. Also, the attack must look real, must seem to involve a large party, while actually exposing the smallest possible number to danger.

The word "plays" appeared in his mind, and almost immediately there was an answering pulse. One of the new memory carriers, containing only the human knowledge . . . He scanned the word and its associated meanings, leaped to three other memorybank units checking out inferences and related data, and the plan he needed started to take form. One of the humans had been an ardent follower of a game common on Earth, one which involved deceptive movement of bodies, concerted displays of strength designed to mislead an opponent, and the hidden movement of an object called a ball to a specified section of the playing area . . . He worked out the necessary details, and swiftly communicated them to the selected units of the people.

Allan crouched low in the rocks and watched the water. The two larger moons were passing slowly through the clear sky, and the beach was well-lighted. He turned away a second to rub his eyes, and when he looked again the beach was swarming with short figures. It was almost as if he had signaled them to attack by looking away.

The seals came running upright out of the water and scurried behind the two walls of rock, moving stiff-legged but swiftly across the open area. From his vantage point Allan could see the leaders starting to twirl their slings. He drew his laser pistol and sent a red beam flaring into the sky.

Instantly the searchlights came on, brightly illuminating the areas behind the rocks where the seals were gathering. The work gang dropped their tools and drew stun guns, and the men hidden in the rocks rose to their feet, searching for targets.

The abortive attack stalled. The seals broke for the sea, fleeing what was obviously a trap. Allan saw the hurrying line of sleek forms plunging into the water, and rubbed his eyes. He would have sworn there were many more of them than now seemed visible.

"Got one!" came an exultant yell, and "Me too!" said another voice. But Allan's attention was abruptly distracted. A seal popped into view less than twenty feet away, twirling a sling and looking directly at him.

He hastily drew his stun gun, fired and missed, cursed himself for a bungling professor who belonged in a classroom, fired again, and saw the small figure drop. The sharp-edged missile clattered to the rock.

The floodlights abruptly went out. There were wild yells as the humans, their eyes slow to adjust back to moonlight, found themselves blinded. Allan groped his way to the seal he had shot and crouched over the body. They should have several prisoners, but remembering the creatures' habit of carrying off their wounded, he was taking no chances.

After a moment someone found the outlet where the power cable had been disconnected—the fitting was a locking type, but had somehow been pulled free—and the lights came back on. The noises of fighting had died away in the darkness, and now Allan saw there were no attackers in sight.

"Hey! My seal's gone!" called the first man who had claimed a hit, as though he could hardly believe it.

"Mine too!" said another voice, and other men began to climb among the rocks, searching for seals they had been certain they saw fall. When the confusion subsided Allan discovered they had exactly one captive . . . his.

The small creature in the cage twitched its long whiskers, stirred, and after a moment raised its head. The eyelids moved, and Allan found himself staring into a slightly protuberant

17

pair of golden eyes. The thick black lips opened as the seal gave an almost human yawn, showing the long incisors of a carnivore's dentition. The mouth closed with an audible click of teeth, and it moved to the bars separating them.

"At close range it even *looks* intelligent," said Phyllis softly, and the captive turned the golden eyes on her. They were alone in the cold room.

I am not intelligent as you humans use the term, said a clear, calm voice in both their minds, in perfect World English. *As a separate entity I exist as an animal, directed primarily by inherited instincts. But I am a member of a mentally interlocked species, and the combined minds which merge in my brain possess the quality of intelligence.*

The two humans turned toward each other simultaneously, and each saw that the other had received the message. There was a brief silence while the stunning implications sank in, and then Phyllis opened her rosebud mouth in a yell of high glee. "I told him! Oh, the thickheaded oaf, he'll believe me now!"

Her enthusiasm was contagious, but Allan forced himself to be calm. A sense of steadily mounting excitement was building up and his breath was ragged, but this was no time to become emotional.

There was an odd quality to the mental voice. It gave a strong impression of a group speaking in chorus, but with the voice of this individual dominating the rest, as a singer dominates his accompaniment.

"How may I best communicate with you?" Allan asked aloud.

As you are now doing. Your immediate thoughts are unclear when you do not vocalize.

"Then first"—his mind shifted into high gear, many events of the past few hours clicking together into a coherent pattern—"first I want to know why you only pretended to attack the work party and deliberately let us capture you."

18

Because we wish to establish face-to-face communication. It is our understanding that you will decide whether these humans now here will leave, or stay and be joined by many more.

"That is my responsibility, yes. But why are you interested in my decision?"

There was a brief silence. Allan felt Phyllis's hand clinging tightly to his arm, and he stared into the unblinking golden eyes, waiting. The creature finally projected, *Face-to-face with this unit is not sufficient for our purposes. It would be better if you would accompany this messenger to a Gathering-Place. The Decision-Maker has decided that he wishes to meet you in the presence of a complete memory.*

Allan turned to look at Phyllis. She was staring at him, wide-eyed. Her expression asked, *Trap?*

He shook his head, and turned back to the seal. It had closed its mouth, and the heavy lips hid the sharp teeth. For the first time he saw how the large eyes, the downward curve of the mouth, the jutting whiskers, gave the seal a tragi-comic look, like the sad clowns of an ancient circus. "I will go with you," he said aloud.

"Your safety while you are here is my responsibility!" Murdock said angrily. "I couldn't possibly permit it!"

"You have no way of preventing me," said Allan, making a strong effort to keep his voice down. Despite the man's bluff friendliness he had not liked Murdock from the first, and this unexpected opposition was too ill-timed to be anything but deliberate obstructionism. "My special commission in the Space Service authorizes me to assume active status at any time I choose. As a colonel, I have the authority to take command of any civilian-operated station. I will do so if I must, and remove you as manager."

Murdock jumped to his feet, stood towering over the smaller man. His face was a fiery red, his big hands clenched into

19

fists. Allan found himself wondering if the station manager would actually hit him. It was true that the authority he had quoted was built into the P.P. Corps's charter, but to his knowledge it had not been invoked within the Corps's short life. And while Space Service officers had no choice but to deal with outplanet situations as they arose, they too were ultimately accountable to civilian superiors on Earth.

"Removing me may not be as easy as you seem to think!" the big man bellowed. They were alone in his private office, and the sound was almost deafening.

"Don't be childish. The station personnel are familiar with the authority of a Practical Philosopher. They aren't going to risk a turn in rehabilitative therapy by supporting you."

"You talk pretty rough for such a little man!"

"Please. Will you simply supply me with the needed equipment without further argument?"

Murdock supplied it. An hour after daybreak Allan and the seal were swimming through the blue water, about ten meters below the surface, heading northwest along the ice shelf. The station's standard underwater gear was a spacesuit with a ducted propeller mounted on the back, with a simple variable speed control installed between the first two fingers of the right hand. At maximum he could move less than ten kilometers an hour, and keeping his head tilted back for vision and his arms rigidly extended for guidance was tiring.

Surrounding them, but keeping a respectful distance, were fighting seals, all carrying basalt spears. Phyllis had assured him she had seen a team of seals kill the largest carnivore in this fresh-water ocean with those sharp-ended rocks.

It was another long and weary hour before his escort projected, *Move toward the ice and descend slightly. Slow your speed.*

Allan obeyed, and after a moment saw a dark shadow in the white wall of ice, a shadow that swiftly grew larger. He turned that way and it became a jagged tunnel. The seal moved ahead, and led him inside.

After a few yards the roof began to recede and he angled upward. Allan rose until he broke the surface, to find himself in a scene of strange but compelling beauty.

It was a large grotto in the ice, at the head of a glacier that had reached the shore and lost its momentum. It had calved in a peculiar way, leaving this great hollow opening, and the sides had grown together again at the top. The ceiling was thin, sunlight pouring in through several long cracks where the joint was not perfect. The yellow beams struck one ice wall and rebounded in glittering fantasms of color, springing from surface to surface in a deceptive brightness that concealed more than it revealed. The massive walls were rough and jagged, with many sharp protruding edges. It was a fairy palace of crystal and glass, of reflected light and softened shadow, and Allan Odegaard thought it the most beautiful structure he had ever seen.

Lying on the little beach, and watching him with unblinking attention, were about thirty adult seals. As he waded out of the water Allan saw that they formed a semicircle, and at its center was the one who could only be the Decision-Maker.

4

The two Decision-Makers faced each other, the golden eyes of the seal meeting and matching the brown eyes of the small Earthman. Allan realized his heart was pounding far more than justified by his exertions, and his breath coming fast. He lowered his gaze to check the suit's environmental indi-

21

cator, then undid his helmet. The air had a slightly fishy smell, but was crisp and refreshing.

We welcome you to this Gathering-Place came a projection, strong and commanding, and again it was compounded of many minds, though the overriding personality was that of the Decision-Maker. *We have brought you here to prove that within the meaning of your terms defining "species" and "intelligent," we are an intelligent species. We want you to declare this planet unlawfully occupied by Earthmen, and order those present to leave and all others to stay away.*

"I have no choice but to grant that as a whole you are intelligent," said Allan slowly. "But if this mental ability is achieved by grouping minds, and as individuals you are something much less than the unified whole, then you are a unique lifeform and will require further study. But for now I would like to know why you want us to leave the planet."

We know what the other Earthmen, those who understand the ways of wind, water, and ice, seek to do here. Three times from the year our group memory came into being the ice has grown, the sea lowered, the area you call Atlantis become half land and half water, the land green with growing things. Three times within memory our people have moved in great numbers on to the land, only to be driven back into the sea when the ice melted once more. We have confirmed, from knowledge found in the minds of Earthmen, what we already felt to be true, that as a species we cannot progress until we have freed ourselves of the environment of the sea. In another eight-thousand of our seasons the ice will begin to form, as it has before. We will move on to the land, as we have before. But this time we will apply what we have taken from the minds of your companions and stored in our memory; we shall master the physical sciences, develop the necessary technology, learn to control the weather as you do. There will be no more flooding of the land.

Listening to the calm, unhurried way the words formed

22

themselves and beat slowly through the neural passages of his brain, Allan accepted the fact these people could do exactly what they said.

"You have taken all the knowledge of all the humans here and stored it in your 'group' memory?"

All except yourself. Yours we will have after a few more nights.

"Since you can read my mind you obviously know that I have a difficult decision to make. It would help me if I knew what your 'memory' is and how it operates. I would also like to know your goals as a species once you are on the land, and how you plan to achieve them."

Those questions are easily answered. Our group memory is an accumulated mass of knowledge which is impressed on the brains of young individuals at birth, at least three such carriers for each memory segment. We are a short-lived species, dying of natural causes after eight of our years. As each individual who carries a share of the knowledge feels death approaching he transfers his part to a newly born child, and thus the information is transmitted from generation to generation, forever.

As for our aims, they are similar to your own. We have achieved—there was a brief pause—economic independence. There is always enough to eat and we require no environmental protection. We have none of the conflicts between individuals, or groups of individuals, which characterize your society. But this is not enough. We seek to improve the life of the individual within the species, and this entails increasing the natural lifespan, eliminating enemies, perfecting a science of medicine—a concept new to us—and achieving the ability to enjoy pleasure, which we now know to be lacking in our lives. All this we can accomplish by means of the knowledge now stored in our memory, once the land is again ours.

And the Earthman has ruined another innocent species, thought Allan with wry bitterness.

23

We can read your thoughts when you project that strongly. You equate "ruin" with increased knowledge of the choices open to an intelligent being, and an inclination to make those choices which lead toward greater personal pleasure in life. Why do you consider this a regressive quality?

"I'm afraid it would be too complicated to explain, and perhaps I don't fully understand myself," said Allan. "For now it's enough to know I must make a decision which will vitally affect your future, and I freely admit I'm going to find it hard to do."

Since you state we qualify as an intelligent species, your path should be clear. If you are now ready, another unit will guide you back to your Gathering-Place. When you have made your decision speak it aloud, and we will hear. Bear in mind that if you decide to stay, we will harass and fight you in every manner within our power.

Allan slowly replaced his helmet. He felt like a man who has eaten too large a meal, and wants nothing more than to crawl into a corner and estivate while it digests. But his meal had been mental, and he might be a long time in torpor before he fully understood all that he had learned.

The trip back was uneventful, and by noon he found himself in Murdock's office, with only Phyllis and the base manager present. He gave them a brief report, and watched the incredulous expression form on Murdock's face. Phyllis, too, seemed a little stunned.

"Do I understand that you have definitely decided an individual seal is not intelligent?" asked Murdock when he regained his composure.

"I've made no decision. This ability to group minds is new to us, and requires a thorough evaluation."

"Because their group intelligence is a unique phenomenon is no reason to consider the individuals within the group as weak," said Phyllis, her voice sharp.

"I'll probably want to talk to you again later." Murdock's

voice was carefully expressionless. "In the meantime why don't you get a bite of lunch. Phyllis, can you stay a moment?"

Allan took the implied dismissal at face value, and rose. He was hungry, but when he sat down to eat the concentrates seemed curiously tasteless. He kept thinking of the refreshing coolness of the air in the grotto, of the beauty of the sun on the sparkling ice, the strange and ancient wisdom he had found in a group of seals. How odd, that as a species they had achieved the goals that had dominated the thought of Earth's best minds for thousands of years, and then had formed the conviction that the needs of the individual were as important as those of the group. There were *still* social planners on Earth who were unable to think of people in any terms except "races" and "classes."

After lunch he put on cold-weather gear and went outside. He walked the beaches all afternoon, hating his responsibility and the necessity for it. When he returned to the station at dusk his thinking had degenerated to vagrant thoughts; loose fragments, impressions, and partial memories swirled through his mind . . . *we have achieved economic independence, but this is not enough . . . "ruin" is increased knowledge of the pleasures open to an intelligent being . . . we will harass and fight you in every manner within our power* . . . The memory of blood oozing from the bitten body of a fish he had seen an escort seal catch on the trip back, the sad-clown faces, the overwhelming inclination to think of them as lovable pets . . . What would it be like, to share your thoughts, emotions and desires with your fellows, to form a composite being greater than the sum of its parts? There was a clear, reasoning power in the Decision-Maker, an intellect of great strength.

When he stepped inside the door the p.a. was calling his name. He walked to Murdock's office as requested.

"Sit down, Allan." The bluff heartiness, the easy, friendly attitude had been discarded, as though the big man knew they no longer served a purpose. His voice was brisk and imper-

25

sonal. "I'm going to give you some information about Sister you won't find in the regular reports. All personnel who are aware of it have been sworn to strict secrecy. Not that that's necessary in your case, of course."

"Thanks," said Allan.

"You are aware, I'm sure, that Earth's supply of uranium is almost exhausted. In the excitement over this new 'sunlight diffusion' method of power generation and propagation, the public has tended to forget the thousands of other industrial and medical applications of atomic science. They think that virtually unlimited power, available anywhere at any time, will solve all problems. Actually, the need for uranium grows every day, and it has proven hard to find in commercial quantities. Sister is a very rich planet. The cores we have taken from Atlantis show extensive deposits of uranite and davidite, as well as some pitchblende, carnotite, and tobernite. The primary concentration of davidite is on a rather high plateau, one which will be above water in five years. I predict that within ten there will be a refining plant there, shipping ore to Earth. I can't overemphasize how important this is."

"That's interesting information, Zip, but I fail to see the direct connection. I'm sure you are aware economic considerations never play any part in a P.P.'s decision."

"Oh, come off it! That garbage about being the 'conscience of mankind' won't wash with me. When word of these deposits reaches certain ears on Earth, they'll have your credentials pulled in a minute if you give us trouble. Let me remind you that the New Roman opposition doesn't accept the Conservationist idea that a planet with semi-intelligent animals has to be left isolated."

"Do you really think you can get me overruled?" asked Allan. His voice was soft, almost gentle. Mentioning the New Romans, the presently "out" political party that believed Man should have free access to the resources of any planet, was the surest way to antagonize any P.P. Murdock obviously believed he had enough influence to win a battle of authority with Allan.

"I'm certain of it. Idealism has its uses, but it can't stand in the way of a genuine need."

"Would this sudden disbelief in a P.P.'s authority be connected in any way with the royalties your university will lose if I rule against you?"

Murdock's face flushed, and he rose to his feet. "Can't you understand that I'm thinking of the good of *all* mankind?"

Allan had heard that pious declaration before. It was the powerful appeal of the New Romans, to whom Murdock obviously belonged. From the viewpoint of obtaining an immediate practical return from space, they were obviously correct. It was the Conservationist position, to which Allan heartily subscribed, that morality outweighed economics. They also believed that in the long run, the benefits of information exchange with other intelligent species would be of far more benefit than any exploitation of their physical resources.

Allan said aloud, "Perhaps you are. And the needs of Mankind influence me, in a way you might not understand. But you're a little late with your information. I've already made my decision. And I'll require that underwater gear again in the morning."

When he was standing in his own cubicle after dinner, Allan spoke into the air; "You said that you could hear me. Acknowledge that you do."

There was a sudden electric sense of presence, as though someone had picked up a telephone in his room and stood holding it without speaking. He waited, and after a moment the calm multiple voice asked, *What is your wish?*

"I would like to speak to the Decision-Maker again, in person. Would you send someone at daylight to take me to the Gathering-Place?"

There was another brief silence, and he could almost hear the ether stirring with the hurried conference. Then the voice said, *It shall be done.*

27

The beautiful grotto seemed unchanged, except that there were several more of the spear-carrying warriors present. They did not trust him, which indicated that their mind-reading abilities were limited. He had prepared no treachery.

The Decision-Maker regarded him sadly from the center of his specie's memory bank, the golden eyes unblinking. *This time you have summoned us.*

Allan took a deep breath of the cold air and paced back and forth on the small beach as he spoke, not looking at the seals. "You said you had no concept until our arrival of the science of medicine. Do you understand the meaning of the term 'gamble'? Because I am gambling with your future, and I can't possibly know how it will turn out. Let me give you my reasons and then my decision, which I have already sent to Earth."

The guards nearest him moved closer, their spears perceptibly rising. He sensed the air of menace in the room, and wondered if he had made a mistake in coming here in person. It would be strange to die in this ice palace, surrounded by so much beauty.

"If you are left alone it will be eight thousand years before a seal again walks the land, but then it will be a safe and certain thing. If we occupy your planet and war comes, you will kill many Earthmen before you are finally hunted down and killed. But make no mistake about it, you will be exterminated. Man is a capable, ruthless, relentless foe, and if he sets out to destroy you your cooked bodies will grace his tables. It will not matter that the brains he shatters contain a memory reaching farther into the past than his own.

"I cannot endure the thought that another thousand generations of your kind should follow the tortuous road of the sea, gaining nothing but the day's food. Neither do I wish war between us. My decision has been to report that you are definitely an intelligent species . . . but that I recommend completing the terraforming operation and starting colonization.

28

I am certain the World Council will concur with this deviation."

There was an instant stir among the seals, a silent shifting of bodies, and those guards nearest him raised their spears and advanced, stood poised, ready to thrust him through. Allan glanced at the waiting warriors, and back to the Decision-Maker, and knew that his life hung on his next words. He had not known how they would react, and his meager knowledge of hive minds did not justify guesses, but somehow Allan had not thought the seals would take an immediate and personal revenge.

"I am an Earthman," he said slowly and clearly. "Sometimes I have been proud of my people, and sometimes ashamed. But the gamble I am taking is based on a knowledge of them, of other species, of yourselves, that you cannot match even with your long memory. If the colonists will follow my recommendations—co-operate with you, help you on land and be helped by you in the sea—there is no reason why the two species cannot progress together. Despite our past history I have enough faith in Man to think he will fulfill his share of the bargain. Will you match my faith, and pledge your people to work with mine?"

The Decision-Maker faced him silently, and Allan felt a secret tug of knowing sympathy for an individual who must decide the course of his entire species. The silence stretched out; the guards standing by him did not lower their spears, nor did the tension in the room abate.

Time crept by on leaden feet. Allan waited, knowing the Decision-Maker was consulting with the elders among his people, scanning the memory banks for data, and that ultimately he would perform his function.

The warrior seals around Allan abruptly lowered their spears and turned away.

The sunlight in the grotto seemed to grow brighter, bringing an increase in an already profound beauty, and the Decision-Maker projected *It shall be as you say.*

29

5

"What's this?" asked Allan as Phyllis walked up to him at the base of the shuttle. He had noticed the extra luggage piled by his own, but been amazed when her small figure, wearing the required spacesuit, emerged from the building.

Phyllis smiled, somewhat wryly. "I'm going with you, Allan; at least as far as Aldebaran XXI. Zip will have to stay until the new manager arrives, but I decided it would be easier on both of us if I left now."

"I'm sorry your university president decided to relieve Zip," Allan said quickly. "Believe me, no such recommendation was in my report."

"No, but the facts were enough to damn him," said Phyllis. "It doesn't matter. I'm just thankful I learned what Zip considers important—his career—while our marriage was still in the trial stage."

Allan helped the shuttle pilot load their luggage—no station personnel were there to see them off—and he and Phyllis strapped themselves in. A few geological samples and a large volume of written reports was the only cargo from Sister. They had a four-minute wait, tilted back in the acceleration chairs, that passed in silence; neither Phyllis nor the pilot seemed to feel talkative. When the flight computer activated the non-radiative rockets and the little ship smoothly lifted off, Allan braced himself against the 3 G strain. It was too bad stasis chambers were impractical in small ships. But the Space Service neverlander they were catching was in a low orbit, and it was only a few minutes before the shuttle smoothly tilted over. In seven more they were out of the atmosphere, and within fifteen had obtained orbital speed. Allan spotted the huge interstellar ship they were overtaking on the forward viewscreen, and ten minutes later the pilot was easing them into the hangar deck.

It was amazing how much space travel had progressed in just the twenty years since Allan had made his first off-planet trip in 2042. At that time a vacation on Mars was still prohibitively expensive, and his parents had saved for it by staying home during their three prior summer leaves. In that same year the stasis region had moved from a theory to a working reality, and the World Council had authorized the construction of eighty-four neverlanders. A final assembly line was built in the Dumbbell, largest of the space stations walking an endless circle around the earth, four-hundred miles above the equator. While Allan was growing into manhood and completing his precollege education, the first of the mass-produced interstellar ships followed their primitive predecessors into the galaxy.

Mankind had accomplished a great deal prior to 2042, doing it the hard way. The Centauri group had been explored in 2035, Munich in 2039, and Sirius A two years later. All were reached by explorers willing to bear the grinding strain of months spent in acceleration and deceleration. Hydrogen fusion provided almost unlimited power, but the human body could not endure more than a 2.5 G acceleration for prolonged periods. Einstein had been wrong in applying the limitations nature imposed on an electromagnetic wave to a self-propelled physical object. The physiologists had been more nearly correct in stating that Man's physical limitations made long trips impractical. It had taken the perfection of the stasis region to overcome that final barrier. Now those first interstellar ships were in museums on Earth, and the neverlanders formed the working body of Earth's space fleet.

Allan's father had been a college teacher and his mother an administrator at a Preparatory School. It had seemed only

31

natural that their only child should follow them into teaching. But that first taste of space travel had aroused a deep and abiding yearning in the adolescent boy. Something of the sheer vastness, the grandeur and mystery of a galaxy now slowly unfolding before Mankind, had gripped and enthralled him. As a young man Allan had tried for the Space Service, and been turned down. His psychological profile indicated too high a degree of introspection, a slowness to action that disqualified him for such dangerous work. After that bitter disappointment he had followed his parents' plan and obtained his teaching certificate, acquiring a wife and two children during his graduate work. Two years after he started teaching, in 2058, the P.P. Corps was chartered. The personality factors that had doomed his previous attempt were part of what the new quasi-military agency was seeking. He had been accepted as a trainee, resigned his position, and returned to school for the required extra graduate courses. And out of that first group of over a hundred, he and eleven more had survived and been commissioned into the Space Service Reserve two years later.

Joining the P.P. Corps had been a traumatic experience. His wife Kay had not waited to see if he survived the intensive academic training. She had given him an immediate choice—decline the appointment or dissolve their marriage. Kay had been very surprised when Allan accepted the separation, and her bitterness toward him had never healed. Both had signed trial marriage contracts a year later, Kay to another teacher who had no ambition to leave Earth, Allan to Secret Holmes, a member of the second group to start the rigorous training. Allan had long ago forgiven Kay her lack of understanding. He had had no choice but to accept the fact she would never forgive him for leaving her for the endless fascination of the unknown.

The number of new planets discovered grew almost daily. When Allan left for his first assignment, Earthmen had already visited over thirteen-hundred solar systems. In the first half of the century space exploration had been almost entirely a research effort, with knowledge the only real commodity returned. The neverlanders changed that. Operated by a crew of thirty, they had the capacity to carry over three-hundred passengers and 200,000 pounds of cargo. Even larger ships were now under construction, ones designed to carry up to five-thousand people in stasis and suspended animation. Planners foresaw the time when up to ten-thousand people a day would leave Earth, never to return. Even this figure would provide little relief to a world groaning under the weight of eleven-thousand million people, but the products the colonists could send back would make life more bearable for those who remained.

Regular schedules had already been established for all stations on planets within eighty light years of Earth, and travelers such as Allan and Phyllis could ride free when on official business. Tourists were not yet permitted on interstellar flights, but that too would be coming soon. A few planets already had small permanent colonies flourishing. It was a period of expansion and exploration such as Man had not seen since the discovery of the American continents.

As always, new discoveries brought new problems. The P.P. Corps was an attempt to answer one of the oldest, how to treat creatures at a lower level of intelligence or civilization. Whether or not their work would be accepted was another matter. The election of 2060 had been a hard-fought battle, the newly formed coalition of parties that called itself the New Romans opposing the older Conservationists. The Party long dedicated to preserving the environment had won, and the P.P. Corps was a logical extension of the philosophy that Man should utilize rather than exploit his planet. But in a galaxy where only *Homo sapiens* had developed a genuine civilization, much less space travel, it was difficult to justify leaving worlds rich in resources in complete isolation. The fact that a world

33

might contain a species in the beginning stages of intelligence simply did not mean that much to very many people.

The shuttle had landed horizontally, and Allan found it a relief to exchange his spacesuit for magnetic overshoes. An efficient military steward led them to the huge hollow stasis chamber in the center of the round part of the teardrop-shaped hull. All three availed themselves of the sanitary facilities adjacent to the entrance—three hours was a long time to suffer from a full bladder—and then deposited the overshoes in a cabinet and floated into the round room. They were the last of the 280 passengers to arrive, and the stasis regional field was turned on within two minutes. The thirty crewmen were strapped in at their consoles, distributed evenly around the outer edge of the sphere, and did not move. The passengers were immediately gripped by the mass-balancing effect of the stasis region. They floated into positions precisely separated from each other and the immovable crewmen, until all loose weight in the room had been balanced. The massive stasis generator, supported on invisible magnetic beams, remained suspended in the center of the circle. The field it produced extended well beyond the walls of the chamber, but faded into a weak interaction field by the time it reached the fusion rockets at the long end of the teardrop. Otherwise their thrust would have been nullified.

By chance Allan had floated to a position not far above the captain's console. Phyllis was almost at his elbow. He glanced down, and saw the officer checking the personnel location grid one last time. Methodically, he consulted their boarding papers, although he knew perfectly well two passengers had been added and none discharged, and added the totals. When the two matched his grid, verifying that every person on board was in the stasis region, he activated the course computer.

Allan was peering over the captain's shoulder at his console viewscreen, showing the surface of Sister. The water below

34

abruptly fell away. The horizon expanded in a rush of motion, then contracted even faster, condensing into a ball. The ball grew smaller, shrinking gradually to a mere marble in space. Capella G came into view, already noticeably receding. The ship was gaining speed at an acceleration that would have flattened them into jelly but for the isolation from normal space provided by the stasis region. Even the massive structure of the ship would have collapsed under the enormous thrust of the series of sustained fusion reactions. To date no stasis generator had failed while in operation.

There was little to do but talk during the three hours before the first relief period, and Allan tried again to apologize for his part in ruining her marriage. Phyllis stopped him halfway through with, "I wish you wouldn't, Allan. It's no fault of yours—you did your job, and I had to find out what Zip's real interest was sooner or later—but I don't much like you for it, either. If you have any thoughts of comforting the grieving woman . . . forget them. I'd be just as happy if I never laid eyes on you again."

Crestfallen, Allan turned away and resumed staring at the captain's viewscreen, now showing the starfield ahead. Once Phyllis had openly stated it he realized she was right; a comforting sharing during the three-week journey to Aldebaran *had* been in the back of his mind.

Allan lifted his gaze and surveyed the great hollow sphere with the 310 mathematically spaced bodies. As usual, the passengers were four-fifths men. Of the few women he could see, none looked like a good prospect for a short-term relationship. He sighed, and turned back to watching the captain and his crew. It was going to be a dull trip. Fortunately, it was also a comparatively short one.

At the end of three hours the rockets were shut off, and after a moment, the stasis field. The ship started a gentle rotation and the passengers floated slowly toward the round walls, some of them steering away from consoles to land on the curving deck. The captain announced that they would start their second period of stasis flight in one hour, and left for his other command post on the bridge. The length of a journey between stars, for nontechnical passengers, could be measured in three-hour stasis periods. Only one more would be required for this flight, plus the two during which they would decelerate.

The speed of rotation increased until the passengers were locked to the outer floors by half a gravity. One-half was the maximum gravity centrifugal force could produce on a ship that diameter without a sickening side-pull. Allan saw Phyllis walk through the nearest entrance. He followed her, but turned aside once out of the chamber and hunted his own small cubicle. The other passengers were going about their affairs.

Phyllis was as good as her word. She did not speak to Allan during the remainder of the trip. The neverlander let her and many other passengers off at Aldebaran XXI, for a two-week wait for the next ship scheduled for Earth. Allan and the rest stayed aboard, and most of the empty spaces were taken by people heading farther out in the galaxy.

Allan had learned his destination before leaving Sister. He faced a five-week journey to a very hot planet named Misery, circling a small star some eighty light years from Earth. His orders had arrived on the same day Zip Murdock had been informed he would be relieved as Station Manager and returned to Earth.

Allan had been in space less than six months, but he was already firmly convinced of one fact. He would be perfectly content never to set foot on Earth again.

6

Allan stepped briskly from the landing shuttle and turned to meet the inevitable reception committee. To his surprise only one person was waiting, a tall woman wearing a wide sun hat, a coolly aloof expression, and an odd one-piece garment obviously designed for the local climate. It left only the face and hands exposed to the muggy, steam-bath heat. The suit's light cloth was suspended from an air-conditioning unit on her shoulders, and pulled tight at neck, wrists and boots. A slight internal pressure puffed loose sleeves, pants, and trunk into semi-cylinders that bent and reformed with her movements. The contrast to the cold-weather gear worn on Sister was dramatic.

"Welcome to Misery, Conscience Odegaard. I'm Jeri De-Witt, the plant manager." Her voice was deep, feminine, and guarded. "Follow me, and we'll get you out of that heavy rig and into one of our light suits."

She turned and walked rapidly toward a foamfab warehouse at the edge of the cleared ground, moving much too swiftly for a short man in a bulky spacesuit to keep pace. Jeri did not turn her head to check on his progress. When he fell behind Allan deliberately slowed to the short-step walk of the spaceman, and followed at his leisure. He had been warned by the ship's captain that this lady executive was a tough customer, and he could expect only forced co-operation from her and her people.

The dirt landing field was on the rounded top of a medium hill. It afforded a wide view of the hot and fecund ocher-green jungle smothering this watery world's one small continent. In terms of land area Misery was similar to what Sister was scheduled to become, but this planet was larger, had a higher temperature, and a wide variety of land-based lifeforms.

A small loading crew emerged from the building, hand-carrying rough wooden crates to the shuttle. The men nodded courteously to their visitor, but did not pause for conversation. Jeri was waiting inside. She helped him out of his spacesuit and into the local clothing with impersonal efficiency. The brief time he was exposed to the ambient heat and humidity was more than enough. He saw that the light, comfortable shoulder unit contained a two-way radio, and had a hand laser and canteen strapped on opposite ends, outside the cloth. The suit's exhaust flow passed in front of his face, providing breathing air that had been cooled and somewhat dried.

Jeri led him out of the single door and off the crown of the hill on to a well-used game trail. They were moving through almost solid walls of greenery toward a larger foamfab building he had seen atop another cleared hilltop about three kilometers away. The tall woman set a fast pace and wasted no breath in talk, though she spoke to subordinates several times on her radio. Allan had to admit that this commercial business was certainly managed with tight economy. He wondered how this cold, driving woman managed to dominate so effectively the men working for her. Little tricks like walking ahead without looking back?

Allan had lived in the neverlander at half-gravity for two months, and Misery was a 1.4 G planet. His legs were starting to tremble when they reached a narrow, laser-cut tunnel branching off to the right. Jeri turned into it and stopped short. He caught up to her, and found himself facing one of the creatures he had been sent to investigate.

The Shambler was standing silently in the trail, apparently waiting for them. It was over three meters high and humanoid in shape, with four very long limbs attached to a slim cylinder of a trunk. The hairless head was also long and slender from

38

chin to temples, but from there up swelled into an impressive cranium size. Its open mouth was only a lipless slit, and the dentition consisted of two bone grinding plates. The ropey skeletal muscles stood out little more than the clearly visible tendons. Each arm and leg segment had only one bone, and the joints were huge and knobby. The skin was a uniform dull green, and innocent of covering; no sex organs were visible. The entire body was trembling, as though afflicted with ague. One shaking hand clutched the strap of a carrying sack, slung over one narrow shoulder, and the other was held before the face, palm inward, in an odd gesture of seeming appeal. Allan saw that the raised hand had three long thin fingers, apparently without an opposing member.

"Back away slowly," Jeri said in a low voice. "This one is jumpy."

Allan was watching the dull brown eyes, which were blinking furiously. "Are they dangerous?"

"They can be. Herbivores, but armed."

The thin body began jerking with an almost spastic violence. Jeri took an easy step backward, reaching slowly for the laser on her left shoulder. In the same conversational tone she said, "Several of our people have been attacked, and by trained pickers, within the past few months. Two were killed. All reports indicate the killer Shamblers were in the grip of some strong seizure, and this could be—*duck!*"

Allan was already diving for the ground. The towering skeleton figure had suddenly released the bag, and as it dropped he took a giant step forward, a hand sweeping toward each human's face. His great stride and length of arm brought him within striking distance in that one motion. The flying hands were slightly offset on their wrists and the forearm bones continued through the base of the palms, forming two long daggers.

Allan felt his hat whisked away as a sharp bone pierced its conical top, and then he was flat on the dirt in the main trail and rolling, frantically trying to find the strap holding his weapon on the unfamiliar shoulder unit. He heard a hiss of heated air, followed by a cry of pain. A long, narrow green foot hit the ground a few centimeters from his nose, and he turned on his stomach in time to see the Shambler fleeing down the path in a stiff-legged, shuffling trot. The awkwardness of its movements explained the odd name. It was holding one thin arm with an equally bony hand.

Jeri was calmly replacing her laser. "Managed to drive him off without killing him. Have to find the cause of these attacks. Getting serious."

Allan got to his feet, and found his legs trembling worse than before. There was a lingering whiteness in Jeri's face, but she lifted the Shambler's bag and swung it to her shoulder with a brief, "Can't let these go to waste."

They resumed walking. When his heart slowed to a less frenzied pounding Allan said, "We know very little about the Shamblers on Earth. How do they reproduce, and where are the sex organs?"

"The Shamblers are oviparous animals; both sexes have retractable genetalia that fold up into a body cavity when not tumescent. You can tell them apart by the color. The female has a mottled green-yellow camouflage that helps conceal her when she drops out of the tribe to sit an egg."

Their moment of shared danger seemed to have melted some of the ice. "Can you give me a little background on them?" Allan asked. "I'd particularly like to know your opinion of their intelligence."

"The adults are definitely below the minimum reasoning level, though the children approach it. Shamblers reach maturity at about ten of our years in age. From the time they come out of the egg until sexual potency, the young grow steadily smarter. A seven-year-old is about the equivalent of a human child of three in innate intelligence. At eight they go through puberty, a painful affair that fortunately lasts only a few days. After the change they start retrogressing, and most old ones are like the male you just saw."

"That's an odd growth cycle. Any explanation?"

"Not even a good guess."

The trail began a steep climb, and Allan needed all his wind. The top of the hill was free of brush, and protected by a charged fence equipped with several gates. The building behind it was obviously both processing plant and living quarters. Jeri deactivated the voltage in the gate before them with a key, and Allan followed her through the spacious yard and into a narrow vestibule. A cloudy sonic insect barrier hid the inner door, which opened into the recreation lounge.

"Put your gear in that rack. I'll be back in a moment."

Allan breathed the thoroughly cooled and dehumidified air with relief. The high-ceilinged room was deserted in the middle of the working day, but looked well equipped and comfortable.

Jeri was soon back, dressed now in figure-hugging tights. Allan had to make a conscious effort to keep the admiration off his face. He had been expecting a tall woman of lean arrogance, but the sun hat and inflated suit had concealed a full-bodied, statuesque Nordic redhead. She might have been designed to be an opposite extreme from small, petite Phyllis Roen. Even in low heels she matched his height of 180 centimeters, and probably outweighed him. She was several years older than he, and strong rather than pretty, but a crackling vitality permeated every pound of her body—which was as shapely as it was large.

Jeri seated herself in a locally made contour chair. "Now what can I tell you?"

"Everything. I know very little about your operation here."

"Simple enough. We're employees of the Exotic Spice Company, operating a station on the planet under a government commercial charter. We extract and condense the spices that grow in abundance in these jungles. Said spices are one of the few products that can still turn a profit after paying the

41

Space Service's exorbitant commercial interstellar freight rates. We maintain a crew of twenty, consisting of myself, assistant manager Dergano, and eighteen technicians, of whom five or six are always women. We recently passed the break-even point after four years developmental work, and are starting to show a return on the investment. And let me add that we didn't send for a Conscience . . . and don't feel we need one!"

"I'm aware that you didn't send for me," said Allan, trying to keep his tone pleasant. "Captain Arcan of the Space Service filed a request that the Shamblers be checked."

"Arcan? I remember that he landed with the shuttle once, and watched us training a new group. He spent some time with the Shambler children, and they do show a deceptive promise, as I've explained. But I'm an animal psychologist by profession, and I've run extensive checks on the creatures. Not one adult has qualified as intelligent."

"Arcan also reported that you pay for work by feeding the Shamblers a local addictive drug," Allan went on, his voice low. "My instructions state that I am to check on this practice, and stop it if Space Service regulations or Earth laws are being violated. Can you explain how you justify such a program?"

7

"Our attorneys will be happy to prove the drug laws do not apply to animals!" snapped Jeri, obviously stung. "Starting the Shamblers on condensed *sorba* milk was my idea, and I had the legalities carefully checked. I didn't come out here as plant manager, Mister. I was the assistant to the psychologist sent to see if the beasts could be trained to pick spices, after it became obvious the plant couldn't pay its way with human labor and the company was about to lose a huge investment. I watched that man stumble around for a year, trying to get work out of the Shamblers. They don't take easily to routine labor. Food is free for the picking, and they're too stupid to want toys and gadgets. The pay-for-labor system failed here, because we had nothing whatever they wanted. But I had noticed that the adults were constantly eating *sorba* seed, though they have little food value. I fed a few adults the much stronger milk our plant produces in the processing cycle, and it sent them into a deep trance state that's evidently highly pleasurable. When they came off it they wanted more. I went to my boss with the idea of *creating* a need using the *sorba* as a drug, and he climbed on his moral high horse and preached for an hour. The station manager let me feed the milk to three, though, and with an effective reward-stimulus available I made productive workers out of them in a week. Now we have every adult in the area working for us, this plant is running near full capacity, and the Shamblers have at least one pleasure in their miserable lives. The only change in their diet is that they drink the milk pure instead of eating the seeds."

"With the drug strength increased by what factor?"

"About thirty to one, but what does that matter? The milk doesn't physically harm the beasts, and the addictive effect is temporary."

Allan let the obviously angry woman cool down for a moment while he examined an alternative that had just occurred to him. Mass production had lowered the price of robots. A hundred, properly programed and working day and night . . .

Jeri summarily disposed of the suggestion. "You can't build a robot with the necessary sensitivity. This world has no seasons. Three identical trees standing side by side can have ripe fruit, green pods, and buds, at any given time. Each tree may support three types of creeper, each of which produces a usable product, with all three at separate points in the growth cycle. A Shambler knows instinctively when any given item is ripe. He eats many of them as his natural food."

Allan accepted the information as valid, and tried a new tack. "Captain Arcan says that you have a Shambler female for a pet, and that she works without reward by drug."

"Oh yes, Tes. That proves nothing whatever. Tes has received intensive training and been motivated to please. Her reward is our affection, and she works to earn it. During one of our first training courses she was almost killed by a contaminated batch of *sorba* milk—one of our techs mixing it had a rare and undetected skin disease—and Tes is deathly afraid of it now. She stayed in our clinic so long we eventually adopted her, and she serves as a messenger or does simple jobs around the station." Jeri stepped to the door of the sleeping quarters and called, "Tes! Come here, dear."

A moment later a thin, stooped figure entered and straightened in the higher lounge. Tes was slightly under three meters in height, and a splotched mustard-green in color. The nude trunk was as featureless as that of a male.

"Tes is everyone's favorite Miserite," said the big woman, her voice affectionate. "I've managed to train her for fairly complicated tasks—cleaning the quarters, for example—but all the tests I've run indicate normal Shambler intelligence."

Allan studied the placid female with deep interest. The brown eyes looked back at him in a manner that hinted of evaluation.

"Her grasp of linguistic concepts is weak, of course, but she responds to many simple commands," said Jeri. "You may go, Tes. Go!"

As the Shambler obediently returned to her work the station manager asked, "What would you like to see first?"

Allan told her, and a few minutes later he was following assistant manager Dergano, a lean, heavily tanned man of indeterminate age, to the working half of the building. A Shambler tribe had just arrived. They were being admitted into a long room that opened on to the yard at the opposite end from the living quarters. The adults were lined up to have their bags weighed and evaluated. Each individual received a quantity of *sorba* milk proportionate to the kind and amount of spice he had brought, then lay down on one of a series of long low cots jutting from both sidewalls. The milk was swallowed in the prone position, and within minutes each Shambler seemed to drift into peaceful sleep. The time in trance was determined by the amount of *sorba* consumed.

The young, Allan noticed, went into a large room adjoining the long one, where a technician locked them in. Before the door closed he caught a glimpse of fruits, vegetables, unbreakable water cans, and some elementary toys.

Part of the crew began working on the spices. They were sorted into types and emptied into hoppers protruding from the inside wall. Dergano explained that the actual extracting and condensing operations were almost completely automatic. The finished product emerged in a pressed block sealed in plastic. Even the *sorba* milk was dried into the crystalline form for shipment. On an Earthman's food it was a harmless and very tasty spice.

There was nothing to see among the somnolent Shambler adults. Allan asked to be let inside the room with the children. After a short argument Dergano shrugged, his face showing his exasperation, and got the key.

There was an audible chorus of grunts and squeals as the door swung open, but it swiftly faded into a dead silence. Allan found himself the focus of all eyes. Several youngsters taller than himself were holding toys. Others had fruit or watercans in their hands. All were motionless and silent, and the lack of activity persisted after he sat down among them. He waited until he was certain they did not intend to resume their normal routine, and then rose and knocked on the door. The assistant manager, who was evidently waiting, let him out.

Dergano saw by the look on Allan's face that the idea had not been a success. "We learned what we know of the young while training the adults in the woods," he said drily. Allan could only nod.

The third meal was waiting when they returned to the living quarters. After eating Jeri brought out the data she had accumulated. Her tests were standards with which Allan was intimately familiar, and he could find no fault in her work.

Jeri had concentrated heavily on Tes, obviously because she was always available. Her scores seemed to vary more than the rest, but averaged out to normal. As he was poring over her records Allan had another idea, and asked, "Jeri, is Tes still on good terms with her tribe?"

"Why yes, she visits them now and then."

"Good. I'd like to borrow two picking sacks, and your pet. I want to see if her people will let me live with them for a few days."

The redhead looked slightly alarmed. "That's very dangerous, Conscience. These woods are full of carnivores, a lot of whom prey on the Shamblers."

"I'll be armed. Don't worry about me."

"I'm not. I just don't want to be blamed if you don't come back!"

Allan watched Tes at her work. The Shambler female moved with mindless and mechanical precision, the three thin fingers grasping a pod and holding it against the opposing bone while she gave a little twist that broke the stem. Since she declined *sorba* milk there would be no reward for her, but the tribe's new life pattern dictated that all adults must gather spices. He picked at a somewhat slower pace, imitating her choices. Most of his attention was on the Shamblers around them. Their organization seemed equivalent to that of a baboon tribe. The mothers carrying babies stayed in the center of the group. They were surrounded by females with walking young and children large enough to pick their own food. The males formed the outer circle, the largest and apparently fiercest ones leading the way. Everyone watched for enemies. There was a fairly extensive range of sounds and gestures which conveyed meaning, and every adult knew them. The children obeyed their mothers without hesitation in times of danger, but otherwise devoted themselves to play. They picked only what they wanted to eat, leaving them much more free time than their parents.

When Allan first appeared with Tes he had received many suspicious stares, but as she set to work and he joined her they gradually accepted him. After two hours he might have been a member of the tribe all his life.

It was only a few minutes before sundown. A grunt originated at the edge of the circle and worked its way inward. The males stopped picking, bunched everyone into a compact band, and began herding them through the undergrowth. In a few minutes they reached a seemingly impenetrable tangle of thorn and briar. The leader twisted his lean form around a bare tree trunk, moved sideways, and vanished. The rest followed one by one. Allan found sharp thorns tearing at his newly dyed green suit, but forced his way along a narrow passage and emerged in a small roofed glade. It had the smell of long years of use, a scent distinctively Shambler.

Two guards took up stations at the entrance; the normal order was broken among the rest, most of the adult males joining their mates and young. There was a low mutter of grunts and groans in the brief minutes before darkness. Allan saw a few couples mating, but most of the males seemed to have little procreative urge, being content simply to be with their families.

Allan dug some concentrates out of his pack, and stretched out to rest as he ate. Tes, who had apparently been accepted as his mate, was already asleep a short distance away.

After finishing his food Allan lay quietly as the light swiftly

47

faded, observing his companions. At the moment he would not have traded places with any human in the galaxy. As a young man laboriously working his way through college—he had been a competent but not brilliant student—he had evolved a philosophy of life that enabled him to endure when others faltered. It was a simple belief that life, for everyone, could be divided into high, low, and routine moments of experience. The routine ones occupied by far the largest part of anyone's time, the low moments were bad but at least provided motivation, and the high ones were the rewards life offered. You were successful at living when you managed to have enough high moments to make enduring the low ones, and living through the routine ones, more than worthwhile.

Allan had joined the P.P. Corps in search of more high moments, which he found woefully lacking in teaching. It was true that traveling through space was terribly boring and time-consuming—the routine part of this job—but there were few low moments, and the high ones were unique and priceless experiences. When he had walked out of the water into that beautiful grotto on Sister, and found himself gazing into the sad wise eyes of the Decision-Maker, he had been too tense for abstract thought. Now, looking back, he could realize that had been a high moment such as he had never known. In this sheltered glade, with the lean green bodies of his companions sprawled like stick-figures across the soft grass, he had the leisure in which to savor the experience as it happened. This was another such moment, and on his personal time scale, sixty seconds in this environment equaled a month of routine life. He had tipped the scales far in his favor.

The dull light of dawn found the tribe on the move. By midday most adults had a full bag, and at some signal Allan missed, the group closed up in a tight formation and started marching for the spice plant. How they found their way through the maze of twisting game trails was a complete mystery, but after two hours fast hiking they wound up the side of

48

a small hill, where the undergrowth thinned, and Allan caught a glimpse of the plant on its higher elevation about a kilometer away.

They descended into an unusually straight trail. After another five minutes, during which the group became scattered as the leaders pressed forward like eager children, they reached the bottom of the hill. The faster pace had dropped Allan to the rear with the young, and Tes stayed with him. When the carnivore that resembled a snub-nosed crocodile burst from the bushes and charged at a tall child, they were only a few meters behind him.

8

Allan recognized the animal as one he had been warned of that preyed regularly on the Shamblers. It seized the selected boy just above the ankle, twisted, and brought the tall form crashing to the ground, screaming. When the terrified cries reached the leading males the column halted, turning back on itself. They were too late to aid the child. As its head hit the ground the attacker dived for the throat in a practiced movement, sank sharp teeth into the long neck, and gave another savage twist. Allan heard the muffled crack of breaking bones as his fingers undid the strap on his laser.

The carnivore, still holding the long neck, threw the body of the dying boy across its scaly shoulders and turned toward the undergrowth. Several of the closer Shambler males, hands high and bones hidden, stood waiting for an attack signal. Someone saw that the child was beyond aid, and a harsh command came from farther up the line. They were not going to risk more lives to recover the dead.

Allan was not taking a risk, and he wanted the body. His stomach was churning, in reaction to violence and sudden bloody death, but he carefully aimed the pistol. Despite a slight shaking in his hand the hot beam burned a hole into the killer's feral brain. The short legs collapsed and it crashed heavily to the ground, teeth still locked in the child.

Both were dead when Allan walked up. He had to look away for a moment to compose himself, then began prying at the closed jaws. They loosened easily and the thin neck came free. There was only a little blood in the wounds, but it was a familiar and sickening deep red.

Allan seized the flaccid knees and spoke sharply to Tes, motioning for her to take the trunk. She hesitated, but finally accepted half the burden. The procession resumed its fast walk. When Allan and Tes fell behind again, a large male dropped back and relieved Allan, and another soon took over Tes's load. Allan used his radio to alert the plant, and requested that the station manager meet them in the receiving room.

At the fence a technician let them through a rear gate, and the Shamblers went directly to the entrance of the long room. Allan, not wanting to interrupt the usual routine, waited impatiently just inside the door until Jeri DeWitt appeared.

The big woman walked casually up to them, glanced at the child's mutilated throat, and averted her eyes. She took their bags, glancing into Allan's. "Not much here, Conscience. This won't earn you an hour under *sorba* milk."

"Spare me the bad jokes. I'd like to take this body into your lab, if I may. I'll run a dissection while the tribe gets its reward."

"Surely." Jeri led them to the lab, which was small and not too well equipped. "Do you need help?"

"I'll manage," said Allan. "Just get Tes out of here. I don't want her to see me carving up one of her people."

Jeri complied, and Allan reached for a vibra-scalpel. Three hours later, when the tribe was ready to depart, he was in the middle of a gory mess. He told the station manager to let them go. Tes could take him back to her people later.

The long day of Misery had ended when he finally stopped. He was almost reeling with exhaustion, and had very little to show for his efforts. The Shamblers were just what they seemed to be, oviparous humanoids with a brain slightly larger than Man's. Their nervous system, digestive tract, and major secreting organs were all found in some known animal. The only outstanding characteristic of the cell tissue was its noticeably alkaline quality, and he had no way of knowing if this was normal or a result of deterioration after death.

Allan forced himself to clean the lab, then bathed and headed for the dining room. He found remnants of a meal on the table. Tes was working nearby in the kitchen. He discovered he was too tired, and too full of the sight of blood, to eat. After forcing down some innocuous green vegetables he gave up the effort. Most of the crew was in the adjoining lounge, but Allan was in no mood for conversation. He went directly to bed.

Sometime during the night Allan slowly awakened, gradually becoming aware of a warm and naked body pressed to his own in the narrow bunk. When he finally realized what was happening he put both arms around that warmth and comfort, drew it close, kissed soft lips with a hunger too long repressed—and discovered he was holding the only woman at the station as tall as himself.

The knowledge that it was Jeri in his arms jolted Allan fully awake. Dergano, in response to a feeler on Allan's part, had stated emphatically that the station manager always slept alone. The other men and women had adopted the form of polyandry common on such isolated stations. Why had the big woman developed a sudden passion for Allan Odegaard? She had seemed actually hostile at first, only gradually warming to a semblance of cordiality. Could that have been a staged act, a psychological gambit to throw him off his guard? If she wanted to influence his decision . . . she had learned at

51

the landing field that he could not be dominated. Fawning would be equally useless. But the gift of her herself, after she had carefully established that it was from nothing more than shared desire . . . he could be misjudging and insulting a lovely woman. Jeri, who looked normal and healthy, probably practiced continence here because even in this enlightened age men still tried to dominate their sleeping partners. If she felt lonely and frustrated, honestly needed to share with a man who would soon be leaving . . .

Jeri sensed his confusion and kissed him again, hard. Allan twisted his head away when their lips parted, and then turned over and faced the wall. He couldn't take the chance. His aroused body throbbed with need and yearning. He ignored its demand, and forced himself into an unyielding stiffness.

She waited a moment, to see if his rejection was final, then got quietly out of bed, dressed in the darkness, and left.

Next morning Tes led Allan back to her tribe without difficulty, confirming his suspicion that their seemingly aimless course was actually a tightly planned schedule. Allan stopped pretending to pick spices and settled down to an intensive study of the children. The ease with which they accepted him, and the fact his preference for their company went unnoticed by the adults, made him wonder if the males had accepted him as Tes's mate, or her child. He noticed that an old Shambler, who suffered frequently from the attacks of trembling he had seen on his first meeting with one, started paying a mild courtship to Tes. He was promptly rebuffed. The male gave up his suit without argument or attempted force. Their sexual drive was apparently as weak as that of an Earthly gorilla. And those former inhabitants of the jungles of old Africa were propagated in zoos by artificial insemination.

Two hours after he started playing with the children, Allan felt certain that Jeri was right; they were far more intelligent than the adults. On the second day he organized some new games, and the ease with which they mastered them caused him to increase the complexity. The children, as if stimulated by the challenge, learned the harder games as fast as the simple. By the third day they had become so interested in what he was teaching them they had dropped all other non-essential activities. Allan found that he was enjoying his brief return to the teacher's role, and accumulating several hours of notes on his minicorder, but scaling their intelligence was a slow, time-consuming process. And his services were urgently needed elsewhere. The P.P. Corps had come into existence with a heavy backlog of cases to decide.

On the fourth day Allan saw a Shambler adult die, apparently of natural causes. One of the older females who was subject to frequent fits fell to the ground, jerking and kicking violently. Somehow the tribe seemed to sense this was the final attack, and four male adults gathered around her. The tribal leader motioned for the others to move on. Allan chose to stay and watch. He swiftly discovered that the normally placid chieftain was going to treat him as he would any other rebellious child. The long fingers curled around the sharp bone as one hand drew back for a slap. Then the tall male remembered Allan's unique status, or the ease with which the Earthman had killed the carnivore. His hand turned, in the peculiar gesture that hid the ever-ready dagger. Allan hastily backed away, reaching for his laser. The leader stared at him a moment, then wheeled around and shuffled after his people.

The female on the ground continued to jerk and twitch, occasionally trying to crawl away. The males held her, and after a time she went into clonic convulsions and died in the middle of a violent spasm. The four attendants picked up her body and carried it as far into a patch of thick undergrowth as they could force their way, finally jamming it deeply into a mass of thorny brush. Then they hurried after the tribe.

Allan followed, somewhat sick from watching the female die, and slightly puzzled. Even the baboons, to whom he kept constantly comparing these people, made more of a ceremony of death than this.

During that same afternoon one of the adults who habitually led the way was caught by a heavy vine net that dropped suddenly from overhead. His companions began frantically trying to free him, but retreated when the weaver descended to his catch. Tes, who was nearby, turned and screamed to the armed Earthman in obvious appeal. Allan unstrapped his laser and ran for the trapped Shambler. The attacker was a huge insect, armed with vicious mandibles and two long, jointed front limbs, tipped with spikes. It had a round body supported by a circle of flexible legs that raised it two meters off the ground. As Allan drew near, the deadly creature bent the stabbing arms and inserted the sharp points into a cavity behind its head. They emerged covered with a wet and glistening green slime.

Allan stopped just ahead of Tes, well out of the carnivore's reach, and raised his weapon. Before he could aim, two long hands pushed hard against his back. To keep from falling he had to take three fast steps forward, and this put him within striking distance of the waiting enemy.

Allan took a voluntary fourth step and dived for the ground. The first sharp spike cut the air where his head had been. He hit rolling and brought up against the circle of legs, directly beneath a bulbous head. The predator scuttled backward, poison-tipped limbs rising. Allan lay flat on his back and brought up the laser. As the huge compound eyes found him again he touched the firing stud. The searing beam burned a hole deep into the tiny insect brain, and the killer collapsed in a tangle of hairy legs.

Allan struggled to his feet, to find himself shaking, as usual. He had not consciously realized the tree-dwelling climber could not see its own feet, but some unsuspected fighting instinct had saved him. He looked back at Tes. She was standing where he had left her, raw hatred on her usually blank face. The Earthpeople's pet had just tried to kill him, in a manner that would reflect no blame on herself or the tribe.

The adults gathered around the dead enemy, grunting in excitement. Allan, who was rapidly recovering his equilibrium, turned away and motioned for Tes to accompany him. Her face had fallen back into its normal dumb placidity. She followed obediently. When they were some distance from the rest Allan asked, "Why did you push me, Tes? *And don't pretend you can't understand speech!"*

The long face became animated again. She hesitated, fingers curling nervously around the deadly bones. Allan waited, holding the laser openly ready. She quieted after a moment, and turned partly away. When she spoke her voice was guttural and slow, but understandable. "I—I kill! All Earthmen die! They—they hurt Shamblers! White-milk bad! Earthmen go!"

Tes's vocabulary was rudimentary, but adequate for a simple conversation. Once the first barriers were broken she seemed almost eager to talk, as if proud of what she had learned from listening to the spice plant personnel.

The rest of the tribe began to move away. The Earthman sat still, entranced. Tes became absorbed in her narrative, and Allan did not even remember putting his weapon away and leaving himself at the mercy of her long bones. When a darkening of the forest gloom indicated it was time to hunt shelter for the night, he was in possession of a strange and mystifying story.

It must have been heart-breaking to a puzzled child, to find early in life that she possessed more reasoning ability than her parents. All around her she saw other children, her playmates, in the same predicament. Habits derived from instinct and custom kept the tribe alive, and the adults' size compelled obedience, but any child over five could outsmart his elders, and knew it. The young had a system of sounds and gestures more complex than those used by the mature Shamblers. All

55

children learned before time-of-the-change that their reason was a temporary gift, one that would fade swiftly after mating. They compared themselves to new-hatched babies, to the oldest adults, and discovered a set and definite pattern. A child was born knowing nothing, learned slowly, reached a peak just after sexual maturity, and started declining shortly afterward. When an adult went into his final fit and died he was a walking idiot.

Tes had accepted her fate without question, having no reason to think the cycle odd. She took a mate shortly after puberty, but he was killed and eaten almost immediately. While she was grieving her tribe was introduced to *sorba* milk, but the first drink almost killed her and she would not accept more. The station personnel nursed her back to health and she had lived with them since.

Tes still saw her people at frequent intervals. She had been forced to watch her generation go through the gradual change from reasoning beings to instinctual animals, dropping their more meaningful vocal sounds and elaborate gestures along the way. Tes remained unaffected, still able to reason, to think. The sickening knowledge that she alone could remember they had once been something more than they now were tore at her mind. She wondered if it was the elementary training received from the Earthpeople that made her different, and tried working with some of the young adolescents. They learned quickly, but the knowledge faded soon after first-mating-time. If a child did not mate the power of reason disappeared anyway.

Allan asked if she had been responsible for the near-idiot Shamblers attacking station personnel. Tes admitted it without argument. The nonthinking adults were near death themselves, but still responded to a strong command to attack. She knew the ancient signals by which to drive them.

"Why?" asked Allan.

"*Sorba* milk bad. It slow big Shamblers. Eat not enough,

make babies not enough. Kill humans, kill *sorba*. Tes . . .
stay humans, be—be *good*, listen, learn, no talk in plant. In
woods say words, try . . . *prac*-tiss! Jeri not know. I do bad
tests. Act wrong, do wrong. Learn more, kill if no one know.
Like try kill you."

Allan asked if she knew why he was on Misery, and when
her answer was negative he told her of his mission, and what
his decision might mean to her people. They started for the
plant, which was close, and as they walked Allan told her
something of Earth's long history of racial and species injus-
tices, and how the World Council had organized the P.P. Corps
to ensure fair dealing with more primitive lifeforms. When
understanding swept across the now expressive face he knew
his life was no longer in danger.

Just before they reached the electric fence Allan told Tes
to behave normally while in the plant. He also asked her to
bring the body of the next adult who died to the lab.

"You help Shamblers, Allan? Make *sorba* go?"

"I can't answer that now. You may be a mutant, a person
completely different from the rest of your people. He hesitated,
wishing he could promise her more, then said, "Get me that
body as soon as you can."

9

Tes brought in an old adult the very next day. Allan, when
he began his dissection, discovered it had been killed by a hard
blow to the rear of the head.

The cracked skull was a good place to start. He peeled back
the shattered bones to expose the parietal area, and found
himself staring at the bane of the Shamblers. He retched,

turned away, forced his heaving stomach back to calmness, and proceeded with his work. It lasted far into the night. When he finally dragged himself off to a shower and bed he had a tentative answer to the riddle of the Shamblers' strange growth cycle.

Next day Allan had Tes take him back to her tribe, and this time he carried sampling equipment. He worked in the woods for two days, and at night took specimens of the soil in the Shambler sleeping glades. Early on the third day he returned to the station for more lab work. When he was satisfied, Allan asked Dergano to bring him three of the humanoids' long cots from the receiving room. Out of the next group of pickers he selected two adult males, one young and one old, and had them take their *sorba* in the lab. When they were deep in trance he brought in a male child from the playroom. Allan ran several comparative tests on the three prone bodies, ignoring the inquisitive stares of the child. That afternoon he repeated the experiment with three females of the same ages. When the results were identical he made a few final notes into his minicorder, and returned to the jungle to complete his field work. He was acutely conscious that the days were slipping away on this comparatively unimportant planet, but he wanted to be absolutely certain that his hypothesis was correct.

Allan was bent over the shallow excavation he had just made in a Shambler sleeping glade, carefully extracting the small open-top box he had buried there two days earlier, when he heard a light footstep behind him. There was something distinctively human about the sound, and he turned to greet his unexpected visitor. Without shock or seeming transition he found himself pitched forward on his face, black shadows beating at the edge of his mind. For a long moment he hovered on the brink of consciousness, slipping over and pulling back, and then his senses steadied somewhat and the dizziness faded.

Allan resisted the inclination to straighten his bent neck and lay perfectly still, while his strength slowly returned. Someone was kneeling by his head; the right arm was pulled from beneath his chest and stretched out ahead of him. The prone man cautiously cracked his left eye, which was partially concealed by the grass. He was just in time to see a round, flat, almost transparent insect drop from a rough wooden box on to the back of his hand. Allan felt the impact of a slick, moist underside as wide as his wrist; by a strong effort of will he kept the extended arm relaxed. The creature froze, and there was no sensation of a sting.

A short distance from his hand, almost hidden in the grass, Allan saw an odd object he finally recognized as a bootstocking. It had been packed with soil and tied closed above the heel. He had been hit with a weapon that left no external trace, and the transparent insect, whose color was already changing to match his hand, was obviously a killer he might easily have touched accidentally.

Allan opened both eyes without moving his head, and managed a quick glimpse of the kneeling man's profile. It was Dergano.

The tableau endured for another minute, and then Dergano impatiently reached for Allan's arm near the shoulder, apparently planning to shake the extended hand and jar the insect into striking. As the fingers closed on his biceps Allan rolled backward, yanking his hand from beneath its slimy burden with all the speed he could muster. He came to a stop on his back, his right hand, which was functioning normally, already freeing his laser. Dergano, after a second of stunned indecision, was reaching for his own. Allan focused his weapon and released the safety in time to shout a command, and the lean Earthman stopped with one hand on the strap.

"Hands up and show your back!" snapped Allan, without moving. Dergano hesitated, then slowly raised his arms and obeyed. Allan got to his feet and cautiously removed the man's weapon. When it was safely in his own vacant strap he said, "Turn around."

Dergano about-faced and lowered his arms without waiting for permission. "What now?" he asked, his voice insolent.

"Now we go back to the station." Allan gestured toward the glade's narrow exit. As Dergano shrugged and turned toward it, Allan swiftly bent and retrieved the box he had dropped when struck. He checked its contents, then followed Dergano back to the main trail, keeping close enough to his captive's back to prevent a sudden leap sideways.

The recreation lounge was deserted, but a few people in the corridors gazed wide-eyed as Allan marched Dergano toward Jeri's office. When they entered without knocking the big woman glanced up from a stack of forms on her locally made desk, as astonished as the rest. Allan closed the door, motioning for Dergano to sit down. If Jeri was acting she was superb at it.

"Would you be kind enough to explain why you're holding that gun on my assistant, Conscience?" the station manager asked, frost in her tone.

"He tried to kill me," Allan said slowly, watching her face. "And he chose a method that would make it appear an accident; a bite on the hand by a deadly insect."

For the first time Allan saw an expression of uncertainty appear on the woman's strong features. "Is that true? Why?" she asked Dergano.

The dark-faced man slumped low in his chair. Without looking at her he said, "I saw you coming out of his room the other night."

Jeri paled slightly, then flushed. "You utter fool! You don't own—" she stopped, full lips pinched thin while she regained control. More quietly, she went on, "We have no trial marriage contract, Dergano. Our agreement was to maintain discipline by keeping our arrangement a secret. I thought you could rise above possessive jealousy."

Allan felt a sharp pang of regret. He had indeed misjudged the big woman, and forfeited the chance for a short but pleasant affair.

"He probably could," Allan said aloud. "That's not why he tried to kill me."

Dergano jerked erect in his chair, obviously jarred. "He attempted murder to stop me from revealing what he somehow already knew, that the Shamblers are an intelligent species," Allan continued as Jeri turned toward him in amazement. "Now he's attempting to make his motive seem personal, to keep from implicating you. The heroic sacrifice is unnecessary, Dergano. I was already reasonably certain you were acting on your own."

Jeri jumped to her feet and hurried around the desk, her executive poise now completely gone. The strong face was as red as her hair, and for a moment Allan thought she might clench her large hand and hit him. Instead she began to pace the floor, and her voice had a biting edge when she finally asked, "Would you please tell me how the Shamblers could be intelligent, and my tests completely wrong?"

"Your tests were correct, as far as they went," Allan answered. "I am rating them at what they will be when a physical disability that impairs mental function is removed."

She could not keep the interest off her face. Allan went on: "A Shambler is born with something less than human potential. This increases steadily until puberty, as you have noticed. At sexual maturity there is a distinct change in body metabolism, along with the more obvious physiological changes. All body tissues convert from an alkaline condition to a slightly acid one. This makes it possible for a certain parasitic worm to live within the Shambler's body. Sometime within a few months after the change a newly hatched larva enters a sleeping adolescent, probably through the anus. It makes its way to the brain, where it anchors and starts eating tissue and blood. It grows steadily for years, while it eats a large open

61

space for itself. During this time the adult slowly deteriorates, and when the damage becomes irreversible, in what should be his late middle-age, he dies. The mature worm then leaves the body by dissolving a doorway into the ear and crawling out. It goes into a short metamorphosis, emerges as a flying insect, and seeks a mate. The impregnated female finds a sleeping glade by scent, lays four or five hundred eggs in the grass to start the cycle again, and then dies."

Jeri stopped pacing, and there was horror and revulsion on her face. "I've learned two facts I think will eradicate it," Allan continued. "One, they are able to live only in their present host. All other animal tissue I've been able to examine is too alkaline for them. Apparently the worm is a fairly recent mutation from some older form not inimical to the Shamblers, since it's destroying the species at a fairly rapid rate. Two, the worm can't crawl through soil. I caught the one in the adult whose skull I opened just as it reached the ear, and buried it along with three eggs just starting to hatch." He showed Jeri the open-top box he had brought from the glade. "All of them died after struggling upward only a few centimeters. The easiest way to eliminate the parasite is to teach the Shamblers—"

"To bury their dead!" Jeri interrupted him.

Allan was able to smile for the first time in several hours. "Correct. I see you also noticed they failed to develop that fear of the dead that started the human custom of locking cadavers in place underground. With the Shamblers it can serve a useful purpose. The parasite's life cycle can be broken at its weakest link; with no other host available it should die out shortly."

"And just how do you propose to start this new custom?" Dergano asked sullenly.

"There's only one practical way. I am going to recommend that your company be authorized to establish at least four more plants here, with the intention of getting every adult

62

Shambler on the planet under the influence of *sorba*." He told them briefly about the intelligence of Tes, who had not been infected due to living in the station, and her mistaken belief that *sorba* milk was the cause of Shambler sluggishness. "Each of your stations will bring in a cultural anthropologist, who will establish the burial custom by rewarding the action with free *sorba*. You'll have to abandon the planet when the worm species dies, but that's far in the future."

Dergano looked stricken. "Then . . . it was all for nothing? I ruined my career for . . . ?"

"Conscience, surely . . ." Jeri held out a hand to Allan in hopeful appeal, and for the first time since he had known her she seemed softly and alluringly feminine.

"Your lover kept quiet about the worm because he was afraid your ethics would overcome your business sense if you knew," Allan went on, hating what he had to say. "I'm sure Dergano was right. I don't know if he was thinking of his profit percentage or you, but it doesn't matter. The fact he tried to murder a Conscience can't be excused. He will have to stand trial in a Space Service court."

Dergano leaned forward and buried his face in his hands. Allan turned and walked out. His head hurt, and he felt drained, tired, and old far beyond his years.

The preliminary report Allan had prepared the night before was in his cubicle. He added a brief statement about the attempted murder and headed for the communications room.

A subradio message for Allan had just arrived from the P.P. Administrator. The giant tarsiers of Epsilon Indi VI had attacked in force, killing several people and placing one new town under virtual siege. The local Space Service officer had declared the tarsiers intelligent and ordered the colonists to leave. The indignant settlers had managed to obtain a high priority, and Allan was to report as soon as possible. Less urgent cases could wait.

Allan sighed. It was a long trip to Epsilon Indi; he would be in space over three months.

The hectic work of the past few days had caused Allan to lose track of flight schedules. He was pleasantly surprised to find the regular neverlander was due in that night. At least he would not have to endure the indignant anger of Jeri and her crew. He left for his cubicle.

As he was packing Allan let his mind wander in a manner he seldom permitted himself. The tarsiers sounded both interesting and dangerous. But beyond Epsilon Indi VI there would be other planets, new fascinating species, and more difficult decisions to be made. Sooner or later, he supposed, the necessary loneliness would get to him and he would grow tired of being a nomad. For now he could not imagine a better life. He had been right when he had given up home and comfort, even love and family, to take to the spaceways.

The tarsiers, like the Shamblers and telepathic seals, somewhat resembled creatures already familiar to Man. Allan wondered where duty would take him after this next assignment, and when he would encounter some species totally beyond human experience. It was a comforting thought with which to face a long dull journey through space.

10

Allan heard a brittle tinkling, a loud warning sounded by elfin chimes, as his pursuer brushed a crystalline flowering plant. He stopped at the end of a small clearing and turned to confront the danger. This deaf hunting animal had been on his trail for several minutes.

It was going to be close. The vegetation was thick and the

carnivore would appear only a few meters away. Allan drew the spare pistol with his left hand and held it ready for a second shot. Bodies composed of siliceous tissue resisted even the cutting heat of a laser. Cappy Doyle, the local station director, had told him the scientists at this isolated research facility always carried two weapons when working in the jungle. The ability to fire twice had saved lives that would have been lost in that five seconds a small laser crystal had to cool between pulses.

The powerful infrared lamp on the helmet of Allan's protective coverall sent a broad beam across the small open space, illuminating the wall of brush on the opposite side. His goggles, ground to accept wavelengths in a narrow band around the $10°$ frequency, kept out all visible light. The infrared beam did not reflect off crystalline or glass surfaces as badly as white light, and he could see clearly.

The sounds of pursuit stopped. There was a slow movement at the rear of the clearing as a large head approached the edge of the brush. The hunter paused, testing the wind, unaware that it could be seen by its intended prey. The huge mouth was open, and Allan saw a round silver snake of a tongue curling over pyramid-shaped teeth of unbreakable glass. And then a strong breeze started behind the human's back and carried his odor directly to the animal. They were so close he could see the skin crinkling around the flaring nostrils, hear the snuffling sound of heavy intakes. And then the wrinkled flesh smoothed out, and Allan knew with the certainty gained from encounters with strange beasts on many worlds over the past eight years that it was not going to attack. To the carnivore his strong scent indicated a mistake. It signaled that he was not only alarmingly strange, but inedible.

Allan had a sudden dangerous impulse and yielded to it immediately, before reflection cost him his chance. He holstered the left-hand gun and pulled down his goggles.

It was like opening a doorway into the softly lighted heart

of a diamond. This planet had no moon, but stars hanging thick and close in the clear night sky provided a diffused illumination. Crystal was a unique world, where life had evolved with silicon instead of carbon as the anchor element. The proportions of hydrogen and nitrogen in living tissue were similar to his own, but the oxygen content had dropped from 76 to 68 percent, and been replaced by metallic elements. Physically this planet, like Sister, resembled Earth, and the structure and activity of its flora and fauna were similar. But what on Earth would have been a tree became on Crystal a giant chandelier, with a trunk of shimmering crystal and leaves of tinted glass. The wind rippled branches covered with innumerable tiny jewels, bending plant tissue where the metallics in every scale of bark colored the light and reflected it from a thousand glistening facets. In the daylight it was blinding, a visual fury of changing light in every color and intensity. A minute of open-eye exposure would burn out the color receptors in the fovea; five would blind a person. No one went outdoors without goggles similar to the ones he was wearing, ground to admit only a few wavelengths.

Even in the softer starlight the display was dazzling. After a few seconds Allan recognized the head of the hunter by the pattern of the teeth, glittering like diamond pyramids in what to the animal's protected eyes seemed deep shadow. And as Allan watched, the mouth that could cut him in two with one bite slowly closed. The head receded, fading from view. There was a low sibilant rustling as hanging vines of vitreous crystal parted, and the fading sounds of padded feet on blades of glass.

Reluctantly, Allan pushed the goggles back over his eyes, and the visually dangerous beauty around him faded. The silence also died as the small jungle creatures who had quietly awaited the outcome of the stalk went back to their nightly business. And Allan had to return to his. He lived for moments like these, when some strange beauty burst on senses dulled by the monotony of months in space, or his work threw him into a situation so startling and new it surpassed previous human experience. But he had a job to do, and little time in which to accomplish it. A neverlander was due next day, bringing World Council Member Celal Kaylin of Turkey, chairman of a subcommittee checking on the work of the P.P. Corps. Kaylin was a member of the New Roman party, and in the past had been critical of the need for the Corps. Allan had been on his way to Earth, for the first time in eight years, to testify before that committee. He was unexpectedly ordered to Crystal because it was on his route home. The scientists here had reported that an elusive creature they had been unable to capture was possibly intelligent. And Council Member Kaylin was going to accompany Allan on this assignment and observe a "Conscience" in action.

As Allan started forward again, hearing the brittle crunch of small plants breaking beneath his thick boots, the Cryer called from close ahead.

Cappy Doyle had played several recordings of the thin, plaintive voice for Allan. It sounded like a high-pitched child who understood a few words of English and used them interspersed throughout a string of gibberish. But one word that had been consistently repeated was "help," and another was "leave." Once they had recorded a clearly heard, "Help us; leave." The voice always spoke from the same area, at night, and when the wind was still. Limited vision and numerous carnivores who killed before they realized their prey was inedible kept night work in the jungle to a minimum. Two heavily armed parties had sought the elusive voice without success, and several daylight searches of the area revealed nothing. Allan was no braver than the resident biologists, but he had dared the night jungle alone because experience had taught him that shy creatures on the verge of intelligence were less likely to flee from a single person. And he did not want to keep the subcommittee chairman waiting while he made that first careful contact with the frightened Cryer.

The sound came again, and Allan pushed away yielding fronds of spun glass and moved slowly ahead. He made no attempt to walk quietly because it was impossible. What on Earth would have been a silent walk sounded on Crystal like a mad giant trampling on greenhouses. But the local fauna were equally noisy; every bird that landed on a branch, every insect blundering into a leaf, spread its own small circle of sound. It hardly mattered for most of them; only a few had hearing organs, and most of these could only detect loud noises.

The wind died and the Cryer called again, a long wail that lasted over a minute. Allan stopped and listened intently. He picked out the words "leave" and "difficult" in the jumble of sounds . . . and received a strong impression there were syllables of other words in the mixture. Then a new breeze started and the thin voice faded.

Allan took a few more careful steps, stopping when he judged himself within a few meters of the creature. He waited, light focused directly ahead. He saw nothing, and heard only the crystalline chiming of vegetation shaking in the wind. The vagrant breeze gradually died away, and almost immediately the sound came again, so close it startled him. He was facing a bush a little taller than himself. Out of its shadows a high voice cried, *"Leave us!"*

Allan felt the hand still holding a laser tremble, and eased his finger back from the firing stud. The distinct words were followed by nonsense, and he strained his eyes to find the speaker. When he still saw nothing he took a step forward. The bush he was searching had a slender trunk and straight branched limbs with only a moderate number of leaves. No animal larger than a very small bird could be hiding there.

Another gentle wraith of a night wind appeared, and the

voice stopped. Allan strained his eyes, and when the breeze faded and the sound came again he finally saw the Cryer.

At almost eye level with the human one branch crossed beneath another. A saucer-shaped leaf, laced with silver threads, hung from the upper limb and grew into the lower; the normal growth pattern on both branches was upward. Two thick coils of silver wire, spun fine as spider silk, hung suspended in the air on both sides. The supple limbs, when not disturbed by the wind, kept the leaf pulled taut to form a crude but workable diaphragm. As Allan stared, almost unable to believe his eyes, the leaf vibrated and the thin voice uttered a string of gibberish.

The leaf and coils formed an electrically operated speaker. The Cryer was the bush itself.

"*A mountain* of silver?" Allan asked, astonished.

Cappy Doyle laughed, his bony frame shaking slightly in the locally made glass chair. A supply ship had failed during the research station's first year and the personnel had almost starved. Cappy, who had arrived middle-aged and plump, had chosen not to regain the lost weight. "Yes, a mountain, according to our seismic readings. This little hill we are sitting on is just the top of the peak, with the rest deep underground. We've done some mining and smelting as hobby work. By using silver instead of lead in stained glass, you can get some very beautiful effects, as you see in our windows."

The research station windows justified the director's pride. The standard dome of poured foamfab had been modified by adding thick but narrow panes of stained glass. If the vibration barrier that surrounded the hilltop failed and a large animal got through, the narrow embrasures behind the windows would not admit it. The heavy coloring in the glass kept the chaotic light reflected by the crystal jungle from penetrating too strongly. From inside, the human eye saw a constant play of

69

movement and color on the exterior of each window, a chromatic, living mosaic almost hypnotic in its intensity.

"We've found silver used in various ways in plant tissue," Cappy went on, "but the one you describe is unique. I suppose you realize that as hardheaded biologists we will have to see this speaker operate before we can accept it."

"I saw it and *still* don't believe it!" said Allan, smiling. "But you'll have to perform your recordings and measurements in a hurry tonight. I want to substitute a better speaker for the makeshift one and try to establish communication."

The thin director shook his head, as though to clear it of incredulity, and got to his feet. "It's your show. But you realize, Conscience Odegaard, that the data we've already accumulated on silicon-based life will keep three Earth universities busy for a decade. And now you throw in a wild factor like possible plant intelligence . . ."

"The hazard of your profession," said Allan, also rising. "Mine is to determine whether a questionable species has developed the basics of intelligence. From the evidence so far this is going to be an easy decision. Now I'd like to get some sleep before our Council Member arrives."

"I'll have a crew ready to support you tonight," Cappy promised. Allan slid open the cloudy glass rectangle of the director's office door and stepped into the open community room. A few late risers were finishing their breakfasts at a long crystal table. Allan spoke to several of the men and women, but ignored an obvious overture to draw him into conversation. He was too tired. The P.P. Corps, as a semimilitary organization, required its members to keep fit. But Allan had landed out of cycle with Crystal and was already behind on his sleep. The circadian disassociation pill he had taken to help him stay awake was now making him ill. And he was worried. The message from P.P. Administrator Wilson had been blunt and clear. Unless Kaylin could be convinced of an urgent need for the Corps, his subcommittee would probably recommend to the

World Council that it be abolished. In its eight years of controversial decisions the official "Conscience of Mankind" had made numerous enemies. The P.P.s had ruled that too many potentially rich planets could not be colonized or exploited.

Allan tumbled into bed without bathing and slept soundly until called for dinner. In the dining room Cappy introduced him to Council Member and Mrs. Kaylin, who had arrived while he was asleep. The C.M. from Turkey was a short, sturdy, dark-haired man, surprisingly young for such an important political appointment. His wife, Gilia, was a small, blond, and very beautiful Russian. Allan noted with approval that the short woman had a full, almost lush figure, with broad hips and breasts that seemed large for her small frame. This unusual field investigation made more sense to him when he learned the Kaylins had signed their trial marriage contract just before leaving Earth, and that Gilia had been, and still was, on the C.M.'s staff. They were enjoying a honeymoon trip, at World Council expense, that only the rich could afford on their own.

"Conscience Odegaard, I have heard so much about your work," Gilia said as they shook hands. "Yours must be the most interesting job in the galaxy."

"And one of the most difficult to justify," Kaylin said, his voice dry. "Each time you throw Earthmen off a planet, the demand to abolish the P.P. Corps grows stronger."

"The returns will more than pay for all sacrifices in the long run, as I hope to demonstrate here," said Allan. "Are you going to accompany us tonight?"

"We certainly are!" Gilia said immediately. Kaylin only sighed.

They ate a meal of carefully prepared concentrates—not an ounce of edible food grew on Crystal—and afterward Allan met Carlson and Manabe, the two biologists who were to accompany them. Cappy had chosen for youth, strength, and a good shooting eye. Carlson was a large blond man with long hair and a drooping mustache, who looked more like a displaced Viking than a scientist. Manabe, a small, lithe Asian, was a specialist in bioelectric systems, and Allan asked his help in preparing some special equipment. It took only a few minutes to assemble the simple device they needed. An hour after dark the small expedition set out.

11

Cappy Doyle had decided to personally safeguard his important visitors, and joined them to make a party of six. All were wearing the protective coveralls and helmets that shielded tender skin from the cutting edges on a great deal of the glass vegetation. Allan led them down the hill to the vibration barrier at its foot, where Cappy used his key to deactivate a gateway. An electrified fence was adequate protection on most planets, but the animals on Crystal were very poor electrical conductors.

All the men except Kaylin were carrying portable equipment. Allan swung his head to both sides as they passed through the safe area. The infrared lamp revealed several surface roots, mindlessly pressing to the edge of the low wire coils. Their tips were being oscillated into free molecules as they grew. The barrier could disintegrate even a large animal, but there was no portable equivalent for a personal weapon.

They had barely entered the heavy vegetation outside the barrier when a carnivore appeared. The wind was blowing, creating such a cacaphony of small noises Allan did not at first recognize the purposeful sound of a large approaching body. When he realized they were in danger it was almost too late to fight. A long snout suddenly thrust through the vegetation only a few meters away, two eyes like giant rubies staring down at them from a head twice Allan's height off the ground.

"Hold your fire!" Allan called quickly, cutting through Gilia's startled scream. His order was unnecessary; the biologists had all noticed the flaring nostrils above the two long U-shaped rows of pointed teeth. They waited, while the dim-witted creature's eyes and nose argued over their edibility. The nose won and it turned away; the noise of its passage gradually faded into the constant small sounds around them.

"That was a close one," Cappy Doyle said, his voice shaking slightly. "We call that large lad the elacroc, unofficially. He's big as an elephant and has teeth like a crocodile."

The Kaylins both laughed nervously, but Allan heard what seemed real fear in the C.M.'s voice. The short walk to the speaker-equipped plant, which was near the barrier but halfway around the hill, did nothing to relieve that fear. As the humans were approaching their destination they met a second hungry night prowler. This one launched itself from a tree where it had crouched in waiting, bowling over Carlson. Allan heard the sound of metallic claws ripping at the fabric of the downed man's coverall, and saw diamond-hard teeth close on the thin metal of the helmet. Then a beam from the laser ready in his hand cut through the lucent skin of the neck, and two more from Cappy and Manabe hit it in the side. Three burns were too much even for the tree climber's silicate flesh. It leaped away, threshing violently in its death agony, and the cacaphony of sound created by shattering vegetation almost deafened the humans. The animal was a catlike creature about twice the size of a man. When it stopped moving Allan lowered his goggles for a moment, and told Gilia to try it. He heard her gasp when she saw a slim pointed head of what seemed sparkling quartz, filled with teeth like two curved rows of pyramidal crystals.

When they arrived at the bush it took the three biologists five minutes to get over their awe, and two hours to film,

73

record, and measure. Allan volunteered to stand guard, and Kaylin and Gilia at first watched the three men work. When they grew bored the visitors from Earth lowered their goggles, and at once were standing in a fairyland beautiful beyond words. Allan noticed the normal jungle noises slowly returning as the smaller denizens resumed their interrupted nighttime routines. He kept his infrared beam in constant motion, scanning both nearby trees and the ground, but saw nothing dangerous.

"If you could transport a section of this jungle back to Earth it would be quite an attraction," said Kaylin, bending to examine a closed flower of fragile beauty. A huge insect, with gossamer wings as large as Allan's hand, fluttered to a landing on the same bush. The C.M. stared at it, utterly absorbed. Gilia uttered a low cry of appreciation.

The three men finally finished, and Carlson replaced Allan as guard. Using a field-sensitive meter Manabe had brought, Allan made a few simple measurements of his own. He needed readings on the operating current to the silver magnetic coils. The wind had been blowing intermittently since their arrival and the speaker had uttered some gibberish in the quiet periods, but no discernible words. Kaylin paid little attention to the biological speaker after an initial inspection, but Gilia seemed fascinated.

It was the work of a minute to adjust the speaker and microphone on the unit Allan and Manabe had prepared to operate on the very low plant voltage. Manabe muttered that so little power would hardly move the diaphragm, and started tying in a spare preamplifier stage on the input side.

Allan was carefully checking the wire in the silver coils; it was insulated by a layer of silicon-based tissue only a few molecules thick. The upper wires emerged from a layer of metallic bark, formed the coils, and disappeared beneath the bark of the lower limb. Allan scraped off insulation and connected the leads from his input speaker on both sides of one coil. A breeze had started and there was no current flowing at the moment. He hesitated, and then hooked the leads from his microphone to the opposite coil in the same way. This was the procedure in which he had the least confidence. The plant should learn quickly that the diaphragm in the new speaker had an automatic return to neutral, and the primitive device of a magnetic coil on both sides was unnecessary. Whether or not it could recognize signals coming in on what to it had been half of a co-ordinated output was another matter.

The breeze died, and almost immediately the receiving speaker on Allan's unit muttered some low static.

There was a pause, and then the sound came again, a little louder; the leaf-speaker was also rattling. Allan took a measured risk. He quickly clipped the tiny wires below his attachments from the input speaker, pulling the silver coil free. The speaker sounded again, now much stronger. The noise continued for a moment while the sounds subtly changed, gained form and substance, became syllables, became words. The speaker said, "You have provided an air vibration device."

Allan felt his heart thumping, and knew his hands were trembling. He heard a harsh intake of air as someone resumed breathing, but the other humans were locked in silence. He reached and cut the silver wires to the plant's second coil, laying it on the ground. Bending his face to the microphone that would feed a signal to whatever circuitry existed inside the plant, he said, "Yes, we have provided you with an air vibration device, called a 'speaker.' This signal is generated by a similar device called a 'microphone'."

The plant was silent, and he repeated the message. There was no doubt of the plant's intelligence, but seeing how quickly it could recognize the incoming signal and interpret the content would be a measure of its adaptability. Allan knew a moment of near exaltation when the speaker said, "I have made the necessary changes to accept your signal. With the two air

75

vibration devices you have provided we may now freely communicate."

There was a low murmur from the three biologists, and Gilia laughed; she sounded on the verge of hysteria. Allan had not realized until then how great the tension had become, or that Carlson was neglecting his guard duty. There were so many questions it was difficult to know where to start. He finally settled on the most basic of all and asked, "What have you been trying to tell us with your improvised speaker?"

"My extraction roots cannot cross beneath the killing barrier you have placed around the local supply of silver. The next source is far away, and I must expend great energy to transport from there. Help me. Remove the barrier."

"Ask it why it needs the silver!" Cappy said quickly.

Allan did, and the voice replied, "I am a multiple-body entity. All forms such as the one before you are a part of my Unity. Each form in the circle of my being connects with all others through a system of underground nerves made of silver protected by my tissue. All young growing parts require silver for the communications and storage matrix that exists in every individual. I must have more silver for young growths in this area."

"Conscience! Ask it if all its individual forms are identical in structure!" Carlson demanded, unable to restrain himself.

The voice they were hearing was toneless and mechanical, without inflection or intonation other than pauses for periods. The excited scientist had spoken loudly enough for the microphone to pick him up. The monotonous voice said, "All my parts are not identical. Some are grown to produce electricity which is distributed to all. Others grow with trunks much larger than the one before you. The extra space in these is supplied with silver in matrix form and used for the storage of accumulated knowledge. Unity draws upon any part as necessary."

"How did you learn to speak English?" demanded Kaylin

76

loudly. Allan had forgotten the politician was there. He looked at Gilia. Her lovely face was almost ecstatic with the joy of discovery. She felt his stare, lifted her rapt gaze to meet his, and Allan experienced a sudden and intense moment of sadness. This woman should have become a Conscience. Instead she would finish her government-paid honeymoon and become a politician's wife on Earth. It seemed a terrible waste of obvious talent.

"All my individual forms have leaves sensitive to slow vibrations transmitted through the air. Other leaves and roots are sensitive to temperature-electrical potential-touch and kinesthetics. I am aware of my own structure down to the level you think of as molecular. When your vibrations appeared in the air I realized they were a new form of slow communication. I transformed all slow vibrations to the faster ones that could be stored in my memory and accumulated them. Analysis revealed the structure of the communication and over several years I slowly learned the meaning of individual words. When I felt ready to communicate I changed the growth pattern of the form before you to create an air vibration device. It is of poor quality, and I have had difficulty in producing the correct sounds. The one you have provided is much more efficient. The signaling device you have attached to my nerves enables me to receive your communication in the electrical form which is acceptable without transformation."

"Why did you operate your air vibration device only at night?" asked Cappy Doyle.

There was a moment of silence. Allan sensed that the question posed a strain for the plant's still limited vocabulary. After a moment the speaker said, "I do not possess the quality you think of as intelligence when my forms are receiving sunlight. All my sensors and storage banks function, but the Unity that is speaking to you does not exist while each individual form accumulates energy. When the sunlight ends and the energy cycle reverses Unity resumes from the previous night."

77

Crystal had several small continents, but only one in the temperate zone; most of the planet's surface was hidden beneath water or ice. Unity was restricted to one plant form on the single warm land mass. So far as Allan knew this creature, like its world, was unique. It was not only the first intelligent plant, it was the first lifeform that covered an entire continent with what must be millions of interconnected individuals.

Unity spoke again; "Will you remove the barrier and permit my roots to reach the silver I need?"

"Certainly!" and "Of course!" Cappy and Allan said simultaneously. They glanced at each other, and Allan gestured for Cappy to speak. The thin biologist said, "Tomorrow we will deactivate small sections of our barrier at frequent intervals around the circle. You may send roots in through all of them. If it would help you, we will bring pure silver here."

"I cannot utilize the process you call smelting," Unity replied. "My roots must absorb silver as it is found in small quantities in the natural state. Open places in the barrier will serve my needs."

"Hadn't we better be getting back?" Kaylin asked suddenly. "You people are paying no attention to guarding us, and I don't want one of those glass-toothed monsters taking a bite out of Gilia."

"Celal!" Gilia protested immediately. "I've never been so enthralled in my life!"

The C.M. was right; they were being inexcusably careless. Allan glanced at Cappy, who nodded. "We will return tomorrow night and talk with you again," Allan said into the microphone. "You have learned a great deal from listening to us; we wish to learn from you. In return we will provide you with better access to our knowledge, which is greater perhaps than you can store in your memory trees. For now we will say good-bye."

"Good-bye," said Unity, its voice still toneless. The term could have no meaning for a creature whose separate parts were always connected by an electrical system, but Unity had learned something of human customs during its eavesdropping.

Allan disconnected his leads from the silver nerves, examined the delicate wires, and decided not to attempt to replace the fragile magnetic coils. After he left, Cappy could provide Unity with a permanent communications system, wired directly into the research station.

There were no attacks by carnivores on the return trip. Allan glanced at his chronometer as they entered the door, and saw to his amazement that it was barely midnight on Crystal. The slow walk and the talk with Unity had seemed to last many hours. The Kaylins said good night and retired to their quarters immediately, but Allan and the three biologists gathered in the deserted community room for some shop talk. Allan's decision was a foregone conclusion—Crystal could not be colonized or turned into a vacation resort for the rich—but there was no harm in the research station remaining indefinitely. Cappy wanted Allan to press for a larger appropriation in his report, and he had no choice but to agree. The P.P. budget and that of the research group were determined by different Council agencies, but a recommendation by a Conscience always carried weight.

At the community breakfast Allan learned to his surprise that the Kaylins were leaving that morning. The Space Service neverlander that had brought them was waiting overhead, and the C.M. wanted to make several other stops on planets where P.P.s were at work.

The Kaylins left to pack, and Allan started preparing his preliminary report. He had another week before a neverlander scheduled for Earth would stop for him, a week to enjoy honest gravity without the constant side-pull of rotation. He wanted to get this decision off and enjoy it.

When Kaylin and Gilia were ready Allan and Cappy carried their luggage to the planetary shuttle, waiting in a clear area behind the station. The C.M. stood fidgeting as the pilot stored their gear, something obviously troubling him. When the compartment door was sealed and it was time to board, Kaylin abruptly said, "I hope you two don't really think you've fooled me all that easily."

Allan felt a sudden coldness along his spine. Cappy looked a startled inquiry at Kaylin. "Oh, I don't really blame you for trying to preserve the P.P. Corps, Allan, or Cappy for wanting his budget enlarged. Everyone does it, though not many come up with as elaborate a game as you two played last night. But if you think I really believed all that about an intelligent plant that covers this continent . . . gentlemen, I'm not that naïve!"

Allan saw the expression of half-angry cynicism on Kaylin's dark face, the weary look of a man subject to constant pressures who had learned not to believe even his own eyes. The C.M. went on, "It couldn't have been very hard to make those coils and that bent leaf, and of course someone was hiding in the jungle and speaking into a mike on the other end of those silver wires. I'll admit it was very impressive, and Gilia certainly enjoyed the show, but I'm not convinced."

"Celal!" cried Gilia, distress in her voice. Kaylin patted her hand, and turned and started climbing the steep metal ladder to the airlock. She stared after him, perplexed, and Allan saw the struggle on her face as she tried to decide if her husband was right. The battle was quickly resolved. She impulsively stepped to Allan, took his hand, and said rapidly, "I'll work on him; between now and home I have four weeks in which to change his mind. He's doing you an injustice, but I hope you can forgive him. If you saw some of the schemes people pull to trick him, you'd understand."

Allan bent and kissed her cheek. "Don't worry about it. I'll be at that hearing when it convenes. I've an idea I think will convince both Celal and all the other committee members that we're worth our money."

Gilia turned and quickly followed Kaylin. She waved at the airlock door, then disappeared inside. Allan and Cappy moved back to watch the shuttle lift off, then walked to the station in silence.

"I'll be going back to the speaker plant tonight, and I'd like to go alone," Allan said as they entered. Cappy gave him a sharp look, but said nothing.

Shortly after dark Allan was on his way through the now familiar but always dangerous jungle, laser ready in his hand. This time he reached the Cryer without incident, and carefully connected the speaking device to the silver nerves.

"Are you ready to communicate?" Allan asked into the microphone.

"I am ready. I have found the inactive areas in the vibration barrier. Some of my roots are already near the silver."

"Good; I hope the harm we have done you will be swiftly overcome," Allan said. "I have a question that is very important to me. Can you impress enough knowledge on one of your storage forms to enable it to live, speak and think as if it was a small version of Unity?"

There was a short silence, as though electrical impulses were rushing from nerve center to nerve center, through a million plants and across an entire continent. The speaker said, "I can accomplish this within twelve activity periods."

"Will you do this for me, and allow me to remove that individual and take it to my home planet, if I guarantee that it will be returned and reconnected into the Unity unharmed?"

This time the silence was shorter. The speaker said, "I will."

Allan lowered his goggles and looked at the dazzling beauty of Crystal for the first time that night. All the deskbound committee members should have come with their chairman. But perhaps they would be like Kaylin, unable to believe their eyes and ears.

Unity had said it understood the structure of its forms down to the molecular level. Introducing a plant as a hearing witness, and having it submit obviously valuable new knowledge

81

as a justification for the work of the P.P. Corps, was a means of bringing something of Crystal to the committee.

Allan chuckled; this was going to make his trip to Earth far more enjoyable than anticipated.

12

As seemed customary for Allan, the planetary shuttle landed at the Interworld Spaceport in Lausanne just as dawn was breaking. He would have been starting his sleep period aboard the neverlander. There was nothing to do but take a circadian disassociation pill and resign himself to a miserable day. At least the aircar from the hotel was waiting, with the open top that he had requested. It was all he and the driver could do to lift and carry the huge pot containing Cryer and forty kilograms of his native soil, but they managed it. Allan had to ask the operator to fly at the minimum legal speed, to keep the pressure of the wind off the plant. At the Interplanetary Hotel he could only fit into the freight elevator, but within an hour after landing Cryer was absorbing sunlight from the old-fashioned balcony outside Allan's window.

"Are you comfortable?" Allan asked, wishing he could take a nap instead of reporting to Siggi Wilson.

"I am comfortable. The air is cold and has too much oxygen, but is acceptable. The sunlight is wonderful! I shall sleep and absorb."

Allan chuckled. Cryer, separated from the Unity plant and undergoing unique learning experiences, was developing an identity and attributes of his own. One advantage to Allan was that the plant's voice was no longer the dull monotone he had heard on Crystal. This tree was somewhat larger than the one which had made that first crude speaker, and contained within its thick trunk a detached portion of the entity's central nervous system. A great deal of accumulated knowledge had been impressed on this portable segment. It was the closest the multiform plant could come to providing an individual containing the basics of its own intelligence and personality. A highly sensitive speaker and receiver unit had been incorporated in the base of the tub. Cryer could hear and talk almost as well as a human.

As Allan closed the balcony door, his chime sounded. He glanced at the screen by the room entrance, and saw the familiar gray hair and rugged features of Siggi B. Wilson, Lieutenant General (Ret.), Space Service, now Administrator of the Corps of Practical Philosophers. Since individual P.P.s were usually called "Conscience" as a title of respect, the Administrator was referred to as the "Chief Conch." No one called Siggi Wilson that to his face.

"Allan! Man, it's good to see you! Why are you late? This is the last day of the hearing and it's going to be touch and go for us," the big man said as soon as the door opened. "We've got two Conservationist subcommittee members on our side, but the third one, Kellog, is wavering; and the two New Romans are naturally against us. So is Chairman Kaylin, but we hope he won't get a chance to vote. Today we have to convince at least the leaner that we're worth our money, or that resolution to abolish us is going to reach the floor of the World Council."

Allan liked the blunt-talking Administrator, whom he had several times spoken to on the subspace radio but never met. Wilson was the third retired military general officer to hold the appointment. Allan felt sorry for any man in the Corps or Space Service who had been permanently anchored to a desk on Earth. Still, he disliked the whole bureaucratic tangle of politics and administration, and being immediately thrust into the midst of it grated on his nerves. He was late because of the time it had taken the plant entity to impress a full set of memories on the matrix of Cryer.

But he was here, and had to be effective if he could. "What's our approach? Are we still taking the high road of moral imperative, or has it got down to justifying our existence by the knowledge we produce?"

"Both, but with the emphasis on knowledge. The big complaint is that we cost money by isolating rich worlds, while supplying nothing of value in return. If we can prove that we've more than paid for ourselves, in the same manner as the research outfits, we've spiked their best gun. So far the other field men and the administrative staff haven't convinced them. I want you to be prepared to speak on every planet you've opened to colonization. Negative decisions aren't very popular these days. The New Romans are claiming we've cost the Colonization Department at least three good planets without adequate reasons."

"When does the hearing start?"

"It resumes at two this afternoon. I'd like to go over your material with you this morning."

Allan threw a regretful glance at the untouched bed, sighed, and dug out his presentation. It contained a summary for verbal delivery and a detailed back-up for handouts. Wilson, aware that few committee members would read the details, concentrated on the summary. After a few minutes he looked up and said, "Why, you've spent most of your time talking about a single lifeform on a world humans can never colonize!"

"True, but I authorized the present research station to stay and expand, provided they arrange for the plant entity to have free access to the silver. Our gain will be in knowledge, as I've explained."

"Allan, trying to impress a committee of politicians with technical knowledge that might be useful twenty years from now is a waste of time. They think in terms of more efficient

84

spaceships, raw materials returned to Earth—though we all know transportation costs limit those to extremely valuable items—that sort of thing. I don't think this will help our cause."

"We don't have time to change it now," Allan said calmly.

Siggi got to his feet, looking tired and old. "I'm afraid you're right," he said quietly. "You'd need to start over. Do the best you can to make it interesting; at least try to keep them awake."

The Administrator walked out, not bothering to take a copy with him. Allan had been going to explain that he had a live witness who would certainly keep the subcommittee members from sleeping off their lunches, but let Siggi go. Five minutes later he was in bed, and when the hotel service computer called him at noon he arose hungry and refreshed. He dressed, punched out a lunch order on his room console, and stepped out on the balcony to check on Cryer.

The plant was gone.

Allan almost felt the shock send adrenalin surging into his bloodstream. He stood frozen, mind racing as he tried to weigh possibilities. The New Romans had the dedicated zeal of the fanatic, and were not above sabotage to gain their political ends. But they would have no way of knowing the importance of Cryer, or that Allan's testimony centered on him. Or would they? If someone on the neverlander had scanned his report during the tedious months between Crystal and Earth . . . legally no one could be a murderer for destroying Cryer, and without him Allan's presentation was as useless as Siggi obviously considered it. He had to have the dramatic impact of having a talking plant with him when he appeared before the subcommittee.

The hotel guard system would have registered the presence of an unauthorized aircar outside his window. Cryer had been removed manually. Since the strong sunlight would have placed him deep in the condition that approximated sleep for the plant, he would have made no outcry. And possibly he had died and his body been fed into a disposal without awakening.

The thought enraged Allan. It also forced into conscious recognition the fact that he had come to like, even admire, a plant. Cryer represented a strange intellect, a product of conditions, aims, and interests almost incomprehensible to a human. And yet they shared a common bond of life and mind, and that bond was stronger than their differences. He had to save the plant if it was not already too late.

Allan needed help. He placed an emergency call to Siggi Wilson and reached him immediately at his office in Geneva. There was no time to explain the situation and the importance of Cryer. Allan invoked one of the bureaucratic privileges he despised and asked for a Declaration of Emergency.

The Administrator reached for a button on his executive console, but paused before pressing it. Face deeply troubled, he said, "I'll have to account for a false alarm, Allan."

"This is real. I need a search party with Right of Entry, immediately. I accept full responsibility."

Siggi pressed the button. In under fifteen minutes an aircar landed on the hotel roof and six men in the gray uniforms of Council Security rode the fast elevator to Allan's floor. He met them in the corridor and quickly explained the situation. Within four minutes teams were at the doors of the rooms with balconies both above and below Allan's. On the five-minute mark they placed vibration charges against the doors and activated them. When the plastic panels disintegrated they stepped inside, dartguns ready.

Allan had accompanied the team going to the upper floor, as the most likely prospect. The room they entered was empty. A quick radio check with the other team revealed equally bad results. If Allan's guess of the thieves location was correct, they had already fled.

Allan stepped out on the balcony of the deserted room. The noon sun was shining over the low railing at an angle that threw the northside juncture of floor and riser into sharp relief. He saw a glitter of silver and mica grains in the interstice.

Heart starting to pound again, Allan hurried inside and punched the console for registration. When the house brain refused to supply the information he wanted he turned it over to one of the security men, who used his override card to obtain an answer. The room they were in had been charged to the number of the Acme Detective Agency. Mr. John Dassinkar, who had been registered in a room just down the hall for two days, was using an Acme charge card for his visiphone calls.

World Council Security was the only legal force authorized to carry arms in the international zone around Lake Geneva, but innumerable private detective agencies performed quasi-legal work for every competing national and private interest. When caught, their actions could be disavowed. When the vibration charge disintegrated the door of John Dassinkar's room they discovered he was not one of the wiser operators. He had a dartgun, and used it. The first security man through the door fell, unconscious in seconds from nerve shock. The second went through the opening at a sharp angle and got off one shot before he followed the first to the floor. The third got Dassinkar.

When Allan stepped inside he saw a small plump Nordic about his own age stretched unconscious on the rug. A husky young Indian stood a few meters away, arms self-consciously high in surrender. Cryer was in a corner, apparently unharmed.

Allan hurried to the plant, and saw at once that the silver nerves to the speaker unit in the tub had been broken. He searched in the sandy soil for the tiny insulated roots, and finally saw them. They had moved to the opposite side of the tub, and now trailed over the edge. He pulled the plant away from the wall, and saw the tiny threads snap at the metal rim. Curious, Allan found the almost invisible nerves on the floor and followed them. They led to the communications jack into which the room console plugged. One wire had already slipped between the plug and the wall; the other was just starting to enter.

Allan had learned that Cryer and all his fellow units had sensors that provided information on temperature, movement and kinesthesia, electrical potential in both air and ground, vibration, and touch. Precisely how these interacted to provide information on the environment, and how the limited "brain" of Cryer interpreted it to form a picture, was impossible for a creature conditioned to visual imagery to understand. The Unity on Crystal had managed not only to recognize the vibrations of spoken words as communication, but constructed a device to imitate them. It had also learned English. The poor quality of the organic speaker had been due to the difficulty of execution, not the concept. Cryer, when taken out of the sunlight, had somehow awakened and realized he was in unfriendly hands. The plant had extended his fast-growing roots, not back to the speakers which his kidnapers had disconnected, but to the house communication system. Obviously he had planned to call Allan for help.

As he worked rapidly to reconnect the nerve ends to the speaker unit Allan heard the remaining security men calling the other team on their reserved radio channel. When they arrived, Allan arranged to have a second aircar come for the paralyzed men on the floor, and commandeered the available one for himself and Cryer. Within ten minutes they were airborne and headed for the Council Building, looming like a rectangular metal mountain across the long blue lake.

Allan glanced at his chronometer, and could hardly believe his eyes. They were arriving several minutes early.

The hearing room was far from crowded, though a few spectators were seated on the front rows. Allan recognized a small but lush figure among them, and felt his breath come faster. It was Gilia Kaylin. The short blond woman saw him at the same time and waved, but did not smile. Allan had a sudden hunch she not only had not succeeded in changing her husband's mind about the discovery on Crystal, but had suffered second thoughts herself. Apparently he had lost an ally.

Chairman Kaylin and two committee members were sitting behind old-style oak tables on a raised platform at the head of the room. Siggi Wilson, who met Allan at the door, whispered that these were the two New Romans. Unless all three Conservationist members returned for the afternoon session a tie vote could occur, giving Kaylin the final say. And there was no doubt in Allan's mind how the young Turk would vote.

Allan and Cryer had caused a buzz of conversation when they entered, Allan pulling the beautiful glass and silver plant on a low truck borrowed from the hotel. A Tri-D camera on a long boom swung in for a closer look at the small tree from Crystal. Allan saw the operator in a booth at the rear of the room, speaking into his microphone. Despite the lack of live attendance this hearing was being broadcast on the networks. And although no less than five-thousand live channels were available to a Tri-D viewer every day, it was quite probable a fair audience was watching this hearing. The P.P. Corps had been founded with little opposition, but eight years of work by a growing number of Consciences had made them a very controversial agency. The Conservationists, with a small majority in the Council, could probably beat a motion to disband the Corps. The party leaders did not want the move to get that far. Siggi Wilson had been informed it was best this effort be nipped at the committee level.

It was an unfortunate bit of bad luck that had enabled the New Romans to capture the chairmanship of this standing investigation committee. All such posts were distributed among Council parties by lot, the number in proportion to the party's elected representation. The New Romans were an amalgam

89

of several older highly conservative parties, and the only one large enough to seriously challenge the Conservationists. Since committee memberships were also distributed in proportion to representation, the leading party had a majority on every committee; but if even one member was out the scales could tip the minority way.

As Allan seated himself in the witness section there was another stir at the door, and the Tri-D camera lifted and swung that way. He turned and saw a tall, grim-faced, very pot-bellied man entering, preceded by a red-haired guard in Council Security uniform. A retinue of aides followed behind. The handsome features and shock of gray hair, standing up like dried wheat, were unmistakable. Siggi Wilson, who was sitting by Allan, groaned softly. "Space save us! It's Blankenship!"

Even Allan was not too out of touch with Earth to recognize the Minority Leader of the New Roman party, Council Member Blankenship of North America. The opposition had brought out their biggest gun for this attempt to shoot down the P.P. Corps.

13

The Minority Leader and his followers settled into the spectator seats. Evidently he was there only to lend the weight of his commanding presence, not testify. Allan turned back to the front of the room. It was almost time for the hearing to start. A door opened on the right side and three men entered, talking among themselves. Siggi Wilson gave a big sigh of relief, and Allan realized these had to be the three Conservationists. Now they had at least a fighting chance. Wilson whispered to Allan that Kellog, the key to the vote, was the man in the lead. The others were Hartley and Dao Chi.

Promptly at two o'clock Chairman Kaylin lifted his gavel and declared the committee in session. Allan was the final witness, his appearance having been slid to the end when he was late. When his name was called Allan rose and walked to the table just below the committee's, pulling Cryer behind him. Kaylin's dark face stared down at him without expression, but Allan thought he detected a concealed dislike. It was going to be hard to convince the chairman he had made an error on Crystal; he resented the fact Allan was even going to try.

Allan had no intention of trying to change Kaylin's mind, or that of any New Roman. If he could convince that one Conservationist who was wavering he would have done his job.

"Welcome to Earth, Conscience Odegaard," said Kaylin, his smooth voice even and pleasant. "I see you've brought one of those beautiful trees from Crystal with you. This one looks a little larger than the one you rigged with a speaker for our benefit that night you were our escort. Are you saying now that you've found a second tree that can make a speaker out of leaves and talk to us?"

Allan had been prepared for skepticism, but the context in which Kaylin framed his remarks put him immediately on the defensive. He had been accused of being a charlatan even before he opened his mouth. Allan took a deep breath, nerved himself, and took the plunge. "No, Mr. Chairman, I am making no such claim. This plant, which I call Cryer, has both a microphone and a speaker built into the tub, both of our manufacture. What I say instead is that the intelligence animating the sound system is that of Cryer. Neither the P.P. Corps nor the scientists on Crystal have done anything whatever to this plant, other than install it in this tub and hook up its nerves to the sound system."

"We will let that statement stand for the moment, subject

to later challenge," said Kaylin, his voice calm and deliberate. "To move on to more immediate matters, what are the claims for this plant that you wish to present to us? Why have you brought it, and of what possible benefit can it be to anyone other than perhaps the biologists already studying it on Crystal?"

Kaylin had unwittingly given Allan a good opening. "Mr. Chairman, let me clarify a point there before I start the more technical part of my presentation. You ask what benefit Cryer can be to anyone other than a biologist. What I want to emphasize here is that the biologists on Crystal, though fine men and top scientists, did not find Cryer. I did. And of course I was able to do this by my training on Earth and eight years of experience in the field. Cryer, and the larger plant of which he is a detached part, form the strangest lifeform we have encountered on any of the thousand planets we have explored. Only the P.P. Corps has personnel with the training and experience to locate and identify these very different lifeforms."

"That's a personal opinion, Conscience, not the type of hard data we are seeking here," Kaylin said swiftly. Allan noticed that the other five committee members had sensed the enmity between chairman and witness and were paying close attention. The small audience in the room behind him listened in silence.

"I understand that all testimony made today is subject to later confirmation, Mr. Chairman," said Allan. "But I submit that my special training and work on previous cases is the type of firm data you are seeking, not a matter of opinion. I merely wish to establish that a regular extresbiologist does not possess the particular qualifications required of a Conscience. I make no claim that one is superior to the other. What I hope to help prove today is that both are needed."

"This committee has been assigned the responsibility to determine that, Conscience Odegaard. Please leave the decision to us. Now we would like to have your presentation."

92

"Certainly, sir. I have a detailed report here, with sufficient copies for all committee members and a few for the news media. The basic report is preceded by a nontechnical summary, which I trust you will all find interesting. What I wish to show you today is from the detailed section, but simplified for easier verbal presentation."

The five committee members were still following Allan with alert attention, and Siggi Wilson's fear that they might have difficulty staying awake was unfounded. Allan noticed they glanced at their chairman more often than seemed necessary, and then back to him. The unspoken conflict had brought an unexpected liveliness to the proceedings.

"Mister Chairman, you were with us on the night we first established communication with Cryer, and heard the first exchanges. If you will search your memory you will recall that the plant stated it understood its own metabolism down to the molecular level. What my report states, sir, is that despite all our advances this is an area of biology about which we remain woefully ignorant. The means by which roots absorb inorganic salts from the soil, for example, are reasonably well understood. But most roots are able to augment their salt absorption by energy-expending processes, and these have defied analysis. Cryer has explained the means to me, and it is in my report. The effects on the science of biology would have justified a Nobel Prize, if acquired in original research. We have received the knowledge free. It will greatly aid a hundred colonies growing Earth-type plants on alien soils, as well as our food industry on Earth. Another example is the regulation of the lengthwise growth of individual cells in the growing parts of a plant, which enables it to grow upward regardless of the position of the seed, or even a change in stem position. The three phytohormones, auxin a, auxin b, and heteroauxin, have long been recognized as controlling factors. I can now report plants have a fourth phytohormone, which determines the *rate* of growth. I believe it has escaped detection to date because its chemical structure is very similar to several substances found in the cytoplasm of many plant cells. I submit that by producing this phytohormone in quantity we can regulate the growth rate of many of our food plants. I need not point out how this will help us obtain the maximum possible amount of food off each cultivated area. And there is much more we have learned, which is here in my report. I submit that it is only a small beginning, though, and the real rewards of being able to ask questions directly of an intelligent plant are still to come."

Allan paused, and finished by saying, "That is all the verbal presentation I wish to make, but I will answer questions if you have any."

One of the committee members leaned forward. Allan recognized him as one of the two New Romans. "I have a question, Conscience," he said, speaking very loudly into his microphone. "I majored in biology in college, and I haven't forgotten everything I learned. My question, is, how do you expect to prove all the incredible statements you've made here this afternoon?"

Kaylin smiled, and there was a nervous female laugh from the small audience. Allan thought he recognized the voice. He looked the committee member in the eyes and said, "I brought a second witness to testify to my truthfulness, sir. May I present Cryer, native of the planet of Crystal, whom I am proud to call my friend. Cryer is a smaller reproduction of the multibody plant that grows throughout the entire temperate continent on Crystal. His vocabulary is still somewhat limited, but if you will confine your questions to the biological area he will probably understand them."

"Very well, Conscience, I'll play your game for the moment," the man replied, and addressed a few elementary questions on biological science to Cryer. When they were answered correctly he sat back and folded his hands. Allan noted with approval that Cryer's voice, while still lacking intonation and shading, was reasonably pleasing.

"Conscience, how are we supposed to know there isn't a radio in that pot?" Kaylin demanded, his voice reflecting the weary cynicism he had shown on Crystal. "Or more subtle and less detectable, a point-focus broadcast to that speaker that couldn't be found afterward by our security people. Frankly, sir, this little charade is even less convincing than the one you staged for us on Crystal. I thought the little leaf-speaker a far more original trick."

Allan pushed back his chair and rose. Looking directly in the committee chairman's face, but knowing that he was actually speaking to Kellog, he said, "Mr. Chairman and committee members, you have heard a voice I think you recognize as nonhuman. You have before you a detailed report on new knowledge just acquired that will have important effects on our lives. I think you will grant me that if the hardest part of my testimony to accept is true, the rest must be also. The hardest part is, of course, the idea that you see before you an intelligent plant. And yet that is precisely the easiest part of my testimony to prove, and I will be happy to do so. Subject only to the provision that he be well cared for, I will turn Cryer over to this committee, to examine and question as long as you wish. You may place him in a radio frequency shielded room. You may take him up in a plane, down in a sub, or out in space, if you wish. You may examine his sound system, and trace the small silver wires you will find to where they enter his body. You may isolate him from possible trickery in any way whatever that you may desire, and he will still speak with you. And that, I submit, will prove beyond any doubt that all I have said is true."

"I don't think any such elaborate test program will be necessary, Conscience," Kaylin said, his voice very cold and formal. "You may take your plant with you."

"I quite agree with you, Celal," said the Conservationist

Hartley, speaking for the first time. "In fact I move the question be called, right now. Let's find out who thinks the Conscience is lying, and who doesn't."

For the first time during the hearing Allan saw genuine anger on the chairman's dark face. Kaylin said, his voice sharp, "I would like to remind the member from the U.K. that voting on the question is scheduled as the last order of business today."

"Yes, and I'm ready now," Hartley replied, smiling slightly. "Then we can go home. Question! Question!"

Dao Chi joined the call. Under the parliamentary procedures by which Council committees operated, Kaylin had no choice but to put the question.

The chairman slowly read the formal resolution that said the committee recommended the World Council abolish the Corps of Practical Philosophers. "All in favor, say aye," Kaylin finished.

The two New Romans looked at each other, and muttered low "ayes." Allan was watching the Conservationists; neither man opened his mouth.

"All opposed, nay," said Kaylin, his voice cold and remote, as though he had no interest in the answer.

Kellog voted with Hartley and Dao Chi to kill the resolution.

"I declare this meeting adjourned," said Kaylin. "Committee members with specific inputs for the report may see me in my office." He tapped his gavel sharply on the table, rose, and walked from the room.

Allan, who was still standing behind the witness table, turned and faced the audience. He had not been worried about the outcome since Hartley called for the vote. The Conservationist had felt certain Allan's testimony had returned the wavering member to the fold. And he had been right.

Siggi Wilson was hurrying toward Allan, rugged features beaming and hand outstretched. Allan saw someone in the small audience with whom he was more concerned at the moment. Gilia Kaylin was walking rapidly toward the door, tears in her eyes and a look of controlled anger on her lovely face. Then Siggi was pumping his hand, and some other members of the Corps staff were crowding around to congratulate him. He mumbled his thanks, excused himself, and hurried after Gilia, catching her in the corridor.

She stopped when he touched her elbow, and turned to face him. The tears had been wiped away, and the anger had subsided. "I'm sorry, Allan," she said immediately. "After I left you on Crystal I tried to get Celal to believe it wasn't a trick, but I couldn't get through to him. Instead he made me doubt you, at least a little, and doubt my own judgment. I won't make that mistake again."

"I wanted to tell you something I should have said on Crystal," Allan replied, searching for the right words. This woman was married to another man, even though on a trial basis. He had met her only once and that time briefly; she should not be affecting him so strongly. "I wanted to say . . . you would have made a fine Conscience. You have the sensitivity, the open mind . . . the benefits that might not mean much to some people would be rich rewards to you, as they are for most of us in the Corps. I wish it could have been."

"I do too. Oh, do I! But the qualifications are so hard, and I'm a poor student . . . is it too late, Allan? I'm going to leave Celal today, that's why I was half-crying. I overheard some talk, I know Blankenship was counting on him to get that resolution to the floor. The New Romans know they don't have the votes to actually kill the P.P. Corps, but they wanted to force a floor debate and dramatize how many planets have been lost to settlement. If he had succeeded, Celal would have been next in line for the whip's post in the party, and a lot of people say he would have been a good bet to replace Blankenship eventually. All that's ruined now. And he knows I hated what he was doing, and we've been quarreling about it, and now I'm going. Allan . . . I've got a deferred vacation coming. Would you like to spend a month in the Martian Red Desert Resort with me?"

The unexpected question caught Allan completely off guard. For a moment he could only gape at her. He also had a vacation coming, in fact had accumulated more of them than he could possibly take. Enough people had qualified as P.P.s to relieve the shortage over the past few years, and there was no need for him to rush back to work. "You know I'd like that," he finally said, hearing the tremble in his voice. "But are you sure? Are you positive it's over with Celal?"

"It was over when he tried to force a vote without making any effort to see if your testimony was truthful. He knew then he was wrong, had been wrong all along, but instead of facing up to it he tried to rush the committee to a wrong decision. He was hoping Kellog would abstain, letting the chairman cast a tie-breaking vote. It would have been excellent publicity for him. No, I don't think he wants to see me again; it's best we part now. You're in the Interplanetary? I'll call you tomorrow."

She turned and hurried away. Allan understood the reason for the sudden departure when a heavy hand clamped down on his shoulder and a hearty voice said, "Allan, I see why you rushed off. I'm sorry to interrupt, but I want to talk to you. Have you heard about the reorganization we have on the boards?"

Allan wrenched his mind away from the most pleasant vision it had contemplated lately, and turned to face Siggi Wilson. "Reorganization? Haven't heard a word."

"Well, you know we've always kept the Corps lean and mean, especially in the field staff where you have those rugged scholastic qualifications. But we're getting too big for our spacesuits, and the outfit's hard to manage. As of next month I get a deputy here, which I've needed all along, and we're going to set up three sector chiefs in the field. I want you to

98

take one of those slots, Allan. The duties would be fairly similar to your present ones, except that you'd have a permanent base and be required to evaluate the performance of your people. You would also intervene when a field man gets overruled by a Space Service general, and try to settle the case before it reaches the World Council. We're getting too many appealed decisions in here. The Council doesn't like it, and the New Romans use them against us. What do you say?"

Allan did not have to think it over. As a sector chief he would be working with even more different lifeforms than at present, and probably visit more strange and unique planets. "I'll take it!" he said aloud.

"Good! Good! Then come by my office tomorrow and we'll make it official. And the wife and I will be expecting you for dinner tomorrow night. She's got the robochef programed to use all those fancy spices from Misery. Food like that you never tasted!"

Allan felt a wry sense of incongruity at the thought of eating spices picked by the Shamblers, but agreed. After a few more words Siggi left to return to his office, in the Space Service building down the street. Allan headed for the roof, where he caught an automatic aircar back to Lausanne and the Interplanetary Hotel. He was debating whether or not he wanted to look up Kay and visit his children. If she was in Europe he would have time enough before tomorrow night.

Allan neither attended the dinner nor saw his children. Gilia called him early next morning. He spent a busy day making arrangements with people he trusted to see that Cryer was safely returned to Crystal and Cappy Doyle, to be recombined with Unity as he had promised, and that night he and Gilia boarded the regular spacebus to Mars.

14

Allan and the eight other passengers gazed through the transparent center aisle floor at the verdant surface of Beauty, visible as a green carpet that seemed to cover most of this lovely planet. The pilot had extended the folding wings of the shuttle and was landing it like an airplane. They had been inside the atmosphere for several minutes, and had already shed most of the heat accumulated during entry. Beauty had an unpaved but adequate runway. On most planets Allan visited, the shuttles had to land vertically on their quadruped legs.

Allan was eager to experience full gravity again. It was a long trip, almost two months, from his new "permanent" station on Arcturus IX to this hospitable planet, circling a star known only by a number. He had been a sector chief for almost a year, and had spent very little time at his supposed "base." The opposition to the P.P. Corps, which he had seen growing steadily on Earth, had moved into space. Siggi Wilson had known what he was doing in creating sector chiefs to try to resolve disputed decisions in the field. Once they reached Earth, political considerations became as important as the actual facts in the case. Allan felt certain at least two worlds which should have remained closed had been opened to colonization.

On this planet Allan was going to have a very personal problem. The Conscience whose work he was to check had been his wife for a year.

Allan's thoughts reverted to his more recent affair with Gilia Kaylin. The month they had spent on Mars formed one of

the best memories of his life. Her trial contract with Celal Kaylin still had six months to run when they left Earth together,
and unlike the regular marriage agreement, a trial license
could not be terminated in less than a year. After the interlude
on Mars Gilia had signed up for the P.P. Corps. She was in
school now, and Allan had not heard from her in several
months. There had been no discussion of marriage between
them. With both in the Corps, any real married life was almost impossible.

The shuttle touched down on a grassy runway. Allan saw
that most of the greenery he had admired from above did
not grow very high, being barely taller than the low craft he
was riding. The pilot applied the brakes, and the shuttle shud-
dered and veered to the side. He brought it back to the center
of the runway and it veered again; Allan saw the foamfab
domes of the colony just ahead. And then the craft rolled to a
stop, and Allan violated protocol by unfastening the door and
letting himself out without waiting for the pilot. When he
swung to the ground he saw a lovely figure running toward
him, arms outstretched. Behind her, several other people were
coming toward the shuttle at a more sedate pace.

Secret Holmes was bare-breasted, and Allan felt his pulse
quicken. She was a trim blonde, weighing barely forty-five
kilograms in 1 G and only 148 centimeters tall. The short
skirt she wore above low open-top boots was made from vertical fibers covered by a thick but light fur, offering tantalizing
glimpses of bare skin as the strands curled and yielded to admit
the wind . . . and there was the explanation of Secret's provocative dress. The temperature was uncomfortably high, but
strong, variable breezes were always blowing, and they were
pleasantly cool on exposed skin.

Secret ran into his welcoming arms, oblivious of the amused
stares of the other passengers, and they kissed hungrily and
long. When she finally pushed against his chest and he reluctantly let her go, the shuttle pilot was opening the cargo

101

hatch. There was a polite cough, and Secret turned to introduce Allan to the colony administrator, a short, dark, plump man named Pasquale Bartolini. He was surprisingly young for such a responsible post, and had the typical political leader's heartiness and quick friendliness. He broke away to speak to a few other passengers, but returned and accompanied them as Secret led Allan toward the round buildings of High Hope.

Beauty deserved its name. The gravity was just over 0.9 G, the sky a clear blue without clouds, and the green of vegetation was everywhere. There were no hardwoods visible, but a riot of ferns, brush, grass and flowers, all plants that yielded and moved with the ever-present wind, hid low rolling hills until they faded over the horizon. The tallest plants he saw were a grove of flower-topped trees, strongly resembling Royal Palms, on the crown of the next hill.

Secret interrupted her own flow of small talk to say, "And congratulations on your promotion to sector chief; among other benefits it brought us together again. My decision was blocked by Brigadier General Timothy Terhune, and the case is already on its way to the World Council. But our beloved chief saw my report, and said it didn't provide enough data to be certain we'll win. You're supposed to find additional evidence to back me up. And after you do, I hope the word will get around and the military learn to keep its nose out of our decisions."

"The trend seems to be in the other direction," said Allan, smiling. "But I agree that this is a serious case. I'd like to at least examine the butterflies before I say you were right, though."

Secret laughed, and squeezed the arm to which she was clinging. Pat Bartolini said, "I'm sure the decision was correct, but the local New Roman leader happens to be Buck Terhune, the brother of the general. Buck doesn't much care about the facts involved, he's determined to stay. Not that

102

any of us *want* to leave Beauty, but most settlers belong to the Conservationist Party, and we try to apply what we believe, even when it personally hurts."

They were at the outer edge of the raw new town of High Hope, and Allan looked around with interest. All the round-topped buildings were of foamfab that had been poured to leave numerous openings to admit the wind. Air-conditioning equipment was far too heavy to justify transport charges. A few people were clearing away the heavy brush and pouring new houses. The workers moved rather slowly, and most were as nearly nude as Secret. They passed a large garden; he recognized several varieties of Earth food crops, growing well among plants native to Beauty.

Allan felt a vague unease. This colony had been established for more than two Eryears, and he had seen more progress on far harsher worlds after a few months. Evidently the heat kept the work efficiency low.

Pat stopped before an open sliding door in a house near the center of the small town. He gestured for them to enter. Allan stepped inside, and Pat introduced him to a blond Amazon named Astrid. The administrator's wife was taller than her husband, and wore only a skirt as short as Secret's. Allan had to make a conscious effort to keep from staring at her magnificent breasts. Women on Earth practiced every conceivable style of dress and undress, but the colonial worlds were usually more restrictive in their clothing habits.

When her guests were seated in comfortable but immovable chairs, Astrid walked into the kitchen area to prepare them drinks. There were no partitions in the small house and all furniture was made of foamfab, including a huge bed protruding from the wall below an adjustable window. Although their hostess looked capable of breeding a multitude, Allan saw no signs of children.

The open interior, sliding doors, and numerous adjustable windows enabled the occupants of one of these homes to chan-

103

nel and control the varying winds of Beauty. These people were adjusting to their new world rather than attempting to change it into another Earth, a good sign.

Secret and Pat, frequently interrupting each other in their eagerness, briefed Allan on Beauty's largest native animal, its forty kilogram butterfly.

An hour later the foursome headed out of High Hope, following a trail through the thick brush to the nearby hill where Allan had noticed the tall flowers. As they approached the grove he estimated the plants at less than two hundred in number, but they were wide-spaced and covered the rounded hilltop.

"We're in luck; here comes a butterfly," said Secret, pointing into the sky.

Allan lifted his gaze and saw a startlingly beautiful creature gliding toward the grove, huge diaphanous wings curling and rippling as it lost speed. Those wings extended well ahead of the narrow body and were a burnt orange in color. They were laced with long black streaks of contractile tissue, and had large yellow and white discs interspersed throughout the orange. As the creature settled into an immense blossom and out of sight, Allan saw a row of little grasping feet running the length of the body. The head, surprisingly large, was round as a ball and covered with thick fur.

"They can't actually fly with the wings," Secret said as they walked into the grove. "They launch themselves into a strong breeze, glide to get back into the jetstream, and ride those around and around the planet."

Allan had studied Beauty's peculiar atmosphere during the long trip from Arcturus. The planet rotated in fifteen hours, and had extremely strong jetstreams around its equator and adjoining temperate zones. These approached to within three kilometers of the ground. Below them was a shallow region of high turbulence, and beneath that a slower but more massive balancing flow of air in the opposite direction. At ground level the many hills interrupted the even flow, while lakes and other areas with temperature differentials created updrafts, breaking the bottom stream into innumerable cross currents and ripples. There was no weather prediction on Beauty; the air currents were too complex for analysis.

Allan noticed that the varying breezes were gone, and they were standing in a steady wind of more than usual intensity. The thick trunks of the flower trees were all bending in the same direction. Pat noticed his puzzlement, and said, "We're in a windbore; you often get these on top of a hill, and sometimes they blow steadily for half an hour."

Secret and Pat were scanning the tops of the tall plants as they walked. "I think that one we saw land is the only butterfly here," she said as they neared the end of the grove. They turned back, picking their way carefully through the underbrush. The steady wind of the bore, which had been at their backs, now pushed against them. Allan found himself leaning forward and walking with his head lowered. He was jarred erect by a loud cry of warning from Pat, and raised his gaze just in time to see a flat green disc as wide as his head flying toward him. It was spinning as it came, turning at an angle that let it rise slightly in the wind. Before Allan could dodge it hit him on the chest, and he saw thorns protruding from its rounded rim. Some of them snagged in the cloth of his light jacket as the wind whipped the flat body against him. Allan froze, and Pat called, "Turn around! Quickly!"

Allan did as directed, and the wind again caught the seed and ripped it loose. He saw it dip toward the ground, then tilt and start rising again as it disappeared. Pat and Secret hurried to him, alarm on their faces. Astrid was a little behind them.

"Did it sting you?" asked Pat. "That's a sin-sin seed and the thorns are poisonous!"

Allan hastily shed his jacket and tunic and examined his chest. The two layers of cloth had prevented the short thorns from reaching the skin. "I'm all right. But where did that overlarge seed come from?"

"That bush," said Pat, pointing to a large one directly ahead. "This isn't the season for seed release, but one sometimes gets torn loose during a bore. My mind was starting to 'float' and I didn't watch where I was leading you."

"I haven't felt anything this time," said Secret. Astrid nodded in agreement.

"When one of the butterflies wants to communicate it uses a form of telepathy," Secret explained to Allan. "That's one reason the person being contacted can't prove he's actually received info from the creatures. The first indication is that you start to feel a little lightheaded, something like the beginning of drunkenness. Only it doesn't get any worse, and you start receiving strong nonverbal sensory impressions."

"I was almost on the verge of understanding this one when I saw that disc flying and was jarred out of contact," said Pat, sounding irritated. "Hey, there it goes!"

The butterfly had launched itself into the air, great wings spread wide to take the wind, and the steady breeze brought it directly toward them. As it passed overhead Allan saw that it was rising steeply. The wings did not flap but they were in constant motion, the bands of black muscle tissue stretching and forming them to provide maximum lift. It was out of sight in seconds.

"You should see them mating on the wing," Astrid said in a dreamy voice. "I've taken up a glider—our favorite sport here, as you can understand—and hovered by them. The courtship ritual goes on for hours and hours, involving all sorts of aerial gymnastics, but when they meet and couple it takes just seconds. I've filmed a whole sequence, if you'd like to study it."

"Certainly, and all the other material you have on them," Allan replied, somewhat surprised. The big woman had seemed more formally correct than friendly up to now.

"Allan!" Secret called urgently.

He hurried to the small woman, where she was crouching behind the sin-sin bush. Secret pointed silently to the ground. There were two depressions where someone had knelt, and several broken twigs. Allan raised his gaze, and found the torn branch from which the seed had come. It was in the center of the bush, surrounded on all sides by more discs. The steady breeze at their backs had all the seeds flattened immovably against the dense body.

"So someone deliberately tried to sting you," said Pat, who had rushed to join them. "The New Romans think they can get Secret overruled, but they're afraid of you. We have an antidote for this poison, but you would have been sick for weeks, long enough for the case to reach the World Council. And since they didn't succeed . . . Allan, you'd better be careful. I think your life is in danger."

"It certainly seems that way," said Astrid, who was breathing deeply with excitement. She seemed thrilled at the thought, giving Allan the impression life must be very dull here for most colonists. He kept his eyes off her heaving bosom.

"And I think I know who did this," Pat added. "Buck Terhune! Maybe if we hurry we can beat him back!"

Allan had no particular wish to confront the known enemy at this point, but he followed the short colony administrator as he set a rapid pace back to High Hope. Pat led them to the edge of town, where they saw a small group of men busily assembling a solar power plant. They were being supervised by a big man with very black hair who seemed older than most. Pat introduced Allan to Buck Terhune, the colony's chief engineer.

The tall man extended a broad hand, and Allan had no choice but to shake it. He noticed that Buck was breathing heavily, but it could have been from helping the other men.

"Buck's group doesn't believe the butterflies are intelligent,

107

although they've had the same contact experiences as the rest of us," said Pat.

"You mean we've all had lightheaded moments we couldn't explain," the burly engineer said immediately, and Allan could see that it was an old quarrel between them. "The fact that all of us get dizzy now and then doesn't prove some stupid, overlarge insect is trying to talk to us. I think it's a very thin gas in the air we haven't isolated yet."

They talked for a moment and then left. The hurried walk back had been useless, as Allan had expected. "The real trouble with Buck is that he wants my job," Pat volunteered when they were out of hearing. "And he may get it, if we don't start moving faster here. Trouble is, it's such a pleasant place no one wants to work!"

Allan did not reply, but from what he had seen he felt that Pat was right. The number of new people that could be absorbed depended primarily on how rapidly the present settlers built houses and planted foodcrops, and the people of this first town were moving very slowly. But if the butterflies were declared intelligent and the settlers had to leave before the lack of progress became known . . . Allan glanced sharply at Pat, but the short man's guileless face gave no hint that he considered Allan's decision important to his future.

Secret had taken Allan's arm as they walked, and he looked down to find her staring at him. She grinned and winked, and he felt a quick stir of blood, thinking that perhaps they would spend the night together. It had been over four years since their paths had last crossed. At that time they had arranged a short trip together, and renewed the fire that had burned so heartily during their trial marriage almost a decade ago. Secret was several years his junior, and had been one of his students when he stopped teaching to try for the P.P. Corps. She had entered directly from college the next year, and they had taken out the standard twelve month contract for the remainder of Allan's time in school. They had got

108

along well, but their chosen careers made a regular marriage impossible. There had been no regrets or recriminations when he left Earth.

Allan left the Bartolinis at their home and accompanied Secret to a guest house, to study her accumulated data. He saw with a thrill of joy that his two battered travel bags had been placed inside. Evidently Secret felt his agitation, for she laughed softly and came into his arms for their second kiss. When she pulled back at last she said, "If you close the doors and windows you have privacy, but the heat melts you into jelly. If you don't close them someone may walk in any second, because they've dropped the habit of knocking here. Or you can restrain yourself until dark. No one comes in when the lights are off."

She knew him better than he liked to admit. It hurt to say it, but Allan managed to get out, "We'll wait till twilight anyway. With a fifteen hour rotation, it can't be too long."

He was wrong. It seemed a lifetime.

15

Next morning Allan dragged himself out of bed to the sound of Secret's cheerful singing in the recirculating shower, and they dressed and left for the communal dining hall. Allan had got little work done the previous day—Secret had deliberately tormented him by her closeness and near-nudity until he had become completely distracted—and after breakfast he settled down to an intensive study of her notes. They began impressively enough, with an area survey of the butterfly population, extensive data on the huge flowers whose blossoms provided their only food supply, and a detailed report on the behavioral patterns of a butterfly ingesting nectar. But after that the quality of the data seemed to become fuzzy, as though Secret had stopped caring. He checked some of her later math and found mistakes in simple addition, and the safeguards she had used to exclude environmental influences on some behavioral experiments were hopelessly inadequate. A report of a full day spent following a particular butterfly about in a glider plane was nothing more than an account of seven idyllic hours in the sky.

Allan pushed the paperwork away, stretched, and walked outdoors. It was already noon in Beauty's short day. He saw Secret returning from an errand to the supply store, and waited for her. She seemed subdued, and handed him a spacegram without comment. He saw that it was addressed to him in care of Secret.

NEW ROMAN PARTY CHAIRMAN CLAIMS SEVERAL
RECENT MAJOR ERRORS ON P.P. DECISIONS,
PROOF AVAILABLE SHORTLY. SECTOR CHIEFS
TO DOUBLE-CHECK ALL DOUBTFUL CASES,
EMPHASIZE P.P.S TO PREPARE UNBREAKABLE
JUSTIFICATION ON ALL ABANDON DECISIONS.

SIGGI B. WILSON, ADMIN
CORPS OF PRACTICAL PHILOSOPHERS

"I don't know what our greedy enemies on Earth are up to, but I realize my report contains too much subjective material," said Secret, sounding worried. "But you have to *be* here, actually communicate with a butterfly once, before you're qualified to judge them. Their thinking is nonverbal, all images/sensations. That doesn't make it any less effective."

"No, we've ruled in favor of species that communicate nonverbally many times," agreed Allan. "But since we're undoubtedly going to be questioned on this one, I think I'd better do a little more work. Can we get a butterfly body to dissect?"

110

"I've never seen a dead one. But there's a story . . ." she paused doubtfully, then tossed her short blond hair and went on, "Oh, the local version of the elephant graveyard legend. There are hot sulphur springs in the mountains to the west of us. Several colonists flying in the area claim to have seen butterflies with torn wings descending into the mist. One man hovered at the lowest safe height and watched for hours after seeing two hurt ones go down; they didn't reappear. And since they normally spend only a few minutes on their feeding plants, and don't touch down elsewhere that we've observed . . ." She shrugged bare shoulders.

"Secret, you know I'm biologically oriented. If you haven't run a dissection then I think that should be our first job. How can we reach these hot springs?"

"We can fly a powered glider to a high-level plateau at the base of Charlemagne, the tallest peak, but we'd have to walk in from there. The tiny powerplants on the fliers won't outpull the vicious downdrafts you find in the mountains. It will take two days."

"That's okay. Let's plan on it for tomorrow. Now what about this film Astrid has? Is it useful?"

"Probably as good as mine." Secret sounded peeved.

"Then let's see if she'll show it to us tonight. For this afternoon I'd like to return to that grove and get a sample of the nectar they eat, since I notice you haven't chemically analyzed it yet. And we'd better check with Pat to be certain we can use a glide plane tomorrow."

"You can check with him tonight," Secret said, rising and moving toward the unmade foamfab bed. "And you won't need my help getting a nectar sample; I don't climb trees very well. I'm not accustomed to these short sleep shifts yet, you kept me awake half the night, and I'm going to nap till the second meal. Have fun."

Allan felt a small surge of anger, but quickly repressed it. He was Secret's official superior, but giving orders to your

111

lover was a difficult business at best, and impossible with her, as he had learned long ago on Earth. He gathered up the sampling equipment he needed, dressed in a light jumpsuit, and left. Pat was not at home, but Astrid agreed to show the film and ask her husband about the glide plane for tomorrow.

The jumpsuit was too warm for comfort, but protected the tender skin of his arms and legs as Allan clasped the bare trunk and slowly worked his way up. The wind was again steady, though from a new angle, and the tree bent beneath his weight and the steady push of the breeze. By the time he thrust his head over the top, the trunk was leaning at a forty-five degree angle. Distrusting the light fronds that branched from the center, Allan kept his legs around the bole. He felt slightly dizzy, as though he had overexerted himself during the long climb, and rested for a moment. When the feeling of vertigo faded he opened the sampling kit on his belt. The stigma were large and soft, and he had no difficulty in tilting a pistil and squeezing the syrupy fluid into his phial. He capped it and reached for another . . . and froze when a huge shadow swept across his face. The thin whistling sound of air being spilled across a wide flat surface reached his ears. He looked up in time to see a gorgeously colored golden butterfly, wings rippling and curling as they shed air, shooting directly toward him. Just when it seemed the huge creature would knock him off his precarious hold the great wings lifted sharply, coming almost together as they lost purchase on the air, and the long body dropped suddenly on to a frond. It dipped beneath the forty kilograms of weight, but held. Allan was staring into a golden-furred insect face not a meter away, where two huge faceted eyes were calmly inspecting him in return.

One of the several reasons Beauty deserved its name was the absence of carnivores large enough to be dangerous, and the colonists did not carry weapons. Allan froze, fervently

112

wishing for his laser pistol. The creature did not appear to have teeth and he might have beaten it away on the ground, but he was almost twenty meters high. The butterfly made no hostile move, and after his initial fright passed, Allan returned the stare with interest. This one had the usual bands of black muscle tissue circling and weaving through the wings, but both body and primary wing surfaces were a colorful riot of varying golds. Short yellow fur covered the entire round head except for the eyes; it did not appear to have ears. Two tubelike projections extended twenty centimeters from the center of the face.

It seemed like an hour to Allan, but could have been only minutes, before the creature abruptly bent its head, inserted the two thin tubes into the fluid accumulated on a stigma, and drank. Through the almost transparent walls of chitin he saw the thick syrup flow slowly upward. The butterfly fed until the cup seemed empty, then calmly shifted to another. It took almost five minutes to drain both. When it was through the golden head lifted, and the large eyes once more met Allan's. Suddenly he felt dizzy again, this time so strongly he seemed to be losing consciousness. Afraid of falling, he leaned forward until his torso lay flat across the yielding fronds. His legs were too weak to grip the bole and an abrupt change in the wind would tear him loose, but dark shadows were flickering at the edge of his sight, ready to overwhelm him. Allan closed his eyes and waited passively for the weakness to either fade or conquer him.

It did neither. Allan became acutely conscious of the sweet smell of the nectar cups, the springy support of the fronds, the pressure of the breeze on his face . . . he realized he had been receiving these sensory messages all along, at a lower level of awareness. Then the smell of nectar seemed to turn into taste . . . he felt the touch of simple sugars on his tongue . . . the waving fronds seemed to move more regularly, as though changed to beating wings . . . he felt the lift of the

113

wind on his body, knew he could hurl himself forward, ride the air currents upward into the high pure sky, clean and free . . . he spread his arms . . .

And the dizziness faded. Allan opened his eyes, vision still blurred, to find his gaze locked on the multifaceted glitter of the butterfly's compound orbs. The blurriness disappeared; he realized his arms were lying limply on the fronds, and with a return of his earlier fear, gripped the rough stems with both hands. The calmly impersonal eyes regarded him without anger or fear. And then the lifted wings lowered and fanned out, caught the strong bore wind immediately, and tore the many clinging feet from their swaying perch. It came directly at Allan, the great spread of the thin wings blotting out the sky. He ducked his head and gripped with both hands and legs, and the small feet brushed his hair as the long body passed directly over him. Allan turned and watched the beautiful insect rising slowly into the sky, wings spread to the maximum. Another appeared from the side and joined it, and abruptly both turned into the wind and began riding it swiftly upward, circling and wheeling around each other.

Allan watched until the two were only small black dots, still rapidly rising, in the vastness of the wind-torn sky. He slowly filled three more phials with pollen and tissue samples, and started down the rough trunk. The windbore had died while he worked and the huge flower swayed sickeningly with every vagrant breeze, making the descent far harder than the climb. Safely on the ground again, Allan drew a deep breath of relief. As a Conscience he had to keep himself fit, but he was not a very good athlete. There were times when Allan wondered if the P.P. Corps had made a mistake in accepting him. But somehow he had lasted nine years while better men and women died in service, and been promoted to one of the three new positions of sector chief.

Allan felt fully recovered by the time he reached the small settlement. The second and last communal meal had been eaten, but the cooks found enough for him. Secret was already at the Bartolini house. He made his way there just as the short twilight faded into darkness, and found the projector set up and ready. Astrid ran the film immediately, and Allan studied it intently. He saw nothing in the elaborate courtship ritual that indicated whether intelligence or simple instinct was at work. On Earth some types of herons went through equally complex formalities before mating, and though the dance patterns were beautiful, he had seen similar ones performed by insects on other worlds.

Both Astrid and Pat stood up when the film ended, and Allan realized this was a direct hint. With only seven hours of darkness available, these people went to bed early. They thanked their hostess and returned to the guest cottage. The second night was even better than the first, and when their clock awoke them at dawn, Allan had to exert all his willpower to get out of bed. Secret grumbled and complained when he shook her, but finally crawled out and into her brief skirt.

After a hasty breakfast they loaded their gear into one of the colony's two powered glide planes and wheeled it out of the foamfab hangar. Two men Pat had sent to help them get off the ground held the light craft by its long wings until a steady breeze appeared. Secret, the more experienced pilot, opened the throttle and ran into the wind. The plane rolled for less than thirty meters before clearing the ground, and though it dipped badly once she managed to keep it aloft. In five minutes they were just below the area of high turbulence that separated the jetstreams from the lower air, and she banked and turned to the west. At that altitude the wind pushed against the plane one moment but aided them the next, and they averaged almost two-hundred kilometers an hour.

Looking down, Allan was impressed again with the fact that Beauty had been well named. There were never any clouds here, and no rain. A very heavy dew condensed out of the air and watered the thronging vegetation every night. The plants lived in constant motion, yielding to each erratic wind, and the petals of uncounted billions of flowers swayed and bent in stately rhythms. The entire surface of the world seemed to be alive beneath the plane.

In a little over two hours Secret started losing altitude, looking for an open place to land. They had passed a few foothills and were over a grassy plateau that abutted a low old mountain range, as green as the rest of Beauty. She found a level spot free of brush and touched down without difficulty. Allan was out of the small cabin the instant the plane stopped rolling, holding the craft by the crossbar between the wheels. Secret tumbled out behind him and hastily drove tie-down pegs at front and back.

Allan's backpack was large, Secret's much smaller. It was a little before noon when they started walking. There were only scattered patches of brush at this elevation and they made good time. The swift twilight caught them just as they rounded the flank of Charlemagne. Secret prepared a hasty meal from concentrates while Allan inflated their sleeping bags. It was quite dark when they finished eating and both were bone tired, but Secret shared his bed for a few minutes before getting into hers. When the sun awoke them after what seemed only a nap, Allan understood why the colonists retired early.

Before noon they were behind Charlemagne, and for the first time Allan saw bare ground on Beauty. It stretched directly ahead of them to several small vapor-covered lakes, apparently fed by the sulphur springs. When the vagrant breezes blew toward them, their noses were assaulted by an odor like rotten eggs.

Allan saw several large stone ridges crossing the valley floor, and the closest lake was bordered by one on the right. The winds seemed milder here and the temperature higher.

Not a butterfly was in sight. Allan decided to start their search at the nearby lake, and picked a path toward it. In thirty minutes they were standing on the shore, staring out over the mist-covered water. The lake was several kilometers wide, but the opposite shore was hidden in the thick haze.

"Allan, there's a cave," said Secret, pointing to the stony ridge. "It's the first one I've seen on Beauty."

Allan looked to their right and saw a low dark shadow extending twenty meters across the face of the rock. At the center it seemed at least two meters high, but was less than one at the water's edge. It was difficult to see through the mist, and the high heat was making Allan uncomfortable. He led Secret toward the ridge at the point where it met the shore, the cave being as good a place as any to look for dead butterflies.

And they found them.

16

The elephant graveyard of old Africa was a myth. The butterfly burial ground was real. Hurt or dying elephants could hardly travel hundreds of miles to a single spot; the butterflies could. A picture had started forming in Allan's mind, and the examination of a few dead bodies confirmed it. Corpse after corpse was dry, drained of all substance, with the cracked eggshells of the eater still clinging to the chitinous exterior. The floor was littered with the dry husks of long-dead adults, and as Allan straightened up from his fourth examination he saw a small, weak figure emerge from the deep shadows at the rear. It was a baby butterfly, crawling slowly and painfully on his hundred feet.

Allan motioned for Secret to leave the crawler alone, and they watched silently as it struggled to the opening above the

117

water, the baby wings unfolding as it neared the light. At the edge it paused, testing the almost motionless air. It was stiflingly hot in the cave, the trapped vapor from the lake providing both heat and moisture. But the persistent breezes of Beauty reached even here, and after a moment there was a stir of air at the entrance. The baby suddenly launched itself out over the water, dipping at first until it almost touched but then rising swiftly as it gained speed and the updraft lifted the light body. In seconds it was out of sight in the mist.

The butterfly life cycle both began and ended here, in one of the few places on Beauty where the restless winds could not steal away the heat needed for hatching. There were probably other caves nearby, and other hot lakes around the planet, but they would only be duplicates. The picture that had been forming in Allan's mind was complete.

Even so, he needed proof. Allan slipped off his backpack and knelt at the head of a newly dead butterfly. He opened the bag, found his laser pistol, and adjusted the beam for short-range cutting. Two maximum length burns cut through the thorax just behind the head. Secret watched in silence as Allan wrapped the round ball in his jacket and stuffed it in the pack, but when he started toward the shore she hastily followed. Once safely on the ground and away from the wet heat, Allan immediately felt better.

"Do you want to look around the other lakes for more hatcheries?" asked Secret. Allan noticed there was a new respect in her voice. "We have enough time before dark," she added.

"Yes, though I'm certain we'll just find more of the same," said Allan. And two hours later, when they turned and started back toward their glide plane, he had been proven right. The other caves were of different sizes and locations, but all were heated by proximity to the water and all contained the bodies of adult butterflies. They had seen one female attaching her eggs to a dead male, and Allan noticed that when her chore was finished she too crawled off into a corner to die. The males

118

returned here solely to furnish food for the young; the females came back as their last act after their egg sacs were fertilized. As with many insect species, that probably meant many more females than males were born.

It was rapidly growing dark, and both were exhausted when they reached the slopes of Charlemagne again. Allan insisted they keep moving until it was no longer safe to travel. The shadows were deep at the point where a ridge from the mountain on their right forced them to follow a narrow defile past Charlemagne. It was the deceptive lighting that saved Allan's life when a laser beam lashed down from high on the slope to their left, burning a hole in the ground behind him.

Allan had been shot at before, and though he was not a soldier he had acquired the reflexes of one. He leaped backward instantly, and the second beam from the ridge on their right seared the air where he had been. Allan continued his motion by catching Secret about the waist and pushing her hard to the side. She lost her balance after two running steps and fell sprawling, but her torso was behind the rock he had selected. Allan left his own feet in a dive, hit rolling, and saw the hot beam burn grass behind him as the first man fired again when his laser cooled. Allan stopped behind Secret and scrambled to her side; the rock was barely large enough to hide them.

Keeping his head low, Allan got to his knees and slipped off his pack. He found his laser, and adjusted the beam to its longest range. Fatigue had vanished, dispelled by a surge of adrenalin into the bloodstream, and his mind was racing. Now that a try had been made to kill two P.P.s, the ambushers had to finish the job and hide the bodies. If the attempt on their lives became known the Space Service would never rest until the killers were found. The would-be murderers had to come after them, and though they had no way of knowing Allan had a laser, they would take no chances.

The twilight gloom was rapidly fading into darkness. Allan

placed his lips against Secret's ear and said, "We'll sneak back into the valley in a minute. Is there any other way out?"

She shifted her head and whispered, "Yes, we can go around Charlemagne on the opposite side, but it would take days. We'd need food and water."

"And you can bet they disabled the glide plane," Allan said grimly. He cautiously looked around the rock on the opposite side, but could see nothing in the dimness. As he started to draw back he heard a faint scraping noise, as of a boot sliding along a rock wall. At least one of their attackers was climbing down to the level ground. It was time to leave.

A new hazard occurred to Allan, and he swiftly muttered some emergency instructions to Secret. They crawled backward, keeping the rock between themselves and the danger in front as long as possible. When he finally stood and took Secret's hand to lead the way he could barely see enough to avoid large boulders. They moved quickly but quietly for several meters, and suddenly a light flared behind them. Allan looked back and saw the area behind the rock that had sheltered them brightly illuminated. There was a yell from the man holding the light, and then it moved and swung toward them. Secret hurled herself to the left as Allan had instructed, while he went right and snapped off a shot at the light. He missed, but had the satisfaction of hearing a startled cry, and seeing the light go out.

"Come on!" Allan snapped, low-voiced, as he reversed himself and went after Secret. He found her immediately and led the way again, walking rapidly but quietly. By the time the man with the light found a secure place and turned on his beam again, they had moved behind a rock buttress and were out of sight.

Allan had been thinking as they walked, considering the alternatives. Knowing now that he was armed, the killers were unlikely to come after them until morning. When they came they would be slow and cautious. They probably knew there was no drinkable water in the valley, and could be certain their intended victims had little left in their canteens. Even if the two P.P.s managed to walk around Charlemagne on the opposite side, they would still face an impossible trek through the dense brush. Unless help came from the colony—and Allan had a strong hunch none would come in time—the killers could hunt them down at their leisure.

Allan stopped, slipped off the pack, and sat on it to remove his boots. He stuffed them and the canteen inside and handed it to Secret. "Cross to the opposite side, climb up among the rocks, and hide. If I don't make it back, wait until they pass in the morning and walk to the plane. You'll have enough water and food to last until help comes."

"But Allan! What are you going to do?"

"What they least expect; go after them," he said, making a strong effort to keep his voice calm and even. He turned and walked rapidly away before she could protest.

Allan cautiously rounded the corner they had just turned, and was not surprised to see the light still on ahead. The hard rock was rough on his bare feet and he bruised himself several times, but ignored the pain. As he drew closer he heard voices, and saw there were only two men and that they were arguing over what to do, as he had hoped. Allan dropped to his knees and crept forward, trying to keep near enough to shelter to dodge if the light should suddenly sweep his way. When he reached the last rock large enough to protect him he crouched behind it, then eased his head and the laser around the right side. The two men were standing where he and Secret had huddled, still talking. They agreed on what they would do just as Allan drew a bead on the one holding the light.

And paused.

And realized he could not deliberately kill a man. It was ridiculous—these two were obviously professional assassins, men who had shot at them without warning and would kill instantly if the advantage were theirs—but nevertheless he could

121

not slay except by bad aim in the heat of battle. His inability had nothing to do with what the men were—it was the way he himself was made.

With an inner sigh, Allan shifted his aim and burned a crippling hole in the thigh of the man with the lamp.

There was a scream of pain, and the light fell and clattered along the rock floor. The second man turned and ran, but there was no shelter handy and the lamp had stopped with him in its glow. He hesitated, then started around the large rock. But five seconds had passed and Allan fired a second time, at the largest nonfatal target he could see. The hot beam caught the man in the right buttock.

Allan sprang to his feet and started for the two downed men. Their weapons were ready to fire and his was not, but it took several seconds for the worst effects of shock to hit a severely burned person. The first man had his hand on his holster but seemed unable to open it. Allan kicked him in the head as he went by. The second had his pistol in hand but was trying to crawl behind the rock, expecting a finishing shot when the five seconds were up. Allan caught the weapon with his toe and sent it sliding across the rock, out of sight. He turned back instantly to the first killer, ready to shoot if necessary, and saw that the kick had sent him on into unconsciousness.

Allan picked up the light, took the first man's pistol, and after a short hunt found the second weapon. A brief search located the standard issue knife each man had in his spaceman's emergency kit. Then he yelled for Secret to join him.

The short blonde stared at the groaning man trying to see the hole in his buttock, and the second one lying unconscious, with something like awe. "Holy life, Allan, I didn't know you could fight like that! I always thought you were a little . . . on the mild side. I mean I loved you anyway, but once out of your classroom . . ."

Allan grinned in the darkness. This was probably the best-handled combat he had ever engaged in, but he was not going to tell an admiring woman that. "I've learned a lot not taught in school during nine years," he said instead. "But save the praise for later; let's find out who these two are."

When he had the would-be assassins awake and propped up on elbows facing the light, Allan learned one interesting fact immediately. Both were Earthmen and neither was from the colony. A brief search while Secret held the light and gun gave him the answer. They were out-of-uniform members of the Space Service.

Allan stared at the sullen men in deep anger. The fact that anyone would try to kill a Conscience was bad; that they were from the force supposed to protect them was far worse.

After an hour of futile questioning, Allan realized the two were not going to talk except under drugs. There was nothing he could do except send a security party from the colony to bring them in. As he had expected, there was a part from the glide plane's power-plant in one man's emergency pack, and a crystal from the radio in the other.

"You two are going to be left here for a couple of days to think over your sins," Allan finally told them. "I don't think you can get far, and I'd advise you not to hide; your packs don't hold much water. The penalty for killing a Conscience is death, as you well know, but since you didn't succeed maybe they'll let you off with deep-trance rehabilitative personality reorganization."

The men refused to answer, or even meet his eyes. Allan finally donned his pack again and led Secret a kilometer toward the glide plane before stopping for what remained of the night. When the first light of dawn awoke them he felt as if he hadn't slept at all, and it took a distinct effort of will to struggle erect.

By noon they were back at the glider. Allan had the stolen parts installed and the machine operable within five minutes, but it was better than an hour before the vagrant winds finally

123

died long enough to let him hastily cut the tiedowns and jump aboard. Taking off on rough ground and without a headwind was very dangerous in the underpowered craft, but there was no other way. The wind started again as the wheels cleared, a strong gust from the rear that immediately cost the plane lift and set them bumping along on the grass. They were near the end of the clear area and had to get airborne at once or try to stop and turn back into the wind, a dangerous procedure. Secret made her decision and kept going. The rough brush that could tear the light craft apart drew rapidly closer, and Allan gripped his seat in horrified fascination. But Secret knew what she was doing. The following breeze died and was instantly replaced by one from ahead and to the left. She swung the plane squarely into it, and almost instantly they cleared and rose ten meters. Within twenty seconds they were fifty meters off the ground. And then they had enough speed to be independent of the headwind, and were safe.

"Are you going to call Captain Schultz?" Secret asked as they settled down for the slow trip back.

Schultz was the commanding officer of the neverlander that had brought Allan. The ship was not on a regularly scheduled run, and was waiting in orbit overhead. But Allan knew every man on board, and their two attackers had not been part of the crew. "No, I want to find out what's happened at the colony first," he replied, and despite Secret's obvious curiosity refused to discuss his plans. Two hours later, as they descended through the lower turbulence to land, he had the satisfaction of confirming an expectation. There was a second shuttle standing not far from the one that had brought him down.

"Brigadier General Timothy Terhune," said Allan, pointing. "I think you can guess why he's here."

17

"Then those were *his* men!" cried Secret, alarm in her voice.

"Don't mention them at all; let me do the talking for the P.P. Corps," Allan said urgently as they descended toward the landing field. "That's an official order as well as a personal request, sweetheart."

Secret was too busy with the controls to answer, but Allan saw the quick anger on her face. It faded as the wheels touched and cleared again in a heavy gust, and she concentrated on getting them down alive. He could only hope she would remember the order after the anger was forgotten.

The wings were caught and the craft pulled into the hangar by two men in Space Service blue. When the door cut off the wind behind them they stepped out, and were asked to report at once to the colony administration building. One of the patrolmen served as an escort, staying slightly ahead of Allan as if only accompanying them.

Inside the low open building where Pat maintained his official desk they encountered several men in Service blue, hurrying about various tasks. The plump colony administrator was sitting on a foamfab couch, his face slightly pale. Behind Pat's desk was a tall gray-haired officer in formal dress, sitting ramrod straight and issuing a rapid stream of orders. One white Space Service star glittered on his shoulder.

Their escort nodded politely at the couch, and they joined Pat and waited for the general to notice them. Within five minutes the building was empty except for themselves and a guard, and General Terhune finally rose and advanced around the desk with hand extended. His grip was firm and his deep crisp voice cordial when he said, "Very happy to meet you, Conscience Odegaard. I've heard nothing but good about you, and was delighted to hear you'd been chosen as one of the P.P. sector chiefs. Congratulations, and I hope you can help me straighten out the mess we have here."

Allan formally introduced Secret, and then asked what had happened since they left two days before. The tall officer smiled and said, "I had received instructions to prepare this planet for six-hundred new colonists before Conscience Holmes declared the butterflies intelligent. They are now on their way. Since I've been hearing bad reports on Administrator Bartolini and the lack of progress here, I came to see for myself. It didn't take long to learn that the situation was even worse than I'd heard. I declared martial law on this planet about an hour ago, and assumed command myself. We intend to be ready for those new people. I'm shipping Bartolini back to Earth tomorrow, along with a full report on the situation and a request to the Colonization Department that he be permanently reassigned. I am going to send Conscience Holmes back with him, but only because she needs to appear before the appropriate World Council committee and defend her decision to abandon this planet. You are free to accompany her if you wish, or resume your duties elsewhere until the issue here is resolved."

"Under Space Service regulations," Allan said slowly, "when martial law is declared, all reserve officers automatically assume their active rank. Secret becomes a colonel, and I am a brigadier general. Therefore . . ."

"Therefore nothing," Terhune cut him off quickly and smoothly. "I am your senior by about ten years, as well as commanding officer of this sector. You are under my authority as long as you work within my jurisdiction."

Terhune was right, and there was nothing Allan could do at the moment. The general had the authority, and certainly the power. "Very well. I am performing an evaluation of Conscience Holmes's report and would like to continue my work. I'll let you know in the morning if I wish to accompany her back to Earth."

"Fine. In the meantime, Mr. Bartolini, I suggest you pack your personal effects, excluding official records which I am going to keep. I'll see all of you again in the morning."

When they stepped outside the sun was setting. Allan and Secret walked the subdued Pat to his house. To their surprise they saw his bags already packed, and Astrid sprawled comfortably on the big couch, swinging one long leg. Buck Terhune was sitting in the solid foamfab chair.

The big woman rose to greet them, and Allan was again impressed by the sheer size and magnificence of her body. "I want you to sleep in the new arrival's house tonight, Pat," she said immediately. "If you insist on staying here I'll go with Buck to his place. To preserve what little respect your friends here may have left for you . . ."

Pat stopped as though struck. Allan glanced at his face, and had to look away.

After a long moment of silence Pat said slowly, "I thought there was someone else, but Buck Terhune, my worst enemy . . . why did you do it, Astrid?"

She glanced uncomfortably at Allan and Secret, obviously disturbed by their presence, but finally said, "I'm tired of mothering a boy; I wanted a man for a change. And Buck will be the new administrator when General Terhune leaves."

"I didn't know the status meant that much to you. Well, we live and learn. Certainly I'll stay in the guest house, I wouldn't want to disturb you two. Have fun."

Pat grabbed two bags as Allan reached for the third, and almost ran from the room. The two P.P.s left the broken man in the halfway house and returned to Secret's quarters, where Allan immediately seized the nectar and plant samples he had obtained two days earlier. He turned to leave again.

"Where are you going?" Secret asked in surprise.

"To the lab; I want to run an analysis on the head and these plant tissues. Try to get some sleep; I may need you before morning."

"But—but what are you going to *do?*" she demanded in exasperation.

Secret was questioning more than his wish to run a chemical analysis. Allan slipped an arm around her bare shoulders and said, "Unless there's a second Buck Terhune around I'm going to keep fighting." And he kissed her quickly and left.

Just before dawn Allan found the answer. He got Secret and Pat out of bed, and with their help rolled the glide plane they had used out of the hangar. He took off into the next steady breeze, wondering if a laser beam would come out of the darkness to send him crashing in flames. None did, and as the rapid dawn paled the sky in the east he set a course for Mount Charlemagne.

Allan found the two military assassins where he had left them, comfortable and with their wounds treated, but with empty canteens. He wrote out a confession for each, and realized when they almost contemptuously refused to sign them that they were expecting to be rescued at any moment. Obviously a shuttle from the general's neverlander had touched down around Charlemagne's flank, out of sight and hearing of the two P.P.s, and they had walked in. Their rendezvous time had passed and the shuttle crew would be looking for them.

There was no way he could coerce the two men into signing. Allan accepted the inevitable, searched their emergency kits again, and left his water canteen when he walked away. Once out of their sight he calmly signed both confessions himself, using the names he had seen on the fatigues they had stuffed into their kits when they donned civilian clothes.

The landing had not been too dangerous—Allan had gained some skill in estimating the probable duration of a ground

128

wind by watching the degree of yield in the vegetation—but the takeoff was more difficult. After thinking it over he redid his ground straps where they could be released by a single tug, and ran lines from each to a rope that he took into the small cabin. In less than five minutes the breeze changed until it was blowing directly at the light plane. Allan opened the throttle and yanked on the release cord. He had to steer with one hand while pulling in the rope and closing the cabin door, and the light craft veered sharply to the right. He corrected just as a long wing almost touched the grass, and picked up enough speed barely to clear the ground at the edge of the brush. Fortunately, the wind held and he was soon safe in the slow air stream below the turbulent layer.

It was only a little after noon when Allan landed again at High Hope. The earlier excitement and bustle had died away, but there was now an armed guard at the hangar. He helped Allan roll the plane inside, and said, "General Terhune would like to see you in the administration building, sir."

Allan nodded, and left for the inevitable confrontation. He was not surprised to see Secret and Pat there when he entered the round building. In the careful game of power politics the general was playing, it seemed unlikely he would have sent them away before learning why Allan had left.

"Good afternoon, General Odegaard," the service officer rose and greeted him with formal correctness. "I placed no restriction on your movements last night, having no idea you were planning a trip. In the future please obtain my personal permission before leaving High Hope."

"Certainly, sir," Allan agreed, glancing around the room. There were no guards present, but the general's adjutant, a colonel, sat at the next desk. "I'm happy to see you haven't sent Conscience Holmes to Earth yet, since her planned trip is no longer necessary. I am reversing her decision."

There was a brittle silence, electric with tension. Allan looked at Secret. She had turned white with shock, but held

129

her peace. The adjutant stopped work and stared at his commander. Allan could almost see the mental gears turning as the general absorbed the unexpected blow. After a moment he said, "Ah, I can't, ah, permit a change at this point, Conscience Odegaard. Since the formal declaration by Conscience Holmes and my override order have . . . ah, already been submitted to the World Council, I . . ."

"I am withdrawing her declaration; there is no need for your countermanding order, sir. To be absolutely clear and explicit I will file a new declaration, stating unequivocally that the butterflies are unintelligent insects."

"And, ah, how did you arrive at this conclusion?" the general asked, as though feeling his way.

"Simple enough, sir. On our trip of two days ago Conscience Holmes and I obtained, for the first time, the head of a dead butterfly. We found it in a hatchery the creatures use in the nearby mountains. I dissected that head last night, and learned that they have the enlarged anterior ganglia common to insects, and not a true brain. It is literally impossible for a butterfly to be intelligent."

Secret jumped to her feet. "Then how do you account for their communicating with us!" she demanded angrily; her face had gone from white to red.

"We'll get to that in a moment," Allan said, his voice controlled. "Please sit down and don't interrupt again."

Secret opened her mouth as though to protest, and Allan turned his profile to the two officers and gave her a wink with the hidden eye. Still disturbed, she reluctantly sat down.

"There's another matter I'd like to bring to your attention, sir," Allan went on. He produced the two handwritten papers from his pocket. "I have here two signed confessions from members of your ship's crew. They attempted to kill Conscience Holmes and me as we were leaving the butterfly hatchery. Both state they were acting on your direct orders, with

130

the understanding that they were to wear civilian clothes and there would be no military record of the executions."

General Terhune, still standing, perceptibly stiffened. The adjutant caught his breath in an audible gasp. Allan saw his hand creeping toward his holstered pistol.

"I used the aircraft's radio to send these charges, in code, to Captain Schultz," Allan went on, his voice shaking slightly. "They are now a matter of record on Earth. I don't know how thoroughly you have your men indoctrinated, but I find it impossible to believe there could be more than a few like the two killers you sent against us. I respectfully request that you surrender your command to me, as next senior officer in the sector, and accept quarters arrest until you can be returned to Earth for trial."

The adjutant's hand was openly on his laser. He looked questioningly at his superior, whose face had turned pale. The general's voice trembled when he said, "I'll see you in hell first, sir!"

"There is no legal way I can force you to surrender your command," Allan continued, his voice becoming steady as he saw how badly he had hurt Terhune. "But I assure you a message will arrive within the next few hours, ordering you to turn command over to your adjutant and report back to Earth. P.P. Administrator Wilson maintains a direct contact with the Secretary of the Space Service."

The general's color had returned. "This is the worst non-sense I've ever heard in my life!" he said in a loud voice, and turned to the adjutant. "Place all three of them under arrest! I want them confined and guarded until further notice."

"Colonel, if you draw that laser I'll charge you as an accessory after the fact," Allan said, turning to the other officer. "It will be the end of your career."

The colonel, his hand already on the butt of the pistol, hesitated. Allan saw calculation on his face as he tried to weigh the odds, and realized the man was not privy to the general's

131

plans. He was not surprised. The Space Service was an elite military force, and not even a sector commander could hide more than a few professional assassins in the ranks.

"I think you know your plan to discredit the P.P. Corps hasn't worked, General Terhune," Allan said to the stiffly erect officer. "It was an ingenious scheme—beautiful animals that seemed intelligent, although your brother had discovered their hatchery and knew otherwise, a ruling by a Conscience that you could override and take to the World Council knowing you would win—but it has failed. You had to attempt to eliminate us after we discovered the butterfly life cycle because you knew I'd countermand Secret's order and ruin your chance to make the Corps look ridiculous. And during my last visit to Earth I heard some talk about you that could explain what you hope to gain. You're ready to retire after thirty years, with no higher rank than brigadier despite all your work for New Roman causes. Your associates in the party promised you a member's seat on the World Council if you discredited us, didn't they? Loomis of Florida is ready to retire, and that's your home state and a safe Roman district."

The way the suddenly stricken man almost wilted before their eyes told Allan his guess had been correct. The colonel's hand had moved away from his holster, and his face showed that he now believed Allan.

"Those confessions will never hold up in court," the general said feebly. "The men will retract them tomorrow."

"Probably," Allan agreed. "But it doesn't matter. You'll retire after the investigation, and you won't run for political office. I realize I can't put you in rehabilitation where you belong, but your military career is over. General—I suggest you start packing."

"You mean the butterflies have to *die?*" Secret asked, horrified.

"I'm afraid so," Allan replied. They were back in the guest-

132

house, where he had been telling Secret and Pat of his discoveries. "The tall trees must come down over the entire planet, and with their only source of food gone the butterflies will vanish. It's always regrettable to see a species die, and of course we'll analyze every molecule in a few specimens to be certain no biochemicals of possible value are lost. But the need for habitable planets is urgent; we do well just to preserve the ones with species that show budding intelligence. And I think Beauty can easily spare the trees. The pollen from their flowers is so fine it passes through lung tissue directly into the bloodstream, where it has the same effect as a mild opiate. Chemically it resembles serotonin, and is almost impossible to isolate once it's in the body. You can fight off the effect— Buck Terhune did—but it takes a lot of will-power. The people here have been working in a light state of euphoria since the colony was founded, which explains why they've accomplished so little."

"And the communication with the butterflies? You haven't explained that," said Secret.

"That was a puzzler," admitted Allan. "I found the answer when I ran the flowertree tissue samples through the analyzer. There were traces of a second type of pollen. I got the clothes I wore while climbing and found quite a bit more clinging to them, on the front side only. It seems these trees are male and female, and only the female pollen gets scattered freely by the wind. The butterflies fertilize them by carrying pollen from the male to the female during their feeding, in the same manner as smaller flying insects. Both are mild opiates, and when you combine them you get a strong hallucinogenic drug, where only a tiny touch will have you hallucinating. When you stand downwind from a butterfly you're very likely to get both at once. The primary effect is to heighten your awareness of bodily sensations from below to above the threshold of consciousness. The images and sensations you feel are those

133

of your own body, not nonverbal communication with a butterfly."

There was a moment of silence. Then Pat said musingly, "So I get to keep my job, even though I've lost my wife."

"I'm afraid not," Allan said, low-voiced.

Pat stood up, leaned forward to place the glass he had been holding carefully on the table, and walked out of the door.

"Allan! Was that necessary?" Secret demanded the instant the plump man was out of hearing.

"I'm afraid it was. Pat is a very nice guy, but no administrator. I'm going to recommend that Terhune's order removing him stand. There's no excuse for this situation having dragged on so long. And I'm going to ask that Buck Terhune be recalled, of course. I could never prove conspiracy, but my recommendation alone should be enough to get him sent back to Earth. I can't prove Astrid threw that poisonous seed at me either, though I'm certain she did it herself or told Buck where we'd be. They deserve each other. And that leaves only you."

"Me!"

"Yes, you. Surely you realize your work on the original decision was something less than satisfactory?"

"No I damn well don't! What do you think you are, a little infallible genius? When I think of the way I pulled you through Alien Psych, and some of the compromises you've arranged on other worlds—why damn you!"

Secret was on her feet facing him, breathlessly angry. Suddenly feeling very old and tired, and with no trace at all of genius, Allan rose and said, "Your performance was poor. You let the Terhune brothers sucker you into the decision they wanted while the facts were in front of you. The New Romans gain seats in every election. This could have been the start of a drive to discredit the Corps that would have ended with a Roman majority in the World Council. I'm not going to recommend any disciplinary action—your past record

134

is too good for that—but I have no choice but to give you a low rating."

Allan followed Pat into the night. But he had taken only a few steps when there was a rush of feet behind him, and a sobbing Secret tackled him neatly around the knees and brought him crashing to the ground.

18

A gentle breeze shook the leaves on the branches hiding him, and Allan extended his nonreflecting binoculars to the edge of the green fringe. The dwarf had given the Earthman's blind several sharp glances earlier, when the glasses inadvertently moved greenery. At the moment this subject was sitting in its high nest, idly searching one lightly furred thigh for parasites. Allan saw that those it caught were discarded rather than eaten. He looked down to make a note, and when he returned to the glasses the dwarf had got to its feet and was leisurely stretching. This male was approximately 120 centimeters tall, with the broad shoulders and heavy musculature of his kind. In one G he would weigh in at over 50 kilograms, and Zwergwelt was a 1.08 G world. Except for the height, the resemblance to a hairy naked man was startling.

The dwarf stepped out of his carefully woven vine basket and dropped to a lower limb. Moving with the easy grace of an animal at home in the arboreal pathways, he ambled to an intersecting branch and shifted to the next tree. The neighboring giant was a nut-bearer, and on a planet without seasons a few seeds were always ripe. The short hominid picked two large ones as he walked toward the trunk. Just as the leaves started to hide the dwarf Allan saw him pause, heft one of the nuts, and suddenly let fly. From out of his sight came a thin scream of fear, overriding the soft ripping sound of a body falling through the vegetation.

The hunter disappeared into the thicker lower growth, hurrying to reach his prey before another hungry predator found it on the ground. Allan settled back, and wrote on his pad that an adult male dwarf had obtained a meal of nuts and meat within two minutes after starting his evening hunt.

Such proficiency should have indicated intelligence of a relatively high order. But the ease with which the sturdy hominid had obtained his meal was due as much or more to a bountiful environment. The slain animal was almost certainly one of the large rodents who lived primarily off the nuts of that particular type of tree. The dwarfs could eat almost any seed, tuber, or fruit in the woods, as well as meat.

Once again, nothing had been proven. Allan stared at his notebook, knowing from long experience that the three days of data would be inconclusive when statistically analyzed. The dwarfs had an extremely large repertoire of situational responses, but so far he had not recorded any actions unambiguously proving intelligence; they could as well be complex instinctual responses.

Allan gathered his gear, slipped on the backpack, and descended slowly and cautiously to the ground. There was just enough time to reach the field station before dark. He set a brisk pace through the moderate undergrowth, glad of the chance to stretch cramped legs. There were few worlds with continents where a temperate year-round climate produced huge trees and little brush. He was more accustomed to struggling through dense jungles or primeval swamps.

One of the several rocky hills in the area was on his left, with a small limestone cliffside that paralleled his path. The trees grew so close to the vertical shoulder that several branches touched it, and a solid curtain of leafy vines almost hid the stone. Allan had passed this way earlier, but at a

136

distance. From this close, something about the rock face seemed odd, subtly wrong. He paused, staring at the thickest cover near the center. After a moment he identified the oddity; the coloring was off.

Allan took a step toward the vines, and froze when a savage scream sounded almost in his ear. A second later a heavy body landed on his back, knocking him to the ground. Short but powerful arms locked around his chest and a hard head burrowed beneath his jaw, sharp canines seeking the jugular.

Allan exerted all his strength and pulled his chin down, at the same time rolling over and trying to pin his attacker. His left arm was free and he brought the hand around to push desperately against a thick jawbone, aware without pain that the champing teeth had already cut into his neck. He heard several sharp clicks as his opponent tried to catch his fingers, and abruptly the creature rolled Allan in turn, swinging its head free. Allan continued the roll and they ended up lying side by side. Very quickly he brought up a knee, planted it in a firm belly, and shoved with all his strength. The dwarf lost its grip around his shoulders and slid a meter away. Almost instantly the short hominid bounced to its feet and launched itself in a dive at his throat, now exposed again. The Earthman doubled up both legs and caught his hairy opponent on the chest with his boots. This time Allan heaved so hard the smaller dwarf went flying back against the vine-covered cliff. Allan made a half-roll away to free his right hip and grabbed for the laser there. It cleared the holster just as the dwarf, which had regained its footing in seconds, ended the combat by darting behind a bush. The creature was visible again a second later, but Allan held his fire. There was a final scream of animal rage, and then it was gone.

Badly shaken, Allan got to his feet and brushed himself off. He was bleeding profusely from several lacerations of the neck, but none seemed deep. He opened his pack for the medical kit, and applied an antiseptic coagulant. When the bleeding stopped he covered the torn areas with plastiskin bandages. His clothes were soaked with blood, but there was nothing he could do about that at the moment.

Allan had recognized his attacker; it was the female who claimed this territory. Whether she wanted him for dinner or was simply defending her land was a moot question. The dwarfs lived alone except for temporary alliances for mating, and the females were fully as vicious as the slightly larger males. It was his own fault he had been attacked; a short detour to the right would have kept him out of her way.

Strange; he would never have knowingly walked into the territory of a female leopard at the time of the evening hunt, but had moved into the dwarf's area without conscious thought. Because they were both hominids and he had the deeply ingrained male chauvinism common to their kind?

The dwarfs did not have a leopard's deadly claws, but their dentition included four long matched cutting fangs. And in addition to throwing nuts and branches, Allan had seen one male use a knobbed stick as a club. Neither of these justified a claim of intelligence, but it did make them fearsome opponents. Although the forest abounded in herbivores three times their size, the omnivorous dwarfs were the only large meat-eaters. His carelessness had almost cost him his life.

Allan walked four meters to the vines against which he had kicked the female, and pulled them apart. There had been no sound of solid impact when they stopped the hurtling body, and he saw why; there was a head-high cave behind the thick cover. The dark opening also explained why he had noticed a subtle change in color from outside, though the leafy growth completely shielded the entrance.

Allan had a powerlight in his pack. He took it out, and with laser pistol ready in his right hand, edged through the vines. Five meters in both floor and ceiling started rising, and then the narrow tunnel widened into a small underground grotto. Allan moved the light around. He was standing in a circular cavern about twelve meters in diameter, with a low concave roof. The room was empty except for a single figure, seated on a natural stone bench protruding from the rear wall.

Allan focused his torch on the lone inhabitant. It was a statue, apparently made of clay, and almost human in appearance. The workmanship was crude, but it had clearly defined features, a normal head, and four limbs. The scale was slightly larger than human. No attempt had been made to indicate hair, the ears were outsized, and the lips were huge and ugly, extending like two halves of a saucer broken in the center and lying on top of each other, the round sides protruding. This was not a dwarf cast twice life size, nor a man.

Allan moved closer and touched the statue, then turned his light and swept it across the chamber floor. The stone was covered with a fine layer of powdered lime; only his own footsteps showed. He had an almost certain feeling this room had not been entered for decades, perhaps centuries. And yet the oddly made crude figure seated on its soft stone bench was composed of simple clay, just as it had appeared, and was not even fire-cured. It should have crumbled to pieces within a few days of its making, from loss of moisture.

Allan shook his head in bafflement, then conceded the mystery was beyond present understanding and turned away. Outside again, he pulled the vines back in place. The grotto was as well hidden as before.

Dusk was falling, but Allan easily found the main herbivore's game trail that led to the local station. He walked the remaining three kilometers lost in thought; on this trail he was safe from attack. There had been many mysteries during his years in space, but this was surely one of the oddest. It was within the physical skills of the dwarfs to have made the statue, but they were not sufficiently advanced in culture or intelligence to have need for a god. And if it had been formed by someone else—who, when, and why? And what kept the fragile clay together?

139

The last yellow rays of Pollux had faded when Allan emerged at the base of a low hill, crowned by the standard foamfab dome of a temporary human structure. Halfway up he used a special key to let himself through a gate in the charged protective fence that encircled the building. Trees that approached the fence from either side had been cut down, eliminating aerial pathways, but new green bushes were growing where the original brush had been burned away.

At the door Allan was met by Victoria Gant, the chief of the eight personnel at this field location. She was a short, dumpy brunette, slightly older than Allan and fanatically devoted to her job. She saw the bandages on his neck, asked what had happened, and insisted on treating the wounds again when Allan admitted to having been bitten. He sighed, and submitted with good grace.

"You know very well you may have left some foreign matter in those cuts," Victoria admonished, when she had seated him in her office and opened the station's large medical kit. "Even if not, these wounds need to be cleaned and flushed better than you could manage yourself."

Allan removed his upper garments, and Victoria opened each laceration, poured on foaming antiseptic, and let the fresh blood and liquid run out on the floor. It hurt when she carefully tucked the torn edges of flesh back together, but Allan gritted his teeth and endured. She opened a new tube and carefully covered each wound with a white gel he recognized as a coagulant and flesh sealant, then rebandaged them after the bleeding stopped.

"We're late for dinner; hurry into some clean clothes," Victoria said when Allan rose. She started cleaning up the small mess they had made on the floor.

Thirty minutes later Allan had bathed, changed, and was eating a dinner made almost entirely of local products. The scientists stationed on Zwergwelt were lucky; the best of concentrated foods started to taste monotonously alike after the hundredth meal.

Two other dinner guests had just arrived, the Director of the Zwergwelt stations, Dr. Boris Magnitsky, and his aircar pilot. The elderly scientist spent most of his time at Main Base in the central highlands, but visited the three outlying field stations regularly. The four buildings were the only human inhabitations on the planet. When the dwarfs were declared intelligent this world had been proscribed except for rigidly controlled scientific work.

"Did you finish today, Conscience?" the director asked, after picking delicately at his food. His voice was deep and pleasant, but had a slight quaver of age. There was a faintly sardonic smile on his wrinkled face. "I'll be returning to Main tomorrow, if you need a ride."

Allan decided to meet the challenge head-on. "Dr. Magnitsky, I haven't uncovered one fact that invalidates the prolonged observations your people have made," he said slowly. "Still, I'm not willing to reverse a prior decision without an intensive investigation of my own. I'm going to stay here a few more days."

"Then you'll have to catch Jacque on the regular supply run next week; we can't spare the aircar for a special trip," said the director, rising. He was a very tall man now stooped with age, the first scientist over a hundred Allan had seen at an out-planet location. Magnitsky was also a giant in modern biology, and when he had reported that the Conscience who had ruled on the Zwergwelt dwarfs six Eryears ago had been wrong, Sector Chief Allan had been dispatched immediately to check on the claim. Politicians were always trying to influence the decision of a Conscience, but Magnitsky had impeccable scientific credentials. There were also several extrespsychologists on his staff.

This problem on Pollux Five had arisen at a bad time. World Council elections would be held on Earth within sixty days, and if the New Roman opposition could prove that a highly compatible world like Zwergwelt had been withheld from colonization by error, the embarrassment could cost the Conservationist Party the election. The P.P. Corps had been quietly doing its job during the six Ermonths since Allan had ruined the plan to discredit them on Beauty. It had seemed reasonable to expect another attempt, but when this new and potentially damaging problem arose, Allan had been unable to blame it on political interference. The reputation of the scientists involved was too high, and the work on which they based their claim of previous error too well done.

Allan had been informed by Siggi Wilson that it was terribly important the original decision be proven correct. Unfortunately, to date he had no proof that would enable him to so rule.

19

The five men and three women finished their meal and started drifting into the common room for the night's entertainment; their Director had brought some new Tri-D discs. "Going to watch the Olympics with us, Conscience?" asked Margarete Olmedo, a pretty, olive-skinned girl who had been more than casually friendly to Allan during his short stay.

Allan was tempted. It had been a long day crouching in his blind, and whether or not you liked sports was immaterial; the tapes showed Earth. But he also needed to start extracting the figures that were going to build to an inconclusive statistic, and tomorrow he wanted to get an early start and construct an observation post near the female dwarf which had attacked him. She had launched herself from an overhead branch when he made a definite move toward the hidden cave. If that was not simply a coincidence . . . Regretfully, he declined, and saw the coldness on Margarete's face when she turned away.

In the small cubicle that had been assigned to him Allan sat on the foamfab bunk and patiently assembled his data into class orders. He ran a preliminary analysis in all classes for central value, and compared the result to the established intelligence scales used by all P.P.s. As he had expected, the dwarfs were a borderline case, with a slight bias on the lower side. Apparently the previous Conscience had been influenced by their biological classification as hominids and their demonstrated competence. Allan could not believe his predecessor had seen the hidden grotto and its god figure; the air of antiquity had been too strong.

Borderline was not good enough. Allan sighed, and ran a comparison check between his own data and the refined statistics gathered by station personnel and correlated by Magnitsky. The two were almost identical when obtained under similar conditions. Unless their more detailed studies were faked, which seemed highly improbable, Magnitsky's case was practically proven.

The idea of delaying a decision until after the next election occurred to Allan, but he discarded it immediately. In the first place such conduct was against his principles. In the second, he considered the commitment Mankind had made to avoid old errors of arrogance a lasting one, not subject to changing conditions. If he was wrong he would as soon learn it with the coming election. Opening up new worlds to colonization was the major platform adopted by the New Romans. They had built a good, practical case for the idea that any planet not owned by civilized beings should be available. So far that meant every habitable world Earthmen had explored.

Zwergwelt had a nineteen-hour day and he had worked

143

through half the short night. Allan tumbled into bed and slept dreamlessly until called for breakfast.

After the excellent meal Allan lingered over a second cup of stimcaf with Magnitsky, who was preparing to leave. The aged scientist seemed to have something on his mind. Finally he pulled a flimsy sheet from a pocket and said, "I received an interesting rumor on the daily activity report from Main Base this morning, Allan. The word is out that you're scheduled to leave here for Earth and become Siggi Wilson's deputy administrator. Also, that you just might break a short tradition and replace Wilson when he retires next year."

Magnitsky chuckled, and Allan realized his face must have shown his surprise. The present P.P. Deputy Administrator was leaving and Allan had been offered the job just before coming here, but the thought he was being groomed to replace Wilson was new. The Corps was now firmly established as a semimilitary agency, and the short tradition of selecting retired Space Service generals as administrators had seemed likely to become equally firm.

What Magnitsky could not know was that Allan planned to decline the promotion. He had been in the field now for ten years, eight as a Conscience and the last two as a sector chief. He found more satisfaction in his present job than anything crowded Earth had to offer.

The two men shook hands and Allan slipped on his backpack. At the door he was stopped by Victoria Gant, who asked where he would be if they should need to reach him.

"I'd rather not take a chance on disturbing the subject under observation, unless it's an emergency," he answered, somewhat surprised.

"Understood; but there may be one."

Allan yielded, and showed her the low cliff on his terrain map. An hour later he was sitting on top of it, hidden behind some bushes near the edge. The tallest trees reached well above the limestone outcropping, and he patiently scanned their upper levels with the binoculars. In ten minutes Allan located the female dwarf. She had built her nest on the second tree away from the edge, in a large forked branch slightly below the level of the cliff top.

The thick brush provided an adequate shield, and Allan decided it would not be necessary to build a blind. He settled down to observing details of behavior and taking notes. This female had no children, and like the males, spent most of the morning napping and occasionally eating local fruits. At noon she left and made a circuit of what was obviously her territory, but returned for another nap. Allan began wondering where the dwarfs got their muscular power. Like male lions in the wild, they received hardly enough exercise to stay alive. Yet in fact both had strength out of proportion to their size.

As Pollux sank slowly toward the green horizon Allan entertained the hope that Victoria *would* send someone after him. At the least it would stir the female into activity; at most, she might exhibit protective behavior if strangers approached the cave. But nothing had happened when it was time to leave, and Allan donned his pack and crept backward, until he could rise and walk down the gentle slope to the north.

Allan reached the main game trail that led toward the station and started down it, mulling over the obviously high but unrealized potential of the dwarfs. For some reason he felt very listless and tired, as though drugged by fatigue. There was no reason for it, since he had spent most of the day lying on the ground in reasonable comfort, but the feeling persisted and even grew stronger as he walked.

Some instinct developed by a hundred brushes with death on primitive worlds alerted Allan to danger. He looked carefully around and saw nothing, but the uneasy feeling persisted. There was an abrupt bend just ahead in the trail, and without conscious intent his hand drifted to the laser in his belt as he started around it. And then he saw the waiting human female ahead and started to relax, and reached for the

145

pistol again when he realized she wore an odd black hood with a front panel that hid her face.

"Hold it!" called a harsh voice alongside the trail, and Allan turned to see a pistol barrel covering him from the shadowed bush. There was a crackling of brush from the opposite side, and a second armed and black-hooded figure emerged.

"Who are you? What do you want with me?" Allan demanded.

"You will know shortly," said the female who had waited in the trail, and Allan could not repress his startled surprise. The voice was muffled by the hood, but he was almost certain it was that of Victoria Gant.

The woman turned and started back down the trail, and one of the two men removed Allan's laser and gestured for him to follow. He had a slight dizzy spell, as though his body was almost too weak to endure excitement, but recovered and walked after her.

The masked woman led them toward the station at a brisk walk, but turned aside into an intersecting trail after less than a kilometer. Allan felt so weak it was all he could do to keep up, but forced himself to meet her pace. Two-hundred meters down the new trail she turned into the brush. Allan followed for a short distance, the two guards at his elbows, and emerged into a grassy clearing, a little delta formed by a sharp bend in a small swift river. Three other masked figures, one of them another woman, were sitting on the grass a few meters from the bank.

When he stopped walking Allan's legs almost betrayed him. He sat down and rested a moment, then looked up at the woman he knew to be Victoria and said, "This is an odd game, and I don't really want to play."

"It is not a game, and your participation is mandatory," the woman replied, her voice cold. "This is a Safeguard Squad, Conscience Odegaard."

Allan felt a small thrill of horror. He had heard the vaguest, most fleeting rumors about a secret society recently active on the outlying worlds, and the word "Safeguard" had been whispered. He had not believed the stories, nor put credence in hints that the recent deaths of two P.P.s had been something more than the accidents they appeared to be. The thought that some of the people he knew and worked with could don masks and become killers was insupportable. The horror he felt now was not for his own safety; it was the realization that the unacceptable was true.

"I have heard of you, but only vaguely," he said aloud. "Please tell me more about yourselves."

"In good time, Conscience. At the moment we have more urgent business. Please sign this."

She extended a single page, and Allan took and read it in the gathering twilight. It was the usual preliminary report filed over the subradio when a Conscience reached a decision, and imitated his writing style reasonably well. It stated that the dwarfs of Zwergwelt were definitely below the minimum intelligence level, and the decision of the previous Conscience was reversed. Zwergwelt was to be opened for full colonization. Allan's name and rank of sector chief had been typed in.

"I may very well file a similar report when I'm satisfied here, but I'll never sign this under duress," he said, handing it back.

"You will sign, and promptly," said the voice he was certain was Victoria's. "I have a hypnotic in this medical case, and its antidote. If I must I will drug you, order you to sign, and then administer the antidote before you stand trial. But in your present weakened condition the double drug dose might be fatal. I advise you to sign."

"Why are you trying to force me, when this is probably the decision I'm going to reach anyway?" he asked.

"Even if you were willing to overrule your mistaken predecessor, which we doubt, you made it perfectly clear in talking to Magnitsky that you intend to delay a decision until it's too late to affect the coming elections. We can't wait; this will be just what the New Romans need to throw the idiot Conservationists out of power, at long last. Now sign, or take your chances with the drugs."

She extended the paper to Allan again; he shrugged, accepted it, and signed. As he handed it back Allan said, "I don't understand the rules of the game. What's to prevent me from repudiating this the moment I reach a subradio?"

"If you are found innocent of Crimes Against Mankind in the trial you are about to undergo, you will be kept isolated in a nearby cave until after the election," said the woman, her voice even and very formal. "If found guilty as charged, you will be executed."

The horror came back, prickling at the skin of Allan's forehead. He had been seconds away from death on many occasions, and was frightened every time. But it was not fear that sent cold chills down his back; it was the knowledge he was dealing with self-appointed executioners. These people were willing to sit in judgment on him for what they alone considered crimes. He had thought such barbarism gone from human society.

Victoria slipped the report in her jacket. In measured tones she said, "Conscience Odegaard, you are charged with Crimes Against Humanity; specifically, with forbidding the colonization of dozens of worlds perfectly suited for human growth and expansion. You may speak in your own defense, and as judge I shall appoint a counselor for you. I suggest you take time to consult with him before the trial begins. I warn you fairly; if you are convicted by this jury," she swept a hand toward the woman and two men who had been waiting for them, "you will be summarily executed. This is not a game, as you referred to it earlier; for you it could hardly be more serious. To lose is to die."

"Just a moment," Allan said, raising one hand. "A minute

148

ago you referred to my 'weakened condition.' How did you know I was feeling badly?"

There was a short laugh behind the woman's black mask. "The salve Victoria Gant used on your wounds yesterday contained a new drug, discovered here on Zwergwelt. It acts very slowly, and weakens without killing. We had already planned to take you prisoner today, and the drug lowered your ability to resist."

It certainly had. Allan was so physically weak it was an effort to hold his head erect. His mind was clear, though, and he caught the illogic at once. "Then you had intended to force me to sign that false report even before you heard the conversation with Magnitsky. Right, Victoria?"

There was a short silence. Then she said: "Your guess as to my identity is not important; think what you wish. And yes, we had planned to take action today, even before we overheard the conversation that gave away your intentions. But enough talk. The jury and I will withdraw. The man on your right is the prosecutor. I appoint the one on the left as your counsel. The trial begins in ten minutes, and I repeat—if found guilty you die. Prosecutor, you may move out of hearing distance. I think he is now too weak to run."

The man on Allan's right followed Victoria, and the two stood talking in low tones a few meters away. The other one turned to Allan and said, "Now listen, Conscience, this trial is real, not just an excuse to execute you. If we win you'll be kept on the drug for a couple of months and released after the elections, just as the judge said. It won't matter then because our friends will be in power. Now the best way to beat this charge is to show what you've done *for* Mankind, to counteract the bad. I've read the folder on you, and it shows a lot of cases where you ruled 'questionable' species unintelligent, opening up several worlds to colonization. We'll throw those at the jury."

149

"Are you saying I can't defend the work of the P.P. Corps *in toto?*" asked Allan.

"Of course not! That's a sure way to lose. The Corps as a whole has done more to hold Man back from his rightful place in the galaxy than any organization in history. Some of those muddle-brained 'Consciences' and their bleeding-heart supporters have ruled us off worlds that could be colonized tomorrow. And why? Because of some dumb animal that just might develop intelligence a million years from now! That's what the Safeguard Squads have been organized to fight, Conscience. You know as well as I do that we need those worlds. But look, let's don't you and I argue; save it for the jury. Now will you do it my way?"

"For the moment," Allan agreed. His body felt as if it had been ravaged by a long illness, but his mind remained clear. Evidently the drug did not affect the nervous system. And his defender, whom he felt fairly certain was one of the local station personnel, sounded sincere. Allan also saw that it would be dark in a few minutes. If he could overcome this debilitating weakness he might find a chance to escape.

20

The defense counsel called to the judge and prosecutor. When they started back, Allan struggled to his feet and walked slowly toward the jury near the riverbank. His appointed attorney hastily followed and the other two moved to intercept him, but slowed when they saw he was making no effort to escape. Allan stopped in front of the woman and her two male companions, who had got to their feet, and sat down again. He was now less than fifteen meters from the water.

"The court is now in session," Victoria said promptly when she reached them. "Is the prosecution ready? And the defense?"

The two men mumbled an assent; apparently neither was accustomed to his role. Allan had been studying the three jurors in the fading light, and was convinced the second woman was pretty Margarete Olmedo. The two women at the local station who had been kindest to him were co-conspirators. He was equally certain he had not met the two male jurors. There was something in the way they moved, the easy but sure physical reactions of men accustomed to changing gravities, that said Space Service. Allan had a sudden grim hunch that one of those two would play a second role if the verdict was guilty; that of executioner. And if he enjoyed such tasks, which seemed likely, there was little chance he would vote for acquittal.

The prosecutor began his presentation, and Allan listened carefully. At first it might have been lifted directly from a hot speech by a New Roman politician, a familiar blend of fact, prejudice, and distortion. The diatribe was directed not so much against Allan as against the Conservationists in general and the P.P. Corps in particular. The charge that they had denied human access to hundreds of worlds was accurate. It was also true that no species had been found with a civilization comparable to Earth's, and with several thousand worlds already explored, there was no good reason to think one ever would. Man was apparently alone in the galaxy, and it was ridiculous and wasteful to refrain from relieving Earth's burdensome population when the means of transport and the empty worlds were available. The Conservationists had taken advantage of mistaken idealism and the gullibility of billions of voters to maintain their hold on power, at a cost to the future development of Man that was incalculable. Since they had succeeded in duping a majority of the voting public until now, a group dedicated to operating in secret for the benefit of

Mankind had been organized. They supported the New Roman party but were not a part of it. The Safeguard Squads were their enforcement arms, and had the vested power to bring known criminals to trial and execute sentence upon them.

The last few items were not part of the New Roman dogma, but Allan felt certain higher-up party officials must be aware of the existence of the Safeguard Squads. It was hard to operate in space without the active connivance of some members of the Space Service hierarchy. He had thought the scheming of General Terhune an isolated incident; now he was not so certain. The general had retired from the service, but was immediately appointed to a functionary's post in government. The New Romans were either actively supporting this extra-legal society or passively condoning it.

It was almost full dark now, and the judge produced a light and placed it on the grass, focused on Allan. Behind the glare Victoria Gant became a dim and lumpy figure, sitting on crossed legs. Only the prosecutor and defense counsel were still standing.

"Your honor, I have a question of legality," Allan said when the prosecutor finished. "Am I to understand that the only possible punishment for a guilty verdict is death? Why are there no lesser sentences? And if someone is found innocent, what keeps him from reporting you to the officials?"

There was a short wait, and when Victoria answered it was obvious she was choosing her words carefully. "There have been only two trials to date, and both produced guilty verdicts. The defendants would have been placed on one of the habitable worlds their own people caused to be isolated, if found innocent. As for death being the only sentence for guilt, I'd like to remind you that killing a Conscience is the one crime for which the Space Service is authorized to hold a field trial and execute upon conviction. It seems only fair that you be subject to the same penalty."

152

"Thank you for that enlightening comparison, your honor," said Allan, unable to keep the sarcasm out of his voice.

"Acting smart won't win you any favor with the jury, mister. Now if you want to live to see tomorrow you'd better start defending your career as a 'Conscience'."

"I'd like to do that, your honor," said Allan's counsel, hastily stepping forward. "I'm happy to be able to defend Conscience Odegaard, since he's certainly one of the better members of his club. I can name at least a dozen worlds where he made the decision that a questionable species was unintelligent, opening the way to colonization. Recently there was the case of Beauty, where he overruled one of his fellows and declared the planet okay after the stupid idiot had ordered the colonists off. He forced one of our friends in the Space Service to retire on that deal, but at least we got the planet. On the world of Misery, not one of the better planets for sure, he gave permission for the local spice processing company not only to continue its work, but to expand. Even on many worlds that he ruled ineligible for colonization, like the silicon-life planet Crystal, he okayed the installation or expansion of scientific stations. I maintain that his record as a Conscience is unusually good, and he should be spared and turned free after the election."

"The defense counsel makes some good points," said the prosecutor, without waiting for the judicial permission to speak. "Odegaard is admittedly one of the less softheaded members of his profession. But I deny that his record is really all that great, since he's followed the same line as the rest in ruling humans off any world where the local animals could so much as throw stones. If he's less guilty than most, it's strictly a matter of degree. Since we don't have any lesser sentence, I say we have no choice but to find this man guilty as charged."

The defense counsel took a step forward and started a rebuttal. Both men had got wrapped up in their role-playing

153

and were working hard; each seemed equally sincere. For the first time since the start of this wild trial Allan could almost believe that it was real. His defense counsel was arguing from a limited viewpoint, but judging by the effect on the prosecutor he was telling heavily. It was true that Allan was known as a hardheaded Conscience, influenced as much by biology as behavior, and he had made more compromises with idealism than most. And where the evidence was statistically uncertain, Allan always followed the guideline that intelligence had to be positively demonstrated. Many P.P.s ruled otherwise, as had his predecessor on Zwergwelt.

The two court opponents argued for almost an hour, while Allan stayed quiet and saved his strength. This world had no moon, and there was a light mist in the air, hiding the stars. Allan had been squinting his eyes for some time, to shut out the light and accustom them to darkness. When the judge asked him if he had anything further to say in his defense, he shook his head.

"Then the jury will vote immediately, since we judge by majority decision and consultation is not permitted," said the judge, picking up the light and swinging it toward the three seated figures. "All who vote 'guilty' please raise your right hand."

One hand, that of the man on the left, shot up immediately. Allan knew with almost certainty that he was staring at his intended executioner. The other man made no move. Margarete hesitated, started to raise a hand, and then nervously lowered it. Her agitation was apparent even through the shielding hood. The judge waited a moment, and Allan heard the relief in her voice when she finally said, "Vote noted. All innocent, same sign."

The man on the right raised his hand, and the woman followed suit. The one on the left muttered something under his breath.

"The verdict is innocent," said Victoria, her voice neutral

again. She swung the light back to Allan. "Conscience Odegaard, you will be held in custody for sixty days and then released, providing we win the election. I am sorry we must detain you . . ." She went into a lengthy apology, but Allan was no longer listening. He had planned to make his break when the judge passed sentence; now he would be risking his life when it was otherwise out of danger.

The ruling Victoria had forced him to sign would be promptly transmitted to Earth, but it was the one he would almost certainly have forwarded within a week anyway. It might well cost the Conservationists the election as anticipated, but that was no fault of Allan's; he had not made the original wrong decision. There was no good reason for him to risk his life, especially in this seriously weakened condition.

And then Allan realized he was ignoring one very important consideration. If he escaped and exposed the Safeguard Squads and their secret supporters, the scandal would very likely keep the New Romans out of power for at least another term. The coming election might be won or lost because of what he did tonight.

Allan tilted his torso and dived for the light, snatched it up, rolled to his feet, and hurled it at the left-hand juror. It caught him in the face, knocking him over as he was scrambling erect. Allan stiff-armed Victoria, sending her sprawling on her back, and ran for the water, crouching and zigzagging. There had really been no contest with his own conscience. It was far too strong to permit any choice but the one he had made.

A laser beam, aimed low, flashed past his legs on the right; he had miscalculated the timing. Allan threw himself at the grass, hit rolling, scrambled to his feet, and darted for the water again. After two seconds he cut hard to the left, and had the satisfaction of seeing a second beam miss by two meters. Then his foot touched water and he hurled himself forward in a long flat dive. In midair he felt a surge of weakness, so overwhelming he almost blacked out. The sudden tremendous exertion against the deadening effect of the drug had brought him to the edge of physical collapse.

A third laser beam burned him across the left thigh as his head hit water.

Allan felt the shock of the wound even through the faintness. The water was unexpectedly cold, and jarred him back to full consciousness. Momentum carried him into the strong central current, and he felt it pulling him down. He had snatched a deep breath as he dived, but it was only a minute before he suffered a frantic need for air. He slowly vented his breath, and managed a feeble stroke or two to keep himself under. Even that small effort brought blackness washing back over his mind. He hovered on the verge of awareness for a long moment, and then felt air on his face; his still inflated lungs had brought him back to the surface. He emptied them and sucked in air in a great gasp, and then a light swept over his head, came back, and as he turned on his face to dive a laser beam burned the air a few centimeters in front of his eyes. The water beyond exploded into a cloud of steam.

Allan managed another feeble stroke that took him down, but again lost his fragile hold on consciousness. For a timeless interval he hovered in the grip of shadows, eyes closed, moving as the current took him, and again broached the surface. The light found him immediately, but from farther away. When the laser beam came it boiled the water where he had just ducked, and he felt the heat before the current dragged him away.

When he came up for the third time Allan was past the point where the light was effective. The accumulated need for air was so great he had to take several deep breaths. The mist had lifted, and bright starlight revealed that the fast water had taken him around a bend.

The sound of someone crashing heavily through the brush reached Allan from the near bank, and he managed a few strokes to push himself farther out. He had submerged by the time the expected light swept the surface toward him. This time he managed to stay down for almost a minute, and when he came up again Allan knew he was safe.

It took a minimum of effort to keep afloat in the swift but smooth current. Allan gingerly felt over his burned leg, and for the first time discovered he was bleeding heavily. The beam had taken away some upper muscle tissue as well as skin. Function seemed unimpaired, but it was a nasty wound.

After another half kilometer a natural eddy swept Allan toward the bank. He recognized the area, and realized there was a place of refuge close at hand. When his feet touched bottom he fought the current to stand erect, finally succeeded, and staggered ashore. The extra effort made him weak again, and he had to lean against a tree. When he recovered Allan went on, hoping he was not leaving a blood trail in the grass. Within a hundred meters he had reached the rocky hill he sought, and walked around it toward the limestone cliffside. If the female dwarf was on the prowl now she would find an easy victim. But only the noises of the smaller animal population disturbed the night, and he found the rock face and its concealed cave without difficulty.

After carefully pulling the vines together behind him, Allan struggled up the slight incline to the grotto. In the pitch darkness inside he sat down and finished ripping off the trouser leg partly burned by the laser. Unable to make a tourniquet, he compromised by wrapping the cloth tightly around the wound, placing his left palm over it, and lying with the weight of his body on the hand.

Instead of recovering now that he was resting, Allan felt the familiar black fingers closing around his mind again; he must have lost a lot of blood. His imprisoned hand was swiftly growing numb, and he could not tell if the bleeding had slowed or was carrying him toward death. But Allan knew with absolute certainty that he could not rise from the powdered

157

limestone floor, that he must live or die on what he had managed to that point. The blackness deepened, grew more threatening, and Allan surrendered his hold on life and let the fingers pluck him up and cast him into a wider, stronger river, where he floated toward a more lasting darkness.

21

"Hey, Allan Trueheart, wake up there!"

Allan opened his eyes, gasped in fright, and shrank back from the incredible countenance bending over him. The huge flattened lips that extended ten centimeters beyond the lumpy nose twisted into a weird grin. "Come on, Keeper-of-the-Earthman's-Burden, on your feet. We're going for a little walk." The voice was high and peremptory, hauntingly familiar to Allan. What he saw was unbelievable. The rough clay statue had come to life and was kneeling beside him, one crude arm extended to help him up.

Allan closed his eyes to the nightmare, but it refused to go away. Instead he felt a large hand pulling him upward, and reluctantly got to his feet. The effort made his head swim and he staggered; only the supporting clay arm kept him from falling. He opened his eyes again, and with blurred vision saw that the little circular cavern was lighted by a dim blue radiance of unseen origin. He glanced at the roughly outlined face, a head higher than his own, and quickly looked away. The sight was unacceptable to the senses. He had to be delirious.

"Come on there, fella, let's take a little stroll and say hello to your friends in the Safeguard Squad. They're looking for you."

One grainy arm moved across Allan's back and a huge

hand clasped him under the right armpit. As the ponderous body urged him forward he instinctively gripped the supporting shoulder, and was half carried to the low tunnel. The living statue had to stoop to miss the ceiling. As they walked down the gentle slope Allan felt the rough clay under his hand. The surface did not move and shift to indicate internal muscular activity. With thumb and forefinger he tried to pinch off some material, and could not. In homogeneity alone it felt and acted like living tissue.

"Leave off trying to steal my corporal substance there, fella," said the slightly high but pleasant voice that Allan knew from long ago. They reached the vine curtain and carefully maneuvered through it. Pollux was almost overhead, its yellow rays high-lighting another beautiful day on a nearly perfect world.

Allan had revived slightly, though dizziness was a constant menace, waiting for a chance to pounce. He recognized the now familiar effect of the drug as a deep and abiding lassitude, but he was also feverish and not fully recovered from the shock of a serious wound. As they started through the woods, moving faster in the open, the exertion brought blackness swirling toward him. Just before it hit Allan finally remembered why the statue's voice was familiar.

"*Clay!*" he gasped. "Clay Forrester!" And then consciousness retreated and hovered, taunting him, just outside his skull. When the dark clouds lifted his companion was chuckling aloud.

"Straight on, fella, straight on. This is ol' Clay talkin', or at least his personality as *you* saw it when you knew him."

"But—but why?" Allan asked, feeling helpless and lost. "If you aren't human what's the purpose . . . ?"

"You'd have a hell of a time communicating with me in my elemental form, junior. And that's a pretty good *yuk!* if you understood it, 'cause it happens I *am* an elemental. And I chose Clay's personality out of the several I could have formed

159

from your memory 'cause this body I'm activating is made of the stuff, and that's just the type of obvious joke he'd like. It also fits in with the fact I've got to lay a few heavy words on you, and Forrester enjoyed nothing more than displaying his superior erudition. So just call me Clay."

The description of his former college friend was accurate enough. Allan remembered Clay with fondness, though he had an exasperating affectation of using expressions that had enjoyed a brief popularity and then died into history. Clay had remained a teacher when Allan joined the P.P. Corps, and to the best of his knowledge, carved out a successful career for himself on Earth.

They had reached the main gametrail leading toward the station, and Allan heard voices around a bend ahead: one was Victoria Gant's. "Yeah, they're lookin' for you, daddy-o," said Clay, the wide flat lips grinning in earthen mockery. "Stand to the side, and I'll hide us by casting a spell that'll dazzle the minds of men."

If this was nightmare or delirium it was terribly real. Allan clung to a sturdy bush and waited, Clay standing by his side. Victoria and two men Allan did not recognize rounded the bend. These strangers had to be the male members of the jury, the Space servicemen apparently sent here specifically to try him. One had a plastiskin strip across his forehead. As they passed, the bandaged man turned and looked directly at Allan. In two cold and remote gray eyes he saw a lingering fascination with the finality of death.

To this point Allan had accepted the unacceptable with numbed acquiescence. When the killer looked through him and searched the woods on both sides, it finally became too much to bear. He waited until the three hunters had passed out of hearing, and said, "I can't believe it any more."

Clay chuckled, a light, pleasing sound. "It took a pretty good tolerance to get this far, dad. But brace yourself, 'cause the worst is yet to come."

160

"If you can keep them from seeing us," Allan said slowly, "can't you do something about my physical weakness? Lend me some of the strength you've got animating that clay figure?"

"Could, but ain't gonna; want you just the way you are, for reasons of mental health you'll understand better later. That's why I brought you out in the sunlight. This would be tough on you in the dark. But let's follow your dedicated friends for the moment. And go ahead and talk; they can't hear us."

They stepped into the trail and started after the three humans. "Who are you?" Allan demanded. "Or perhaps I should ask, *what* are you?"

"I told you *what* I am, Allan; an elemental. We were there before your ancestors swung that first bone club, and will be there after your descendants have mutated themselves up the ladder, probably. But just to keep from making this too simple, only a small part of my consciousness is in this sloppy form supporting you. Most of it is back on the old home grounds, Mother Earth and environs."

"Then you're . . . God?" whispered Allan. The concept was alien in his scheme of beliefs.

"Naw, that's too simple also, Allan baby. There's nothing anthropomorphic about me in my basic form."

It was too much. Logic and reason failed, and a trained mind was useless. And then with a flash of insight Allan saw his way clear, and *accepted* the fact he was dealing with matters beyond logic and reason. There was a soft chuckle beside him, and he realized Clay was reading his thoughts as they formed.

"Yeah, keerect, dad. They do have to be *expressed,* though. Not even I can follow the subprocesses that eventually produce a mental verbalization."

For a moment Allan had managed to forget his physical weakness, but was reminded when dizziness again swept over

161

him and his legs abruptly buckled. Clay supported him without slackening their pace. After a minute of foot-dragging the spell passed, and Allan could walk again.

"I think I've made the quantum jump," he said aloud. "Okay, I'm in a new universe. But I'm lost. Guide me."

Clay chuckled again. "That's what I'm here for. Tell me, Allan, when you were a small child and looked at the sun, what did you see?"

Allan thought for a moment, then said, "A big white ball in the sky that made your eyes water."

"Very good. And when you were a teenager in Preparatory?"

"A mass of gases heated by atomic processes in the central core, the source of all energy in the solar system and probably all matter. An understanding that the sun is an incredibly complex mechanism, and only specialists can ever know it in depth."

"And when you became a partial 'specialist' during your astronomy courses in college?"

"I moved from external large basics into fundamentals, more details. I learned how and why the hydrogen-into-helium fusion process works, how other elements are created, the complete life cycle of a star. I also learned there's a great deal we still don't know, and may never know."

"Right. And during these years that was the same sun sitting out there, not changing any appreciable amount. Your *grasp*, your *understanding* of it changed. Now as to what I am . . . you're just at the small child stage, Allan. You've got a long ways to go to reach Preparatory, much less college."

"Then . . . you're a higher intelligence. We've found a more developed being in our own solar system." After he had said the words Allan realized they sounded distorted, as though he had missed the real point and they lacked meaning.

Clay sighed, loudly. "No, dammit, I'm *above* intelligence!

162

The term is meaningless when applied to me. I told you I'm an *elemental,* as much a part of Earth and the sun as the gravitic force that binds them together. Use the previous analogy but substitute intelligence for the sun, and you'll have a better idea of what you really know on the subject."

That hurt. Allan rebelled against such a condemnation, but the conviction that he had just heard an unyielding truth slowly swelled and grew, until it overwhelmed him. His voice was dull when he finally acknowledged the bitter fact. "Then . . . my life has been wasted. I've specialized in the study of intelligence, and what's more, I've made a hundred decisions that vitally affect whole species, based on what I thought we knew."

"Wrong again. Those first protective tears teach the small child not to stare directly at the sun; that's learning by immediate personal experience. In school he switches to a new class of learning techniques, the manipulation of symbols and concepts. Here he loses immediacy, but the volume grows tremendously because of the nature of the working medium, the ability of symbolical representation to condense a tremendous amount of knowledge into a form that can be quickly absorbed. In dealing with intelligence, *Homo saps* is still in the personal experience area, and is going to be there for some time. You learn as you grow, doing the best you can with what you know at the particular moment. You can't refuse to act because you know a deeper understanding will come after you've advanced to a whole new class of knowledge."

The changes in Allan's personal orientation to life were too rapid, too profound for absorption. The hurt eased into numbness, which slowly changed into indignation. "Then why are you telling me about the heights I'm never going to reach? What do you *want!*"

"Well, laddiebuck, now that we've cut the watermelon rind we get down to the juicy heart. You've finally strayed from the straight and narrow by making a wrong decision, and

163

you're about to compound the error by following it with a second one. I'm here to change your mind on both, if that can be done without actual interference. We elementals have our own rules—there's no such quality as total freedom any-where in the universe—and one is that we don't interfere with 'lower' lifeforms. Sound familiar? But if you choose a new path when we finish our walk, especially considering that you're only going to half-believe in this conversation tomorrow anyway, then I haven't bothered you any more than your re-search stations bother the dwarfs. And to hit 'em in reverse order, that's the second wrong decision you're about to make, that our short look-alikes aren't intelligent. They are, Oh Homologous Hominid, they are!"

"Not as I understand intelligence at my child's level," said Allan stubbornly, feeling a helpless certainty that he was wrong.

"Oh, technically and temporally you're quite right, but you've got a short-term perspective. I was on this planet about forty-thousand years ago, for reasons that are none of your business, and at that time the dwarfs would have passed your tests. Your own ancestors were scavenging carrion for a living back then, incidentally. That's when these long-toothed shorties made this statue of the form I took. I kinda' liked it, and told the clay to hang together. Then this world warmed up a little and it turned entirely too lush on this con-tinent. The result was that earning a meal became too easy, and they got lazy. All they really need are some hard times, and they're coming within a thousand of their years. This con-tinent is going to dry out and wrinkle up like an old apple. Five-thousand years after that they'll be finding some of your artifacts and writing learned papers on the unexpected metal-lurgical abilities of their primitive ancestors."

"I don't have any choice but to accept that, as I accept you," Allan said slowly. They had caught up with Victoria and her two companions, who were standing at the river's edge

164

discussing the possibility that he had survived the swift water. He learned they knew the laser beam had caught him and considered it likely he had drowned. Two other squadsmen had launched a raft upriver and were poling it toward them, searching the banks for his body.

Allan had reached a temporary equilibrium with both drug and fever, and for the moment was having no difficulty clinging to consciousness. "What's the first mistake, the one I've already made?" he asked the hulking figure beside him.

Clay sighed again. "Now we get down to the real nitty-gritty, Allan. Brace yourself, 'cause you ain't heard nothin' yet!"

Allan had already heard more than enough, but he followed the advice and tried to compose himself to accept the worst.

"You've already made a firm decision to reject that Deputy Administrator's job," Clay said, his slow voice indicating a careful choice of words. "You did this for purely selfish reasons, the fact that the life you lead now is a hell of a lot more interesting and exciting than anything Earth can offer. I want you to change your mind. The P.P. Corps will need you in that top spot when Siggi Wilson leaves, and despite all its faults it's a good organization. Some of my fellow elementals in other systems—including this one, incidentally—want the work you're doing to continue. And on the personal level, you're about spoiled for field work anyway. Take the bigger job and quit while you're ahead."

The world turned dark again for Allan, but this time he recognized the encroaching blackness as a frantic defense against believing what he had just heard. He forced the tempting oblivion back, and cried, *What do you mean I'm spoiled for field work?*

"I'm sorry this has to be hard to take, Allan, but keep in mind that the cut a surgeon makes to operate could kill a man, if that was the intent. Instead it's the first step in the

165

healing process. You have more than a touch of arrogance in you. It's a common fault of the competent. With all the good intentions possible, you're beginning to think and act too much like these Safeguard cats looking for you . . . becoming a man who knows for *certain* that he's *right!* It's a dangerous and unforgiving attitude. I think you'd better move on up the ladder, and let a younger and more idealistic person take your place."

Clay turned and began walking back down the trail, still supporting Allan. "I don't think they're going to find you in my little hideaway, and when the fever eases you won't have much trouble getting food and water. Just stay away from my hairy girlfriend with the built-in protective drive who guards the joint. Your friends at the station will be guarding the shuttle from Main Base next week, but you should manage to sneak aboard somehow. Competency is a virtue as well as a vice. In any case, it's your problem."

Allan was silent on the short trip back to the cavern, trying to digest what he had learned. It was too much to take in at once. Being on his feet for almost an hour had finally drained his strength, and he was losing his precarious hold on full consciousness. Despite the confusion in his mind he remembered at the cliffside to ask a final question. "How will I find you on Earth? You can't just show yourself to us and then disappear, as you did with the dwarfs. Where *are* you in our solar system?"

Clay chuckled. "Man, you're centered on the geographical and temporal location bit, strictly centered on! Look, dad, I don't want you hunting for me, and this little chat has to be strictly confidential, not that anyone would believe you anyway. Mankind has to *grow* up to us, not find us. Think about that, and when you recover try to remember this as just a vivid fever dream, where maybe you gleaned a few pearls of wisdom from your subconscious."

They passed through the vine curtain, and it was the last thing Allan saw for two days.

Allan awoke to a knowledge of serious bodily dehydration, but his mind was clear and the fever had run its course. He staggered outside, hoping that vicious female dwarf was not at home. After drinking from a forest pool and eating some thoroughly ripened fruits he felt much stronger, and returned to the cavern. In the darkness he made his way to the clay figure at the rear and carefully felt over it. The statue was as lifeless as when he had first examined it, but seemed to have slightly shifted its position. With only memory as a comparison guide, it was impossible to be certain. Without a light he could not even check the floor for large flat footprints.

Allan remembered a verifiable point, and attempted to pinch off a bit of material from an arm. His fingers slipped from what felt like ordinary dry clay without making an impression. The material in the figure was still obeying the elemental's command to "hang together."

Clay had refused to relieve Allan's dizziness for reasons of "mental health." He had said it was best that this experience be remembered as a dream, even though the lessons learned were to be heeded. Which meant that Clay, godlike though he might be, was far from omniscient. There was no slightest doubt in Allan's mind of the reality of his experience. He did not even feel the need to return with a light and examine the floor.

But the elemental had also said Allan was on his own. He had to reach Earth and expose the Safeguard Squads by his own efforts. And Allan had a strong hunch that Clay had made his single contribution by speaking to him, and would not interfere again even if the Conscience died before he could utilize the new knowledge.

Four days later Allan crouched behind a thick bush only a few meters from the charged fence protecting the station. The aircar from Main Base was just settling to the ground, and he saw with approval that it was going to shield him from the laser-armed "gardener" working at the rear of the build-

167

ing. When the pilot stepped outside and was also hidden behind the aircar, Allan picked up the heavy stile he had made and walked rapidly to the fence.

Without cutting tools or power Allan had been forced to use dead branches and vines to construct the inverted V-shaped stile, but it would get him over the two-meter high wire. He held it by one leg and carefully tilted the other back and manhandled it over the top strand; each leg had lashed side braces to hold it erect. Allan had practiced climbing up and over, but not where a slip would result in a severe shock. He moved carefully up the vine-tied cross pieces, and had just reached the top when a low voice called, "Nice try, Conscience."

Allan froze, then slowly turned, keeping his hands carefully in sight. The out-of-uniform space serviceman with the dead gray eyes was standing a few meters away, a laser pistol rock-steady on Allan's chest.

The two men looked at each other. In the coldly controlled face below him Allan saw the need to confront the victim that had delayed his death for a few seconds. Without conscious thought he let the genuine fear he felt show on his face, and when the hot beam did not come seeking his heart, let the expression grow. The killer drank it in, his mouth opening slightly. When it started to close Allan hurled himself to the side in a horizontal dive over the fence, and felt the burning touch of death in the air above his ribs. He landed on top of a young green bush, growing amid charred stalks where the old undergrowth had been burned away.

The breaking branches cushioned Allan's descent to the ground. He curled into a ball as he fell and landed almost on his feet. Coming instantly erect, he spotted a shallow depression just behind the bush that partially hid him, and left his feet in another long dive. This time he hit rolling and was out of the killer's immediate sight when he stopped. But the man had held his fire, and could easily see Allan from two steps up on the stile.

Allan changed his escape plan. He opened his mouth and yelled for help at the top of his lungs.

There was a startled cry from inside the aircar. A second later a surprised face appeared in the nearest window, staring down at Allan. He had forgotten the safety rule that required two men aboard all flights extending more than fifty kilometers from Main Base.

Allan swung his head, and saw the face of his intended executioner rising just above the top of the stile. The man hesitated, and for the first time Allan saw indecision on the usually impassive features. And then the killer realized it would be impossible to hide the fact of naked murder, and unwillingness to risk his own death won. He stepped down and silently faded into the woods.

For a moment more Allan remained where he was, then crawled to the end of the shallow gully. By that time the man in the aircar had swung to the ground, and was approaching him at a trot. Allan recognized him as Jacque Flomain, the pilot; the man who had entered the station must have been a passenger. Jacque was holding a laser at the ready.

The pilot kept his gaze on the quiet woods outside the fence, and called, "Run for the aircar, Conscience; I'll cover."

On a world where a Safeguard Squad existed, where the highest local official was a member, and at least two space servicemen out of uniform roamed at will and one killed on command, it was impossible to know friend from secret foe. Allan had planned to try to reach Magnitsky, of whose honesty he felt certain, without trusting another person. The cleverness of the Safeguards in planting a dummy guard inside the fence, while the real killer stayed outside, had exposed him. Now he had to chance Jacque and the man with him being trustworthy, as well as the laser beam that could still come seeking him from outside the fence.

169

Jacque had advanced to the head of the shallow gully, where he stood with his pistol pointed at the woods, and Allan had not lost all faith in his fellow man. He pushed erect and, crouching low, ran for the opposite side of the aircar.

"I don't understand!" Magnitsky said sharply. "You're certain the masked judge was Victoria. You are fairly sure one juror was Margarete Olmedo and you think you know both the prosecutor and your assigned 'counsel.' Why won't you prefer charges?"

"Lack of any proof better than my word against theirs," replied Allan. The aircar had brought him back to Main Base immediately, and they were seated in Magnitsky's unfinished but comfortable office. Allan had just had the dubious satisfaction of seeing someone as shocked and hurt as he had been. "Besides, prosecuting Victoria and her immature crew would make them too happy. Fanatics are always willing to die nobly for a 'great cause.' I think it was Wilhelm Stekel who said it best two-hundred Eryears ago: A mature man wants to *live* humbly for what he believes. If you had been at the trial you'd have seen how little Margarete and Victoria wanted to kill me, even though the roles they had adopted might have forced them into it. I suggest you transfer all of them back to Earth, where they can work for the New Romans in more legitimate ways. I'm more concerned with the Space Service officer responsible for those two roving 'jurors.' After the election we have to start rooting out the bureaucrats and officers who support these extralegal activities."

"Of course I'll send Victoria and the rest back, that being the only punishment I can administer if you won't prosecute," said Magnitsky. "In the past I've had some reservations about the mission of the P.P. Corps, but now that I see what would happen if exploiters like the New Romans took power, I'll vote Conservationist."

"So will a few billion others, when Earth hears about the

Safeguard Squads," said Allan, rising. "And I *am* filing charges against the two spacers. We can't have killers like that gray-eyed fellow roaming loose. We have Jacque's word to back mine on the ambush at the fence. From those two the Inspector General can work his way up."

They shook hands and Allan headed for the landing field, where a planetary shuttle waited to lift him to the neverlander in orbit overhead. At the entrance port he paused for a last look at the lush and verdant woods of Zwergwelt, wondering how often he would be able to escape his new office and walk again through such primeval beauty. Not frequently, once the bureaucracy got him in its grip.

Allan gazed in the direction of a small hidden grotto, where a crude clay figure sat in lonely but majestic splendor. There was still no slightest doubt in his mind of the authenticity of his experience there, and it was not going to affect his mental health in the slightest. "I hope to God you're satisfied," he murmured, and entered the shuttle.

22

Allan stepped into the aircar, glanced at the two other passengers, and punched out his destination, the Space Service building in Geneva, on the small console. He seated himself in an empty safety chair, and felt the gentle but firm restraining arms lock across his thighs and chest. No one entered behind him, and precisely on schedule a minute later the door locked with an audible click. The aircar performed its automatic self-check, a series of green lights that flickered across the console face for ten seconds. Allan watched the "Passengers Secured" light come on above them and remain steady. It was followed by the "Operational" light, and two seconds later the eight-passenger car lifted off. It had been on the ground less than three minutes.

The aircar accelerated rapidly to enter the main corridor across the long body of Lake Geneva. Allan risked a strained neck by turning around to watch the next aircar coming in. It was almost directly below them, decelerating to land at the spot they had occupied at the Lausanne Spaceport. He would have much preferred to board that car. It was headed for Bern, and to the best of his knowledge Gilia was still in school there. They had kept in touch, but it had been almost two years since they had enjoyed that almost idyllic, legally unsanctioned honeymoon at the Martian Red Desert Resort. The only advantage Allan could see to his new job was that he would at least get to see her again before she left on her first assignment.

It was only an eight-minute ride from Lausanne to Geneva, and they were already halfway there. Allan stared at the snowcapped peaks in the distance, and down at the cold blue water . . . and a tinny voice said loudly, *"Alert! Passenger alert! The powerplant has failed! Prepare for emergency landing!"*

The quiet hum of the craft's two motors died. A ducted fan aircar had no wings, but its tub-shaped body provided aerodynamic lift. A landing in the water would be rough but comparatively safe. And then to Allan's amazement the normal forward tilt became almost a dive, and their descent speed increased. They were going to hit the water at a sharp angle, while moving at a speed he estimated as better than 200 kilometers an hour.

The other two passengers—both were old women—had sat as though frozen after the announcement of an emergency. When the aircar tilt increased they screamed together, and fell silent again almost as if reacting as one. Both turned to look at Allan, and for the first time he realized they were elderly twin sisters. He had not noticed earlier because they

172

did not dress alike. It seemed odd, inappropriate, that a man who had survived a decade of very dangerous adventures on alien worlds should die on Earth, and in such prosaic company.

Something else about this mechanical failure was odd. Allan found the seat restraint emergency release button, and pressed it. The padded bands across his legs and chest retracted into the chair. Internal power at least was still on. He heaved himself to his feet and took two uncertain steps to the console. Even as he moved he saw that its face reflected only two lights. The green "Operational" was still burning; the "Passengers Secured" light had turned to amber. And just to confirm his suspicion, a recorded voice said: "This is a fully secured flight. All passengers will remain seated. Repeat; all passengers remain in their seats."

There was no pilot's chair at the low console, but a panel padded on the inside was recessed into the face. There had been little change in Earth's most popular form of personal transportation during the past ten years, and Allan still remembered the emergency instructions he had learned as part of his pilot's training. He pulled on the release handle, and the panel swung down and locked into place. In the opening behind it was an emergency control stick. On an inner wall was a small red switch with two positions, "Manual" and "Programed." Allan moved the switch from the Programed to the Manual position as he seated himself and grasped the stick. Almost instantly he felt the glide angle change, easing into a less direct fall. Another recorded message came on and warned him he was not authorized to operate an aircar.

The aged twins, still together, started to babble questions as Allan increased the glide angle to the maximum and began shedding speed. He held up a restraining hand and they obediently fell silent. There were a few other controls inside the tiny compartment. Allan pressed the button marked "Emergency Restart," and was not very surprised when the two

173

powerplants almost instantly began humming again. He felt the drag as the four fans began fighting their downward momentum, and glanced ahead out of the curved windshield. The water was close.

The aircar was still moving much too fast for a safe landing. Allan held the stick all the way back, feeling a heavy weight in his stomach as they started pulling out of the dive. The small movable control surfaces on the fat aircar body provided little actual lift; the real control was in the fans. The duel between momentum and opposing power continued for long seconds, while Allan held the control stick at the maximum and waited to see if the airfoils would hold. They were only a few hundred meters high, and slowly changing the angle of descent while rapidly approaching the surface. And then the aircar reached the bottom of its new curved path, flew level less than fifty meters above the water for a few seconds, and started ascending.

Allan released the breath he had not realized he was holding, eased the stick ahead, and glanced at the other controls. They were designed for simplicity and ease of operation, and in less than a minute he had slowed their speed and was turning toward Geneva.

Belatedly, the emergency visiphone came on. A sharp-faced gray-haired man looked up at Allan from the tiny screen. "This is your emergency operator. Do you need assistance? Why are you on Manual?"

"What does your recording equipment show?" Allan demanded instead of answering. "We've been on an emergency status for two minutes!"

The emergency operator disappeared, but was back shortly, wearing a puzzled expression. "Our record shows nothing out of the ordinary until you activated the manual override about three minutes ago, sir. What was this emergency of which you spoke?"

"Does your system record your own actions, or only these

fed back to you by the monitors in the aircars?" Allan demanded, again without answering.

"Why . . . only the monitor input, sir. But my predecessor should have received a signal and taken action before I relieved him. I don't know what happened here."

"I do. And I'll take care of it shortly after I land," Allan said, his voice grim. "Now give me directions for a manual landing on the roof of the Space Service building."

"Sir, I shall have to report this . . . incident."

"So do I," Allan replied. And then he was busy maneuvering the small aircar through the bustling traffic of Geneva. In three more minutes they were settling toward the nonsked landing area on the tall blue spire that housed the Space Service. As they disembarked, Allan turned to the twins and said, "Ladies, I want you both to know I think you would have made good spacers. Your nerves are better than mine."

They gave him grateful smiles, and shy thanks for saving their lives, and Allan caught an elevator down to the 89th floor. His first appointment was with the adjutant to the Inspector General, External Operations. Allan stopped at a visiphone in the hall outside his office and dialed the security section of the P.P. Corps. When he had the correct official on the line, Allan briefly explained that an attempt had been made to murder him by crashing the aircar in which he was riding. An emergency operator had been bribed to assume control and wreck the craft in such a fashion it would appear an accident. Allan was certain now that the first supposedly recorded emergency warning had been a fake. A very human operator had spoken those words, while actually taking control of the vehicle and putting it into a steep dive.

Allan supplied the P.P. official with the flight time, origin, and destination of his aircar, which would enable Council Security operatives to locate the specific emergency operator on duty at the time. The relief who had spoken to him might report the incident as he had said, but Allan was taking no

175

chances. That man had been willing to kill two passengers in whom he could have no interest in order to eliminate a planned victim.

The two attempts to kill Allan on outworld planets had been forceful and direct, by men with lasers. On Earth the means chosen were more subtle, and even less conscienable; innocent bystanders were involved. The incident only confirmed Allan's preference for duty away from Earth. Only special training received long ago had enabled him to survive. And if murder was now a political tool, there might be more attempts on his life. If so, sooner or later one was bound to succeed.

Three minutes later Allan was explaining the circumstances of the weird trial on Zwergwelt to Colonel Bagnulo, adjutant to the Inspector General. The photographs of all spacers in the Pollux system were ready, and Allan quickly identified the two men who had served on his "jury."

"I was afraid of that," muttered Bagnulo, a tall, lean African of Nilotic extraction. "The one you call the psychotic killer is Hardtack McComber, who has three medals for bravery and four busts on his record for insubordination. It only figures he'd join a secret society that promised a little extra danger and excitement. The other man I know nothing about; probably just a sidekick. We'll have them both brought in for questioning and formal charges."

Allan considered telling Bagnulo about the second attempt on his life just moments ago, but refrained. It had nothing to do with the Space Service directly, although Allan would wager a year's pay that the same persons were responsible if you went high enough. Someone had not wanted him to reach Bagnulo. Possibly they did not want him to reach his second appointment, which was with Siggi Wilson in this same building.

Allan stopped at the public visiphone again after leaving the colonel, and looked up Gilia's number in Bern. She was not there, and the home secretary had no recorded message.

In Wilson's office Allan asked that the conversation be recorded, and then quickly informed the heavy-set administrator of all he knew about the Safeguard Squads. Siggi listened carefully, tilting back in his executive chair with his massive chin resting on a clenched fist. When Allan was through he sighed, put his feet on the floor with a loud thump of spaceman's boots, and said, "Most flagrant and best documented case I know of illegal assumption of authority. I agree with Magnitsky, not you. All participants should have been prosecuted to the fullest possible extent."

Allan shrugged, and said, "Why waste time on the knaves? I'd like to get at the king."

"That isn't so easy," said Siggi, frowning. "Well, I'll turn it over to our legal and political staffs. The latter have less than two weeks to make the most of what we know before the election. Your story isn't the first we've heard, just the clearest and most complete. I've had suspicions about those two 'accidents' you mentioned for some time. Both were highly experienced P.P.s who had got out of worse scrapes without a scratch."

"Do you think it will swing the election to us?" asked Allan.

"No doubt about it, in my mind. Which brings up a point, Allan. There may be an equivalent of the Safeguard Squads here on Earth. We have your testimony safely on tape now, but they may still feel you're a bad lad to have around. I think I'd better ask Council Security to assign you a guard."

"You're a little late," Allan said, grinning. He told Siggi about the aircar failure.

"Holy Space! Why didn't you tell me earlier?" demanded Siggi. "The situation is even worse than I thought!"

Siggi calmed down after Allan explained that P.P. Security had been notified. The P.P. Corps did not have a security force of its own, but had recourse to that of either the Space

177

Patrol or the World Council. A full-scale investigation was probably already underway.

Allan considered also telling Siggi about his encounter with the consciousness called Clay on Zwergwelt, but decided against it. Siggi had most of the characteristics of the good administrator, but a totally open mind was not one of them. He would find the story hard to believe . . . and highly upsetting if he finally came to accept it!

"These killers seem very efficient at knowing where you are and what you're doing," muttered Siggi. "The Space Patrol has obviously developed some rotten spots. We'll cut them out after the election."

"Yes, and in the meantime I have some personal business I want to attend to," said Allan, rising. "I'm going to take a few days off, if you can spare me."

"Of course, Allan. You're at the point where you have to start deciding your own hours, you know."

Allan accepted the small rebuke in silence, and turned away. Most high government officials worked long hours, but also took long vacations, where they could not be reached except for emergencies. He would have to get used to the same refuge from overwork. But for the next few years he had a strong hunch he would be seeing more of the long days than the privileged vacations.

Allan caught the next flight to Bern. Gilia was not at home, and there was no door message. While in space he had wired ahead on subradio that he was coming; it seemed strange that she had apparently dropped out of sight. With some foreboding, he called the school where she was enrolled for her P.P. courses. The attendance clerk informed him she had not been in class for a week.

The message he had sent was probably on her home secretary, unread, if she had left a week ago. That might explain why she was not here to greet him, but not where she had gone, and why.

Allan decided to use his new authority as Deputy Administrator, and put in another call to P.P. Security. They agreed to attempt to trace Gilia Kaylin, but asked that he come by the office and sign the official request as soon as possible. Allan had not actually been sworn into office, but he had no reason to think his interview with the World Council committee that passed on P.P. appointments would be more than a formality.

Allan debated looking up Kay and visiting his children, but decided against it. His years in space had compelled a clean break; best keep it that way.

For the rest of the day Allan occupied himself with the mundane chores of renting a living unit and getting his baggage delivered. He chose, for the time being, to stay in Lausanne, near the spaceport. Geneva was nothing but a complex of business and government buildings, where apartments were not allowed. The Lake Geneva International Zone covered not only the water but all land for more than fifteen kilometers on every side. The area bordering the lake was thickly covered with living buildings and commercial enterprises, though all the old cities had retained their separate identities. Most higher government officials and well-paid executives lived in chalets out of the Zone, perching thickly on the mountains on every side. Supporting the World Council was now the major business of the state of Switzerland. The Zone and its satellite cities formed a complex containing more than eighty million people.

Allan felt restless after unpacking his few belongings, and wandered out into the night. As in most urban complexes on Earth, virtually every legal and illegal pleasure known to man was available if you had the money. He enjoyed a fine meal at an excellent restaurant, one that proudly advertised its spices from Misery, but passed up the many other forms of entertainment. Instead he took a long walk after dinner, ignoring the moving pedstrips in favor of his own feet, exploring some of the older streets and byways of the city. Lausanne had not

179

erected an environmental dome, and the October air was crisp and smelled of mountain pine. He was approached several times by women who offered companionship and/or sex, but each took the refusal gracefully when he declined. Allan would have enjoyed the company, and perhaps sex as well, but hoped to find Gilia shortly.

The suspicion that something had happened to Gilia Kaylin was very much on Allan's mind. It did not seem like her to disappear without a trace, even though she had apparently vanished before learning he was coming to Earth. He was mulling over the problem when a small voice said, in international English, "Mister? Mister, will you help me get my father inside?"

Jarred into full awareness, Allan glanced down at the speaker, who was standing against the wall of a house a few meters away. The bright streetlights revealed a small elfin-faced girl, supporting a large fat man apparently far gone in drink or drugs. He was leaning against the wall, barely erect, one heavy arm across the girl's thin shoulders.

She inclined her head toward a set of tall steps just down the street. The daughter did not look more than twelve, and the big man was a heavy burden on her slender frame. Allan suppressed a small sense of distaste, and walked to them. He saw that the man's eyes were closed, and heard his heavy breathing.

Allan moved to the father's left side and slipped a massive but slack arm over his shoulder. Locking it in place with his left hand on the inside of the man's elbow, he passed his right arm around the thick waist and pulled the heavy frame away from the wall. The man sagged at once, but then caught himself before his full weight fell on Allan. The girl supported the other side as best she could, and they took several staggering steps to the first riser. There Allan had to shift his grip and urge the man to lift a foot, but he finally seemed to understand, and started slowly up the stairs. His footing became more steady, and Allan and the girl had no trouble supporting him up the steps to the landing. There she pressed her palm against the recognition glass, and the door opened. The father sagged again, as though exhausted, and Allan muttered under his breath and took the burden on his shoulders. Almost lock-stepping to support the immense weight, he followed the girl down a short hall and into a room on the left. The light was off, but came on as the door shut behind him. At the same time his charge drew himself erect and lifted his arm off Allan's shoulder. He stepped away, and Allan found himself staring into the tiny barrel of a dart pistol, held rock-steady in the hand of the slim girl.

23

"Please don't move, Odegaard. You'll wake up tomorrow with a nasty headache if I have to shoot." Her voice was suddenly deeper, more mature. Even the facial expression had changed, though the figure was as girlishly thin and youthful as before. She was a grown although quite young woman.

"What do you want with me?" Allan demanded.

"*We* don't want you at all. We've been paid to deliver you. And you do make it difficult, I must say. I'd think a bachelor just in from a two-months trip would be lonely enough to take *one* of the women we sent you. But every man has his weakness, and we finally found yours." She smiled pleasantly, as though pleased to find he was human after all. "Now this will be much easier for all concerned if you stay docile. Just put your hands behind you and don't argue about breathing from this bottle."

Allan took a quick look around, trying to memorize the

181

room, but it seemed only another living unit out of ten-thousand similar ones in Lausanne. And then his hands were being tied behind him with tape, and when they were secure the girl placed a palm over his mouth and held an open phial beneath his nose. He had been neatly and competently trapped, apparently by another of the quasi-legal detective agencies, and for the moment Allan saw nothing he could do but submit. He breathed the fumes without trying to turn his head. In only a few seconds his vision blurred, he was assailed by a strong sense of disorientation, and consciousness moved outside his skull and hung there, looking back into eyes he knew must be glazed and blank. And then he became a creature of physical senses only, as though alive just from the neck down. He could feel himself walking, knew when they reached the cool outside air again, felt the steps when they descended to the street, even realized some time later that they were flying. But he had no control at all of his body, and no awareness of where he was or what was happening around him.

"You should be back with us by now, Odegaard," said a strange male voice. Allan realized that his senses had been slowly returning for some minutes. He still felt his nose stinging from an inhalator they had made him breathe, obviously an antidote to the mentally disabling drug. And then he was aware enough to make a conscious effort, and shook off the last effects of the mind-numbing chemical.

Allan looked around. He was in a small, almost bare room, sitting on a narrow bed. The only other item of furniture was a combination lavatory and water closet below a mirror in the corner. The fat man had vanished. The thin young woman was standing by the door, ready to leave. Bending over him was a pudgy, gray-haired man with a lined brown face and very black eyes.

"Good, good; you look awake." The brown-faced man turned to the girl and said, "That's all we need from you,

182

Nina. Good work. Pick up your bonus from Klaus on the way out."

The girl nodded, and left. Allan saw that beneath the child's short skirt were slim but mature hips, which swung with provocative grace as she walked. There had been no such swing when she was being a little girl.

The man turned back to Allan and said, "You can call me McCoy, Odegaard. This is a jail, and I'm the head jailer. We have a very important recording lined up for you tomorrow . . . or the next day or the next, whenever we get you to the point where you can say your lines without giving away the fact you're on drugs."

"And just what are my 'lines'?" asked Allan. His tongue felt thick, but he was able to speak clearly.

"Oh, nothing complicated. Just a confession that your statements in Siggi Wilson's office about the Safeguard Squads on the outworlds were politically motivated lies. Plus an acknowledgment that you were promised a promotion to Deputy P.P. Administrator as your reward for the slander. And of course the usual request that your home state accept you for rehabilitative therapy and make a decent citizen out of you again."

"You have drugs that can make me say all that while looking more than half alive?" asked Allan. "The chemists must have discovered some new ones while I've been away."

"Oh, they have indeed. We can make a man do everything up to and including shooting himself, and sound as if it was all his own idea. But we won't go to that much trouble with you. During the talk you're also going to reveal that you've been a *kinzie* addict for years, and within a week you're going to be found dead in your living unit from an overdose. You should have stayed in the outworlds, Odegaard, where you belong. When the P.P. Corps is disbanded after the election, perhaps you could have found something useful to do."

183

Allan was silent for a moment, and then said simply: "I didn't know there were so many people like you."

His captor stiffened, first defensiveness and then anger playing across the fat brown features. Anger dominated, and he almost snarled when he said, "I hate a damn' bleedin' pure'art! I really do, I hate 'em! So damned smugly sure they're right, with never a thought to the common man! You blinkin' snobs—" He stopped abruptly, paused, and when he resumed his voice fell back into the bland tone he had used before. "Yes, I suppose you fellows get rather good at looking after yourselves, out there in the wilds. If you can shake up an opponent, make him lose his temper and his self-possession . . . I admire you, Odegaard. Too bad you couldn't have put your abilities to better use. Sleep sweet; you'll need your strength tomorrow."

McCoy turned and followed Allan's kidnaper out of the cell. The door shut behind him with a finality that denied any possible hope of escape.

The pudgy jailer had been seeing too many badly written space adventure Tri-D programs. Allan had said exactly what he felt, with no ulterior motive in mind.

With a feeling of almost hopeless certainty that it would do no good, Allan rose and explored his cell. The bed was anchored to the floor with heavy bolts, and the water closet did not have a movable top. The flat light fixture overhead was slightly recessed into the ceiling, and he could be reasonably certain it contained a wide-angle monitoring camera he could not reach to disable. The air vent was only twenty centimeters square and the room had a slightly musty smell, as though circulation was poor. The door fitted flat into the wall and had no inside knob. There was a small space beneath for air movement.

Allan gave a mental shrug, and accepted the inevitable. He shed all clothes but his underwear and crawled into the

184

narrow bed. Turning his face up to the ceiling he called, "Would you turn off the light, please?"

When there was no response Allan pulled a corner of the cover over his eyes. In five minutes he was fast asleep.

Allan was awakened by the opening of the cell door. It took a few seconds for him to remember where he was, and then he quickly sat up in bed. An old man who seemed so short he might almost have been a dwarf, but who also appeared made entirely of muscles, deposited a tray of hot food on the foot of the bed. He turned and shuffled out without a word. The door closed behind him.

Allan struggled out of bed, feeling distinctly groggy, and bathed his face and hands. Though the chemical they had used did not have the long-lasting effects of the one rubbed into his wounds on Zwergwelt, he still felt shaky. He examined the food, wondering if it too was drugged. He was ravenously hungry, and there seemed little point in starving himself. They could force him to swallow the drugs that were supposed to turn him into a lively seeming puppet, if they were not in the food. Allan ate his breakfast.

An hour later the muscular short keeper returned to pick up the tray. He brought Allan a depilatory cream and a brush, and took away his wrinkled clothes. Allan performed his morning ablutions in his underwear, checked his appearance in the mirror, then paced the floor for half an hour before his clothes were returned. Not long after he was dressed the door opened again and he saw a different but familiar face. The cold, remote gray eyes and the frozen expression were unmistakable. But now Allan had a name to go with them.

"McComber!" he gasped.

The lean, glacial features split into a thin smile. "Good morning, Conscience. I see you remember me, even though I'm out of uniform."

"You I could never forget!" Allan said fervently, backing

185

into the cell. Hardtack McComber carried a dartgun in one hand and a laser in a hip holster.

"My . . . associates here on Earth tried to prevent you reaching the Inspector General's office and identifying me," McComber went on. "If they had succeeded I'd have remained in the Service; it's a fun job. But the powers-that-be sent me here on the next flight after yours, just in case I had to drop out of sight. Now I have, of course, and my only consolation is that I'll get to finish what I started on Zwergwelt." The thin smile widened, and Allan saw again the lust for death that made this man a walking anachronism among civilized beings.

"You were born too late, McComber," Allan said aloud. "Two-hundred years ago you might have found your niche . . . as a traveling hangman! Why don't you turn yourself in for deep-trance rehabilitative therapy?"

McComber laughed, a brittle, frozen sound. "I like my present personality, Conscience. I have more fun than people like you. Now move out!" He gestured with the dartgun. "It's time for your medicine."

Allan stepped outside his cell into a long corridor, lined with apparently identical doors on either side. This group, whether New Roman or another splinter force, was well organized and had elaborate facilities. McComber followed him, gesturing to the right. Allan walked to the end of the cell corridor, turned right again into an intersecting hallway, and soon reached a small dispensary. A man who appeared to be a paramedic—he did not have the competent ease of an experienced physician—gave Allan injections in each arm, using the standard pressure gun. He did not bother to roll up Allan's sleeves, as required by good medical practice. Then the captive was marched back into the corridor system and they made several confusing turns before passing through two doors in quick succession, this time into what Allan recognized as a small recording studio.

186

There were already four people in the narrow room. The recording technician sat in a corner, facing the table that occupied most of the floor space. A camera mounted on an extension boom rose out of his console. A blond young man with the smooth and polished look of the professional interviewer sat at the table, facing the door through which they had entered. In chairs pushed back against the wall, next to the technician, were two people Allan did not know. One was a beefy, red-haired man of indeterminate age. The other was a rail-thin gray-haired woman with a big nose and birdlike features.

Allan had an excellent memory for faces, and though he was certain he had not met the red-haired man, he seemed familiar. As McComber gestured for him to be seated across from the interviewer, memory clicked and Allan placed him. He had seen that strong form once before, at the hearing where Allan testified before Celal Kaylin's investigations subcommittee. This was the man, wearing a Council Security guard uniform at the time, who had preceded New Roman Party Chairman Blankenship into the hearing room.

Allan felt his breath catch and his heart beat faster. McComber placed some papers with large type in front of him, and said, "He'll become suggestible in about ten more minutes." Allan's mind was racing, and he barely heard the controlled killer. Unless Red-hair had changed jobs, which seemed unlikely, he was a direct link with Blankenship. The Party Chairman had not stood as aloofly above the dirty work as Allan had expected. Which meant he was not as invulnerable as Siggi Wilson had feared.

A seductive lethargy was slowly creeping up from Allan's toes, but he fought it back and concentrated on the new thought. If he could obtain some documented proof this man was still associated with Blankenship, and an actual party to this kidnaping . . . in one long jump the Conservationists

187

might reach from knave to king, and bring down the New Roman house of cards.

Those were brave thoughts for a man whose body was swiftly sinking into numbness, but Allan clung to them as his senses faded. If it took two or three sessions with the drug before it overcame a normally stubborn man's resistance, he would try for four.

The world around Allan became fuzzy and dim. He heard voices speaking but could not distinguish the words. He seemed to withdraw inside himself, fighting to protect some inner core which was being assaulted by battering winds. He tried to huddle in on his own consciousness, concealing its naked heart, and after a time the winds died away. His last genuine memory was of a vulture-like face peering into his own, big brown eyes blinking. And then for all practical purposes, he slept.

When Allan awoke he was back in his cell.

Allan struggled to his feet, and discovered to his surprise that he had been sitting upright on the edge of the bed. Only his mind had been asleep.

He had no certain memory to sustain such a conviction, but Allan felt sure he had not performed as they wanted him to. There would be more drug doses, followed by questions at the interview table.

Since he was still mentally fuzzy and physically lethargic, Allan decided to exercise and see if he could eliminate the drug's physical symptoms. He stripped to his underwear and started some light calisthenics, gradually working up to more vigorous ones. Ten minutes later he was breathing heavily while running in place, and feeling better. Allan took a short rest, and resumed with push-ups. He felt almost back to normal by the time the door opened and the pudgy McCoy entered with a tray. Behind him in the hall, Allan glimpsed McComber leaning casually against a wall, his hand playing with the handle of the laser in his belt. It was so obviously a calculated pose Allan wondered whom McComber was trying to impress. And then he realized he knew; the man was impressing himself.

McCoy put the tray on the bed and said, "Second session in half an hour, Odegaard. Eat well." He turned and walked out, avoiding meeting Allan's gaze.

The food was of the substantial type usually eaten at dinner, not a light lunch. Two of the items were portions from what had obviously been a larger dish. Allan guessed that he was eating the same food as the crew that manned this secret prison, and that noon had passed while he was in a daze. Evidently it took several hours for the drugs to wear off.

McComber came back alone to escort Allan to the dispensary and the studio. Allan noted that the paramedic, again, gave him the two shots directly through the cloth of his shirt, and an idea dawned. The man's sloppy workmanship was a weakness of which he could possibly take advantage.

The group in the studio was the same as before, but this time the thin woman did not wait until the drugs had him almost out before coming forward to start the conditioning process. Allan still had more than a trace of consciousness when she said, "This morning you were a free spirit, floating in the clouds. We are going to take another trip into the sky, but this time you will observe your body still on the ground more clearly, see it perform in the play you have entered. Are you looking forward to playing your part? You do enjoy the acting, yes?"

"I enjoy it, no," Allan whispered, and that was the last thing he remembered.

When he came out of the drugs a second time he was in bed, wearing only his underwear. The light cover had been pulled up around his neck and he was quite comfortable, except for the awareness that his mind was not functioning normally.

Allan stirred, shifted in bed as though restless, turned on

189

his side, and drew the cover over his eyes. Despite his partially dazed condition he remembered what he had decided to attempt, and time might be short. He waited a moment, then lifted the cover higher over his face. He turned again, until he was lying with his mouth just off the edge of the pillow. The back of his head was to the spying eye in the ceiling, and he had one corner of the single coverlet folded back in under itself, the free end near his mouth. Trying to keep his head from moving while his jaw worked, Allan started biting through the top edge of the material.

It took him several minutes because of the slowness with which he moved, but Allan eventually stripped several centimeters both ways from the corner, gaining access to the inner sheet. As he had expected, it was the standard thin but impervious material found in virtually all bedding. The pressed plastic had no weave and could not be torn in strips. Allan patiently worked a large section out of the corner and started biting, making a continuing series of teeth impressions downward some twenty centimeters from the edge. He had to use his front teeth only and they were not accustomed to pressing against each other. It was irritating and somewhat painful work, but he persisted. Patience and perseverance were two qualities he had had no choice but to develop. Occasionally he had to move his head to shift position, and near the bottom of the cut had to draw the cover upward until his feet were exposed, but hoped his monitor would accept that as normal behavior.

Allan finally reached a point he judged twenty centimeters into the sheet, and stopped. He had to know now if the material was going to tear. Curling himself up into a ball, Allan managed to get both hands under the cover and in front of his face. He paused to calm his breathing, lying perfectly still for several minutes, and then seized the inner sheet on each side of his toothmarks and pulled hard. It resisted, and he knew a moment of panic; then the worn places slowly parted

190

at the top. Allan stopped again, this time as much to gain control as fool his guardians, and then continued to pull. It took great physical effort, but the tear moved downward for the full length he wanted. When he paused to rest, Allan found that his drug symptoms had vanished. He was fully awake and alert. Tension and excitement could stimulate as much as physical exercise.

Allan shifted back to the edge of the material, twenty centimeters down from the corner opposite his cut, and repeated the slow biting process. He had just reached the intersection with the first cut when his cell door opened and the silent dwarf entered with his breakfast.

The short man placed the tray on the foot of the bed and left as usual. If they followed yesterday's schedule, Allan had almost two hours before McComber would be there to take him to the studio. He ate hurriedly, then placed the tray on the floor and went back to bed, feigning exhaustion. It had been easy enough to keep his work hidden by turning under the torn corner, but it took several shifts of position before he finally was able to get both hands on the sheet and start the tear. He had been too hurried with his teeth and it was even tougher than the first one, but he eventually had a square of material in his hands.

It was difficult to judge time, but Allan felt that only a few minutes had passed since breakfast. He should have time to complete the last cut before the dwarf returned for the tray. He folded the square in half and started the slow process of biting down the doubled edge. The smaller piece was easier to handle and he made good time. He was in possession of two 10 x 20 centimeter strips when the cell door opened again. Hastily, he tucked them in his undershirt.

Seeing him still in bed, the dwarf crossed the small room and shook Allan by the shoulder. He sat up, rubbing his eyes, and got out of bed when his jailer gestured, carefully hiding the open corner of the cover. When he staggered to the lavatory and reached for the depilatory, the short man turned and walked out.

Allan bathed slowly, pretending to be weak and shaky on his feet. When he looked presentable again he walked back to the bed and made it up, keeping his body between the revealing corner and the overhead light. He left his work hidden by turning the entire top cover edge inward in a five centimeter fold. He had also made up the bed the day before, and with a normal flat ending to the coverlet, but if his monitors noticed the change they gave no sign.

Allan had been wearing a conservative one-piece jumpsuit when captured. He slipped into the legs, then stopped, as though dizzy, and staggered hurriedly to the bed. At its edge he sat down in an awkward posture, facing inward, bent forward as though very weak, holding his head in his arms. He held the position a moment, and then slowly reached for the left sleeve and fumbled to get his hand inside. With his right hand he quickly slipped one of the two laboriously cut strips out from beneath his undershirt and positioned it around his left biceps. It was impossible to completely hide what he was doing, but neither was it obvious to anyone looking down from the ceiling. He did the same for his right arm, and then sat up and pressed the suit's self-locking edges together down the sides. The form-fitting garment held the thin bands in place around his arms. He walked over to the mirror and checked; the slight bulge they created was almost undetectable.

The door opened and McComber gestured for him to come out. The timing had been fearfully close.

The careless medic was no more conscientious than before. Allan docilely submitted to the shots through his sleeves, this time feeling the liquid run down his arm and soak the material when it could not penetrate the protective bands. The quantity was small, and he did not think the wetting would show.

McComber marched Allan to the studio for his third en-

192

counter with the bird-faced conditioning expert. The former spacer was an excellent guard, always just out of reach of a sudden jump, alert and ready for trouble. He no longer carried his dartgun in hand, but Allan felt certain McComber would have practiced until he could draw and fire in tenths of a second.

They entered the studio, and Allan felt his heart sink. The redheaded former Council Security guard was not present.

24

Allan's plan to both save himself and expose Blankenship had been nebulous at best, but at least the first part had worked. For the second, he had to have positive proof someone closely associated with the political leader was a party to this forcible detention. Now his hopes were shattered.

Allan remembered, with wry self-mockery, that first Secret Holmes and then the elemental Clay had accused him of starting to think like a little tin god. And they had been right. Instead of being concerned with saving his own neck, as any sensible man would, Allan was worried because his plans to topple the New Roman party chairman were not working out. It was mental arrogance of the worst sort. His first aim should be to escape . . . and after acknowledging this, Allan admitted to himself that he still wanted to drag Blankenship right off his political throne, if he possibly could.

The skinny woman Allan had come to think of as "The Vulture" gestured for him to be seated at the table. He did as he was told. She waited a moment, watching him, and Allan realized he did not know how to act to persuade them he was under the drugs. McComber seated himself against the wall, tilting the straight chair back and crossing his legs. He looked comfortably bored.

The woman smiled at Allan and said: "Today I am going to coach you until you learn your part perfectly, and then you will give your first performance. Now don't be nervous: this is just for your friends. We are all your friends, helping you learn your role. Just relax and try to be natural when you say your lines. Ready? Then let's begin with the first scene, right after your introduction to the audience and your bio. Your first words are, 'I'm here because I can't live with myself, Mr. Dupleis. I have to tell the truth or burst.' Now say the first sentence. 'I'm here because . . .'"

"I'm here because I can't live with myself," Allan dutifully repeated, keeping his voice dull and monotonous. He was watching McComber, who seemed to be almost dozing. Neither the interviewer nor the technician appeared to have weapons, and if the woman had one it was in the bag by her chair.

"That's fine, just fine, Allan; you have the words perfectly." The narrow face split into an encouraging rictus that exposed large and spotlessly white teeth. "Now let's work on the emotional tones. Say it again, and put more life into it. Act as if it was really very, very important to you to tell the truth. Your *conscience* is bothering you, you want to make a clean breast of your fraud, ask the world to forgive you. Now once more, and go on into the rest on your cue."

She signaled to the technician, who activated his camera and moved it toward Allan. He saw by the little red light on its face that this response was going to be recorded. Allan tried to put enough more life into his voice to indicate he had complied with directions, but not enough to pass for normal speech. He saw by the disappointed look on her face that he had succeeded.

She leaned forward to coach him again, raising her hand to stop the camera as her face moved within its range. Be-

194

hind her, the door opened and the red-haired man entered and quietly took his seat by McComber.

Allan felt his pulse quicken, and something of the excitement he felt entered his voice on the next try. The woman smiled, satisfaction on her face. She moved back out of range, gesturing for Dupleis to ask the first question and signaling the camera on for a take. The red bulb brightened, and the smooth-voiced man across the table asked Allan why he had come to International News.

"I'm here because I can't live with myself, Mr. Dupleis," Allan said, and rose and hurled himself across the room at McComber, all his weight behind the fist that he planted solidly on the lean killer's slightly pointed chin. He felt the jaw tear loose beneath the impact. The former spaceman had started to lean forward when Allan moved, his mouth open to yell. He was slammed back against the wall and bounced off it without uttering a sound, instantly unconscious. Allan tore the laser pistol out of its holster. While the Vulture's startled scream was still ringing in the air he whirled to face the others, his hand thumbing off the familiar safety. Red-hair had jumped to his feet, but froze when he found himself looking into the red jewel at the base of the laser barrel. The technician, mouth agape, was simply staring at him. Dupleis had risen to his feet, his polished features suddenly pale.

Allan noted with satisfaction that the camera light was still on. The start of his jump had been recorded, although he had moved out of range. "Turn the camera on me," he ordered, gesturing with the pistol. When the operator did not move, Allan lifted the barrel in an aiming motion. The man hastily swung the instrument around. The Vulture realized what he was doing and turned her face away at once, but Red-hair was still mentally stunned and only gaped at the recording eye. Allan grinned at him and said, "I'm sorry I can't go on; forgot my lines. Would you like to say a few words instead?" When the man did not answer Allan turned back to the table.

"Then perhaps our glib friend here would like to talk. Dupleis! Come here!"

The interviewer quickly rose and walked around the table, his eyes on the laser. Allan pointed to the wall between the Vulture and Red-hair, almost above the unconscious form of McComber. "Just keep that camera recording," he called to the technician, backing away a few steps while staying within range of the lens. "Now would you people like to sing a song, do a dance, or maybe act a part such as the one you were teaching me? Here's your chance at fame. And you, O Ugly Bird, turn and face the camera. I don't shoot to kill, but I have no objection to burning a hole in your thigh. Raise your eyes and look at me!"

The woman slowly did as bidden, her face filled with hate. She no longer resembled a bird. At the moment she reminded Allan far more of a snake.

"I think this little change in the script will put a lot more truth into the story," Allan said with satisfaction. "Operator . . . turn it off and take out the recording disc. Put it in the protective box and hand it to me. And if you touch it any-where but on the edge, you're going to lose an arm."

"You'll never get out of here alive, Odegaard," Red-hair finally said, his voice hoarse. Allan motioned them away from McComber and retrieved the unconscious man's dart pistol. The former Security Council guard had recovered his equi-librium, and although he obeyed orders he was obviously poised to jump. "That laser can only get off one burn before we'll have you."

"True, but you aren't going to be the one to risk dying," Allan told him. Red-hair, like many men who carried guns regularly, had come to depend on weapons rather than him-self. The only truly dangerous man in the room was McCom-ber, and on Zwergwelt even he had overcome the killing lust when gratifying it meant exposure.

The technician walked toward Allan, carefully extending

the magnetic disc in its protective case well ahead of his body. Allan held the pistol on the man's stomach while taking it, but saw by the white face and protruding eyes that he was in no danger of being jumped. He motioned with his head for the operator to join the others . . . and shot him in the back with the dartgun just as he reached them.

The hapless technician gave a loud gasp of pure fright, and when he fell, Allan was uncertain if it was the fast drug or a faint that had taken him down. He hoped terror had not caused a heart attack. Before the first man hit the floor Allan had shot Red-hair in the chest, and quickly made a choice and shot the Vulture next. He looked into the frightened face of Dupleis, no longer smooth and controlled . . . and holstered the dartgun and lifted the laser.

Wild terror replaced the fear, and Allan knew he had guessed correctly. "Now, Mr. Dupleis, I don't have to hesitate in using the laser, because there will be no one to jump me after I burn you down," Allan said in a conversational tone. "As I mentioned, it's against my rules to kill people . . . but you'll spend the rest of your life walking on artificial legs if you don't tell me what I want to know. And don't try to lie; you wouldn't be good at it except in front of a camera. Tell me where I am, and the best way out. Talk!"

Only a quick-witted and self-possessed person could have thought up a convincing lie when compelled to speak without preparation. Dupleis was not such a man. He babbled out immediate answers to every question, and Allan felt reasonably certain they were truthful. This prison was in the sub-basement of a large old former government building in Geneva. It had been sold to a right-wing lobby that had its own broadcast stations. They operated legitimately on the upper floors, and kept the basement sealed off to all but a select inner circle. There was only one entrance, and it was always double-guarded.

197

"Does Blankenship ever come here?" demanded Allan. "What's his connection with the lobby?"

"He's never been here," answered Dupleis. "Dawson, there," he nodded at Red-hair on the floor, and for the first time Allan had a name, "Dawson always seemed to me just a messenger, but the wheels here listened to him; I think he spoke for someone very high up." They had been talking for several minutes, and Dupleis's initial fright had started to fade. Allan suddenly realized the man's expression had become almost guileless; he had regained enough control to start lying. Allan holstered the laser and shot Dupleis with the dartgun.

There were two ways to break out of a prison; stealth and force. Allan briefly considered turning the other prisoners loose and attempting to take over the basement and then the building, but rejected the idea. That single exit might be impossible to attack from below, and he had no idea of the prison's current population. There might not be enough able-bodied men to be of any real help. Stealth seemed the better choice.

The building location and description had been given while Dupleis was still shaking with fright, and Allan felt he could rely on them. He removed McComber's gunbelt and holstered both pistols. The extra gun made him feel ridiculously conspicuous. Dartguns were seldom used away from Earth; on unknown metabolisms they might either kill or be ineffective.

The studio door had an upper glass panel. Allan dragged all the unconscious bodies close beneath, where they could not be seen from outside. He had no way of knowing how long it would be before someone would come looking for one or more of them, but since his previous recording sessions had taken several hours, he should have plenty of time.

Allan walked through the two isolating doors into the main corridor system, and turned right. He passed two people in the hall, and both looked sharply at him but made no effort to interfere. Possibly they thought he was the new man, Mc-Comber. There were cell doors lining both sides. The single stairway to the main basement was in the center of the area, and he reached it after one more turn. A bored-looking old man sat behind a small monitoring desk placed in front of a heavy steel door, a sign-in book in front of him.

Allan walked briskly toward the guard, who glanced up from a faxmag and gave him a disgusted look. "Christ, don't you know better than wear a thing like a weapons belt out of here?" he said irritably. "Go back to your room and take it off."

"Don't have time," Allan said, keeping his voice cheerful and light. "Can't you put it in a drawer for me?"

The guard looked even more disgusted, but shoved the sign-in book toward Allan and opened a desk drawer, searching for room. Allan ignored the book, instead undoing the clasp and taking off the belt. The guard extended one hand, and Allan quickly flipped open a holster, drew the dartgun, and shot him in the chest.

The surprised man surged ahead in the chair, his mouth open and eyes bulging. But then the drug hit, and momentum carried him forward so that he collapsed across the desk. Allan opened the right side of his suit and slipped the dartgun inside the elastic band around his waist, at the rear. He walked around the desk. There was a small grill in its top, with a black button below. He pressed it, imitated the older man's voice as best he could, and said, "One new boy coming up."

Allan released the button and a bored voice from the grill said, "Roger." He reached beneath the desk, found the single button, and pressed it. The steel door behind him slid aside. It moved rather slowly. A red light came on beneath the speaker grill, and a green one went out. Allan debated a moment, then pressed the button again and jumped for the door. It seemed most likely a similar status system was built into the upper desk; it would look suspicious if the red light stayed on.

He had trapped himself between heavy steel doors if he

199

failed to overcome the upper guard, but that was a chance Allan had to take. He briskly climbed the spiral stairs inside the enclosure, coming out on a landing four meters up, where a second guard sat before a similar steel door. This was a younger man with better manners. He looked up and smiled, but then the expression froze on his face. It was obvious he recognized Allan; he had probably been on duty when they brought him in.

The young guard pushed his chair back and started to rise. The landing was narrow, less than three meters wide, and Allan was almost on him when he emerged from the stairs. He covered the remaining distance in two steps and hurled himself across the desk, his shoulder carrying the seated man back against the wall. The guard got out one good yell, but Allan was hopeful there was no one inside with them to hear it. They went to the floor in a tangle of arms and legs, jammed against the wall in the narrow space available. The inexperienced guard made a mistake; he attempted to draw his dart-gun. Allan, who had concentrated on regaining his balance, caught the younger man with a hard right to the cheek. He then managed to get one knee under him and put most of his weight into another blow with the same fist. This one caught the guard on the temple, and his eyes glazed. The pistol was in his hand, but he seemed unable to raise it. Allan took his time, set himself, and knocked the man out with a hard left hook to the side of the jaw.

Allan pulled the same trick as before with the slowly moving steel door, knowing this time he could not be trapped. After jumping through, he saw that he was inside a walk-in closet. It even had some clothes hanging on racks. The outer face of the steel door formed the back wall. Allan walked out of the closet door without worrying about being seen, and saw that he was in a small but luxuriously furnished lounge. It was empty. He spared it only a brief look before heading for the door. Outside, he glanced back at the panel. A discrete at-

tached tag said: EXECUTIVE LOUNGE: ADMITTANCE BY IDENTI-
FICATION ONLY.

The information he had frightened out of Dupleis had been
accurate so far, and Allan felt reasonably confident he could
rely on the rest. He shifted the dartgun to where he could reach
it in seconds by opening the side of his suit, and headed for
the elevators. The passenger carriers were all busy on the upper
floors, but the freight was available. Allan entered and asked
for the main lobby. A respectful robot voice acknowledged
his request, and the door closed. Three minutes later Allan
was walking into the street, a free man . . . for the moment.

There were several things Allan needed to do, but he decided securing what he had gained was most important. There
was a branch of the Zone postal system on the corner. He
went inside, looked up P.P. Security in the government di-
rectory, and mailed them the recording disc. With that in-
criminating evidence in the right hands the next election should
be secure, even if a laser beam caught him unawares. And
that was no longer a remote possibility. These well-entrenched
enemies would be desperate to recover that disc, once word
of what he had done spread throughout the organization. He
would be safe only after the recording was released and there
was no profit in killing its originator.

All of the main streets in downtown Geneva were equipped
with two-speed pedstrips going in opposite directions, replacing
what had formerly been highways. The one nearest the side-
walk rolled at six kilometers an hour and the inner one at
twelve, making a twenty-four kilo change of speed across a
narrow dividing space. Jumping from one to the other was
strictly forbidden; tunnels provided a means of changing direction. As Allan stepped from the slow to the faster walk, watching his footing, he heard a low cry. He raised his gaze and
looked into the face of Gilia Kaylin, her mouth open in delighted surprise. She was on the opposite track, being carried
swiftly in the direction from which he had come.

As Gilia passed Allan turned his head to follow her, and a block away saw the wide doors of the building hiding the underground prison disgorge seven or eight men. They immediately split into two's and headed in both directions, as well as into the tunnel leading under the street.

Allan and Gilia were already several meters apart. He started toward her at a hard run, watching the distance between them widen. When he was moving at his maximum speed, Allan jumped. His feet shot out from under him on the opposite strip, but he had been moving fast enough to counter more than half the differential speed. Allan fell, feeling the bruising impact of the hard steel mesh, and almost rolled off on to the slower strip. He recovered and scrambled to his feet, to see Gilia running back to him. But his action had brought him to the attention of the prison guards. The two who had been sent in the correct direction were now dashing toward them, drawing laser guns. There was a fair crowd on the strips and Allan's illegal transfer had drawn several disapproving stares, but no one actually spoke to him.

Allan regretted the impulsive jump. There was an excellent chance the guards would not have recognized Gilia, and she would have been perfectly safe. But it was too late for hindsight. He seized her arm and hurried on to the slower strip so rapidly she almost lost her footing. Gilia was trying to ask him a question, her fair face flushed with joy and excitement, but her words were lost in the confusion. Allan glanced at the rapidly approaching guards, unable to shoot because of the people shielding them, and chose to ride the strip for a few more seconds. Then they were opposite a tunnel, and he pulled Gilia off and almost dived into it. That took them out of immediate firing range, but also put their pursuers only seconds behind. They would certainly jump the strip as he had.

At the end the tunnel angled back and descended to run under the street, but also connected to another, slower moving belt into the building the tunnel faced. Allan hurried Gilia on to the new strip, hushing her questions with a raised hand and insisting they walk rapidly. She fell silent as she sensed the urgency, and followed Allan into the store. He led her immediately to the elevators, and they were lucky enough to find one on the ground floor. Before the door shut behind them Allan turned to face the main room, and saw a man hurriedly enter from the tunnel; one hand was concealed in his pocket. The hunters had split up, and if he had been seconds later in hustling Gilia through the store they would have been seen.

Allan hurriedly checked the elevator register and map. This commercial building had no aircar landing on top. He saw that there was a bridge at the 28th level, connecting with the Transportation Ministry across the street, and there would certainly be an aircar facility there. He asked for that floor, and the bland recorded voice acknowledged his instructions.

At the 28th level they hurried down the hall and into the bridge, Allan finally having both breath and time to tell Gilia whom they were fleeing. He saw her lovely face grow pale when she realized he had been very close to death. "And we're not safe yet," he concluded. "If the fellow on our trail is shrewd, he'll be only a few seconds behind. I've led us on a very logical course since leaving the pedstrips."

"Maybe he won't think logically," Gilia said hopefully.

"And maybe he will," Allan replied.

In the Transportation Ministry they had to wait over a minute for an elevator to stop, but when one finally did it was empty. They stepped inside, Allan asked for the aircar landing, and then took Gilia into his arms for a long and clinging kiss. The two-year separation vanished as though they had never been.

It was a little before the noon hour, and to Allan's surprise the aircar landing area was deserted. As a precaution, he undid the right-hand seal on his suit, slipping his hand inside on the dartgun handle. He also moved away from the direct sight of the elevators, standing to one side. As he watched, the light clicked on above the door next to the one they had ridden. A second later it slid back and a man stepped outside. He carried one hand tucked into his suit.

Allan had had only a brief look at his pursuer through the crowd in the store. He could not be certain, but thought this was the same man. If not, a dart produced only a pinprick wound and several hours of unconsciousness, unless a victim was hurt while falling. Allan drew his gun and calmly shot the stranger in the side.

Geneva, like most modern cities, had no security force personnel walking the streets. Every area of public accommodation, from the pedstrips to the rooftops, was covered by a camera system tied into a central computer. Most stores and other private businesses paid a fee to connect into the guard system, placing their main rooms and money-handling areas under constant surveillance. The computer was programed to recognize most obviously illegal acts and bring them to the attention of human monitors. Each camera had a disc that could contain a week's recordings. When a crime was committed, the reusable disc was removed and preserved as evidence. With any luck at all, the computer had recognized the guns drawn by their pursuers and alerted the security monitors. They should have also recognized Allan's ambush of the stranger at his feet as an illegal act. Security patrol cars were in the air at all times, for the fastest possible response to an alert by the monitors. By now they should have arrived at the scene of the first encounter, and be looking for himself and the guards. They should also be here within two minutes of the new alert.

There was a humming sound behind them, and a gray security car settled to the nonsked landing deck. Two men jumped out, dartguns in hand. It had been less than one minute from the time Allan pulled his trigger.

Allan paused to shift the heavy backpack where a strap was cutting into one shoulder, and wiped sweat off his forehead. His physical condition might decline in the future, when he became a harried bureaucrat, but at the moment he was in much better shape than Gilia. For the first two nights she had been so tired she had responded only feebly to his lovemaking. On the third one she had tried, and on the fourth finally enjoyed full participation. This was their fifth day in the Cascade Mountains of Washington State, and the snowcapped peaks of Mount Baker had finally dropped out of sight behind them. They had crossed the upper Baker River just north of the frigid waters of the lake of the same name, heading deep into the Cascades. There was no particular hurry—it was only sixty straight-line miles to Mazama, the little town where they would emerge, and they still had eleven days—and he had let Gilia hold them to a very slow pace.

Allan looked back and down from the small summit he had just climbed. Gilia was toiling up behind him, bent forward under the weight of her lighter pack. These Northwest mountain slopes just below the Canadian border were cool in October, but still green and beautiful. On every side, tall fir and spruce trees aimed their narrow, cone-shaped tops at the blue skies. To their left, purple asters grew in massed banks in a small meadow. Just down the slope ahead a spreading phlox plant lifted five-petaled violet flowers to the sun, now streaking the sky with gold as it sank slowly toward the southwest. Several varieties of thrush kept the air filled with song, and in the distance they could hear the intermittent hammering of a woodpecker, seeking his final meal of the day.

This was the first time Allan had been on a camping trip in an Earth forest since his college days. He had forgotten how sheerly beautiful his native world could be. Despite the burdensome population and intense crowding in the large cities, there were still millions of acres of virgin wilderness such as those around them. The Cascades extended far north into Canada, and these western slopes were warmed by proximity to the Japanese Current, just off the coast. Winter would still cover these highlands with a blanket of white, but the cold would not be as extreme as that on the eastern plains side of the range.

Gilia reached Allan and stood by his side, breathing deeply but evenly. The sense of beauty around them was so strong Allan impulsively bent and kissed a flushed cheek, and saw her quick, almost shy smile of pleasure. Gilia had refused his proposal of marriage, and he had had a difficult time even persuading her to accompany him on this much-needed vacation. She seemed to feel unworthy, as though her failure in graduate school had disqualified her not only as a Conscience, but even to love one.

Allan had been torn between joy and sorrow when he learned the reason for Gilia's mysterious disappearance. She had been at her parents' home in Moscow, recovering from the bitter knowledge she could never master the hard-science part of the P.P. curriculum. He hated to see her fail—in all other ways Gilia would have made an excellent Conscience— but was happy that she would not be leaving Earth. During the hectic final two weeks before the election, Allan had spent all the time he could manage between Tri-D political telecasts with Gilia. But beneath that soft and sensitive exterior lurked a will of iron. He had been unable to change her mind.

Gilia also caught the beauty of the scene, and Allan saw her face grow subdued and quietly contented. She reached and took his arm, leaning on his shoulder. When Gilia recovered her breath she said, "I think it would be a good idea to make vacations in the woods compulsory for people like Chairman Blankenship and Celal Kaylin."

Allan chuckled; no answer in words was needed. One of the disappointments of the recent election was that the Conservationists had not been able to defeat Blankenship. Allan's high hopes of ruining him through association with Dawson had come to nothing. The redheaded former Council Security guard had been employed by a private detective agency for over a year, an agency owned by a prominent New Roman supporter. The fact that he actually worked for Blankenship, and had undoubtedly been drawing two salaries since he became closely associated with the politician as a guard, had been well concealed.

Allan's disclosure of the Safeguard Squads, and the extremist organizations on Earth who were supporting them, had been enough to send the New Romans down to a sound defeat at the polls. It had not ruined the party, or even disorganized it as much as he had hoped. The pressure group that owned the underground prison beneath the Tri-D station had been broken up and all its broadcast outlets sold, but they had been bought by a wealthy New Roman sympathizer. As soon as new licenses could be issued they would be back in action.

Allan led the way down the slope, and on to a wooded tongue of land between two rocky, almost barren cliffs. Once past the narrow tract of level ground they turned to the right and walked through unusually heavy brush, following the right-hand rock wall. They had gone only a few meters when they heard faint cries ahead. A moment later, and somewhat closer, there was an outburst of the short, excited barking of hunting dogs following a scent that was getting warm.

Wary, Allan stopped beneath one of the few mature trees in the area, behind a thick Cascades Azalea bush. The ground

207

immediately ahead was treeless, covered by some brush and many large rocks that had fallen from the rearing cliff face on their right. It was better than a hundred meters to the next stand of spruce. He motioned for Gilia to join him. There were no dangerous animals in these woods, except for an occasional stray grizzly bear, and they were unarmed.

They stood in silence, listening to the approaching sounds of the hunt. In less than two minutes Allan, looking straight ahead, saw movement in the brush beneath the trees on the opposite side. He placed a cautionary hand on Gilia's arm. They were well hidden, and would see the hunted animal when it emerged.

The noise of the dogs grew louder. They were only a few hundred meters away, swiftly drawing closer. The creature at the edge of the open area hesitated, obviously disliking leaving the sheltering trees, but the hounds were coming fast. Abruptly the concealing brush swayed aside, and it leaped on to the nearest rock. It stood there a second, erect, almost as though posing for the watching humans.

Allan heard his own gasp as he involuntarily took a deep breath. The sound seemed so loud he was afraid he would be heard. Gilia gripped his arm so tightly it was painful.

They had not known what to expect, but the creature before them would have been last on any list. The fugitive from the dog pack was a huge, naked man, almost two-and-a-half meters high. He had a protruding belly, and was covered from head to callused feet with a thick blanket of coarse white hair, making him seem even larger. Allan's trained eye immediately saw several more subtle anatomical oddities. A massive supraorbital ridge protruded above slightly recessed eyes. The forehead did not slope backward as severely as in the gorilla, but but was less prominent than that of *Homo sapiens*. The chin receded, but though he could not be certain at this distance, Allan thought its structure indicated progression past the need for a simian shelf. Despite its impressive height, the torso was blocky and the limbs thick; it would weigh close to 180 kilograms.

After that brief pause to select the next rock, the hairy figure jumped to it without touching foot to the ground between. He continued across the open ground in the same fashion. After forty meters he made a sharp turn to the left, leaping a space between rocks that must have extended three meters. It was almost too long a jump for the heavy form, and he lost his balance and fell forward. The rock on which he had landed was wide enough that his hands came down on its surface, but the impact must have been painful even to palms as hardened as his. And for the first time Allan saw the long dark streak of a bullet wound across the back of the right forearm, and the red blood that had matted the hair heavily on both sides.

Allan also had a good look at the man's feet during the seconds he was stretched prone across the almost flat rock. It took a large surface to support a bulk that massive. The local name for this shy, almost legendary creature, whose footprints had been reported many times over the past two hundred years, was "Bigfoot." The title was well deserved. The broad, nearly flat feet had close to three times the area of a man's.

As Bigfoot scrambled erect and searched for his next jump, Allan made a logical connection. This surviving branch of early man was almost certainly the even more fabulous "*yeti*" of Himalayan fame. The scanty, fragmentary descriptions that had come out of the small high countries over the years fitted him perfectly.

After two more successful jumps Bigfoot was at the cliff face, and started climbing. The wall sloped gently inward at that point and he moved rapidly at first, but slowed as he had to angle to the right to bypass an overhanging small prominence. He was still in sight when the first yelping dog burst from the brush, and ruined Bigfoot's careful effort to throw him off the track by catching his scent direct. The hound lifted his gaze, saw his prey, and dashed across the rocky ground, yelping in triumph.

Two more dogs were right behind the first. All three gathered at the base of the cliff, trying to climb it and constantly falling back. Their early barking changed to a frustrated snarling and snapping when they tumbled into each other. Bigfoot ignored them. He had to work his way carefully around the point where the overhang ended on the right, which would put him past the shoulder and out of sight for the moment. There were very few handholds to cling to, and his progress was slow. He was still visible when two running men broke from the woods and spotted him.

"There it is!" shouted the first one, a short, apoplectically red-faced man dressed in expensively tailored hunting clothes. His companion wore an elaborately beaded Amerindian buckskin outfit, and appeared to be of Indian origin. The hunter was carrying a 30-30 rifle, the heaviest weapon considered "sporting" when hunting the deer in these woods. The guide had a laser pistol strapped to his waist.

"I've got 'im!" the hunter called to his companion, raising the rifle. He drew a bead on the slowly moving Bigfoot. Allan saw that he actually intended to shoot the fleeing man.

"Hold it!" Allan yelled at the top of his lungs, and walked hastily around the azalea bushes shielding them. Gilia followed him. "Don't you idiots realize what you're chasing?" he called as he walked toward them. They turned and waited, surprise and hostility on the hunter's face. When he drew near Allan saw that the man was breathing deeply, apparently as much from excitement as exertion.

"What's it to you?" the hunter demanded angrily, lowering his rifle so that it was pointed in Allan's direction, though not directly at him. "What the hell are you doing on my land? This is private property, mister!"

The Amerindian guide, who was watching Bigfoot's slow

210

progress, drew his laser pistol and took careful aim. Allan started to protest, but stopped when the guide held up a cautionary hand. The laser beam burned into the rocks just ahead of the primitive man's next gripping point, and Allan saw him recoil from the heat. The Amerindian called aloud to the climber, who paused, but then started his sideways movement again. After the obligatory five seconds the guide fired another beam, this one just above and to the right of the hairy head. The huge man stopped, and when the Amerindian called again, turned a blank, impassive face toward them. The man on the ground motioned vigorously for the climber to return, pantomiming that he must descend. Bigfoot turned and looked at the two laser burns; one had hit a dead root, which was still smoldering.

Some primitive fear of fire seemed to lurk deep in the early man's psyche. He had endured the pain of a rifle bullet and kept going. This new weapon that spat fire seemed his undoing. He hesitated, then started slowly angling to his left and back toward the ground.

Bigfoot's fear of fire probably meant he did not have control of that tool. Allan wondered how he survived the winters in these mountains, or the far worse ones in the Canadian wilderness to the north from which he almost certainly came. His fur coat seemed extremely heavy, and judging by his bulk, overlay a thick covering of fat. He probably had a deep, still cave to crawl into during storms.

"Sir, I'm sorry to interfere in your hunt," Allan said to the richly dressed hunter, who was hauntingly familiar. "But surely you realize that's an early form of *man* you were about to shoot. His value to science is incalculable. We've had recorded stories of a species of such men in this area for hundreds of years, but none was ever captured before. You'll go down in history as the man responsible for bringing us into contact with them."

The hunter did not seem impressed. "Just who the hell are you?" he demanded.

This was the type of man to whom title meant more than name. "I'm Deputy Administrator of the World Council Corps of Practical Philosophers," Allan said, disliking such an identification but knowing there was no other way. "My name is Allan Odegaard."

"Odegaard! By God, no wonder your face seemed familiar! Well! Well!" There were sounds of tramping feet behind them, and another foppishly dressed man, followed by a second Amerindian guide, emerged into the open. The hunter called, "Hey, Bill! Look who we got here! It's Odegaard, the kook who cost us the election!"

Memory clicked, and Allan finally recognized the first hunter. This was Thomas Doughtery, a Council Member from Washington State who was chairman of the powerful Appropriations Committee, the most important Council chairmanship the lottery had thrown to the New Romans after the recent election. And although a peaked hunting cap hid the wheat-colored mane that usually elevated him to an imposing height, Allan recognized the protruding belly and long horse-face of Bill. It was C.M. William C. Blankenship, Chairman of the New Roman party.

26

"Are you going to put them all in there together?" asked one of the Amerindians. Allan, Gilia and Bigfoot were standing in front of a small sturdy outbuilding that contained supplies for Doughtery's hunting lodge. The windows were barred and the wooden walls constructed of heavy timbers, to keep bears away from the food when the lodge was unoccupied.

"There's no room in the lodge for 'em, even if we had a place the big fella' couldn't break out of," said Doughtery. "Yeah, throw 'em all in there. Maybe the big ape will break Odegaard's neck and rape his girlfriend."

Gilia gave an unladylike snort of disgust. The guide gestured with the laser, and Bigfoot docilely stepped forward. Despite his size the primitive man seemed more timid than aggressive. If his sexual awareness was aroused by the presence of Gilia, though, that could change in a hurry. Even male deer fought each other when in rut. Doughtery's speculation could easily come true.

"This has been the damnedest day," said Blankenship, who was standing beside Doughtery. His face was also flushed, and Allan had learned the reason on the short walk here. Both men were drinking heavily from hip flasks, ignoring the hundreds of harmless intoxicants available in favor of alcohol. It was typical of what they considered "manly" behavior, as were these guided hunting trips where they carried light rifles. The guides were armed with lasers against the occasional bear. Gilia had known of this lodge, though not its exact location. The Washington C.M. was famous for inviting New Roman politicians here. "Yessir, the damnedest day," Blankenship went on. "I take a shot at what you thought was a bear, and it turns out to be some kind of a hairy ape-man. We turn the dogs loose on it, catch it, and just like fate, who steps in but the big defender of the damn' dumb apes all over the galaxy, Mr. Allan Odegaard, pronounced Odd-God." Blankenship guffawed at his own humor; Doughtery alone laughed with him. "But what the hell are we going to do with them, Tom?"

Doughtery, who did not appear quite as intoxicated as Blankenship, said, "We can't turn this big ape loose, Bill. I'm no scientist, but it seems kinda' obvious the P.P. Corps would have him declared intelligent . . . and maybe throw us off the planet!" He laughed, and it was Blankenship's turn to join in. "No, if word gets out that we have a form of primitive man living right here on Earth with us, it would strengthen the P.P. Corps' hand so much we'd never get rid of 'em. We've got to see to it he gets mistaken for a bear again, this time with somebody better than you doing the shootin'. As for Odegaard and Celal Kaylin's ex-secretary, we'll have one of our boys in the Truth Lab do a little of that brain-burning and deep conditioning that permanently knocks out things you don't want remembered. Of course the IQ never quite gets back to what it was before the treatment, but Odegaard was always too damn' smart for his own good anyway."

"Sounds like a winning program!" said Blankenship, again laughing heartily. He took a final drink from his flask and threw it away. "You know, I enjoy getting my hands into the real work for a change. Makes me feel a lot more like I'm actually doing something for my fellow man. Shuffling paper and chewing out your help can get mighty old. You keep an eye on them, now"—this to the Amerindians—"and call us if the big one starts after the girl."

The two world leaders walked toward the lodge, arms around each other's shoulders in happy camaraderie, still laughing and sharing the last of Doughtery's flask. Allan watched them in benumbed wonder. It was incredible that such men should have a mighty hand in shaping the destinies of billions, and yet it was true, a fact that had to be faced. The democratic process had elected them, and they honestly represented the thinking of many of their constituents.

The guards interrupted Allan's thoughts by motioning for the captives to enter the small building. The door locked behind them with the solid sound of heavy timbers meeting.

One of the Amerindians immediately went to the window, as instructed, and stared in at them. Bigfoot looked around, tentatively tested the bars through the open window opposite the guard, sniffed at some of the smoked meat hanging from

214

hooks in the ceiling, picked up and examined apples in an open bin by the wall, and then sat down. He stared at his fellow prisoners with alert attention, but no hostility that Allan could see. There was no indication that Bigfoot found Gilia sexually attractive.

Allan had been trying to identify Bigfoot more closely since first laying eyes on him. As part of his P.P. training he had taken intensive courses in physical anthropology, and was intimately familiar with every form of early and pre-man known. Bigfoot fitted none of them. The closest Allan could come was the large, very ancient vegetarian, *Australopithecus robustus.* That branch of hominidae had faded away while his smaller, meat-eating cousin, *africanus,* survived. And yet there were obvious differences. The structure of Bigfoot's skull indicated the brain was larger, and the long-past herbivore had never reached such a height . . . and what almost had to be the truth dawned on Allan. *Robustus,* one of the first two creatures on Earth from which *Homo sapiens* could descend, had indeed died out . . . but not before mutations produced the larger hominid before him.

Bigfoot opened his mouth in a wide, slow yawn. Allan saw two U-shaped rows of massive grinding molars, set behind reduced canines no sharper or longer than his own. Bigfoot was a vegetarian.

The lost story of how this child of Africa had wandered into Asia, and later across the land bridge to North America, would be one of the great untold epics of anthropology. The migration had obviously occurred not too long after the line was established, since to date no bones had been found in Africa. An added jot of intelligence had enabled it to survive, though it could not compete with the meat-eaters and had been forced to hunt sanctuary in the less-frequented areas of the world. And there had been no *yeti* seen in the Himalayas in many years, of which Allan was aware. Reports of Bigfoot sightings had persisted in the temperate mountain ranges around them, but they were rare and scattered over both time and space. Quite possibly this was the last of the species, sitting quietly in front of them.

Bigfoot got to his feet, towering like a living mountain over the seated humans. He walked to the apple bin and helped himself to three. Quite calmly, he started eating.

"Allan, I take back what I suggested about exposing Blankenship and Celal to the beauties of nature," Gilia said, her voice shaking a little.

Allan discovered he still had the ability to laugh. Gilia joined in, and after a few seconds the thin edge of hysteria faded and she was experiencing a deeply felt release from tension. Bigfoot sat and looked at them, his placid features expressionless. Allan saw the guard staring at them through the window, his dark face perplexed. After a minute he went away. His head appeared only at infrequent intervals thereafter, as he became convinced the three captives were not going to provide a show.

"At least we won't go hungry," Allan said as he got to his feet. He helped himself to an apple, and offered one to Gilia. She declined with a grimace of distaste, saying her stomach was not up to food.

Allan ate the apple and prowled around the interior of the cabin, stopping when a face appeared at the window. The walls and bars were so heavy not even Bigfoot's obvious strength could break them—they had been built to withstand assault by a hungry grizzly. But the strong little structure had been designed to keep animals out, not people in, and after a few minutes Allan found its weakness. The walls rested on a concrete slab, to keep burrowing animals from tunneling in. The interior was unfinished, the heavy joists and beams exposed and no flooring installed above the concrete. The two cross timbers to which the vertical risers attached were locked down by four simple bolts embedded in the slab. The shafts of these bolts passed through holes drilled in the timbers, and the securing nuts were in plain sight.

Allan carefully rechecked to be certain he was right; he could see no other hold-downs. With those four nuts off, the entire cabin could be moved . . . providing one had the strength to lift such a massive weight.

Keeping a wary eye on the windows, Allan bent and examined one of the nuts. It was almost five centimeters in diameter, a standard hexhead of the type that had been in common use since the dawn of the industrial age. All he needed was the proper tool.

Obtaining a wrench presented a problem. There was undoubtedly a large toolbox around somewhere, but since there was little need to guard it from animals it was not placed in the reinforced storehouse.

All personnel who spent much time in space or on other worlds, where the technological resources were invariably limited, learned to improvise. It was rapidly growing dark in the small hut, and the blackness hindered Allan, but hid what he was doing from the guard. He had noticed two left-over pieces of concrete reinforcing rod, both over a half-meter long, lying in a corner. Several of the crates of food were held together with heavy baling wire. He had the parts from which to construct a tool.

Allan first picked up the two two-centimeter diameter rods and moved them to the darkest corner. With his bare hands he managed to remove forty centimeters of wire from the nearest crate. He laid the rods parallel with each other and touching the nut on each side, with ends extending past the steel. Then he moved the ends farthest from the nut apart, to allow for the slack that would inevitably occur, and bound the ends just past the nut together with the wire. What he achieved was a large, crude nutcracker, fitted to the outside diameter of the steel nut. When he squeezed the free ends together, the parallel bars locked against two sides of the hex with satisfying firmness.

Gilia had watched intently as he worked. Now she giggled, and said, "If that's the best modern science can do, Allan . . ."

"Sufficient unto the task be the tool thereof," Allan misquoted, laughing with her. He hid the nutcracker under a crate. After a few more minutes it was completely dark in the small room. Bigfoot sat as still as before, ignoring his companions. When he felt it was safe Allan replaced the tool around the nut, working by feel alone. He pulled it toward him until the wire touched the outermost hex, then locked the free ends firmly together with his hands and pulled.

Nothing moved. Allan squeezed the handles more tightly together, and pulled harder. The tied ends stretched apart until the rod ends in his hands met, and the steel pressing the sides of the hex slipped around the nut without turning it.

Gilia heard Allan's low curse, and asked what had happened. Before he could answer the door abruptly opened and a light flashed inside. Allan had time to drop the tool before the beam reached him, though he was caught leaning forward on his knees.

"You two can go in the house and use the bathroom," a surly voice said from the darkness. "We'll take the ape out in the woods for a minute, and I just hope he tries to run."

Allan got to his feet and looked at Bigfoot in the faint light. He pantomimed a man squatting to have a bowel movement, motioned to the open door, and, hesitantly, reached and placed gentle fingers on the wound on the back of the hairy arm. Bigfoot recoiled at the last gesture, but slowly brought the arm back and let Allan touch it.

The huge hominid had clearly understood the use of weapons, and that the guide's laser could kill him. To this point he had been a docile captive. Allan could only hope that Bigfoot knew what he meant by touching the wound, and

218

would continue to respect the slaying ability of the smaller humans.

The Amerindian guides were gone. The two men who escorted them to the lodge were obviously part of the serving staff. Two others marched Bigfoot out of their sight, staying at a respectful distance and covering him with both lights and ready lasers.

Bigfoot was already back in the storeroom when they returned, sitting as silently as before. Allan found his nutcracker and rebound the ends, this time pulling them even closer together to allow for yielding when the flexible wire pulled taut. He moved to one of the other three nuts, on the theory they might not all be equally tight. With a low but intense screech, the one he had selected turned when he pulled hard on the improvised wrench.

Allan stopped, went to the open window and closed it, and tried again. By moving very slowly he discovered he could turn the nut with a minimum of noise. He worked carefully until it was no longer tight and tried it with his fingers; the threads were too rusty for him to remove the nut by hand. Using the clumsy wrench was slow and awkward, but Allan persisted, and in a few minutes had that one off.

The first nut on which the nutcracker had failed was the worst of the four. It was late at night, and after a painfully prolonged struggle which Allan often thought he would lose, before it finally yielded. He sat and held the rusty key to freedom in his hand, physically and emotionally drained.

The guard—there was only one now—had continued to flash his light through the windows at intervals, but the four corners where Allan worked were out of the way. He was never caught. Gilia and Bigfoot had curled up on the floor and gone to sleep, the giant hominid's face only a few centimeters from her stomach. The plethora of fictional treatments of Bigfeet that had appeared over the years invariably had them returning to the edge of civilization to capture a human mate. The fact

219

seemed to be that Gilia appealed to him as a sexual partner about as much as he appealed to her.

Allan decided it would be best to make their try at escape just before dawn. Blundering through these mountain woods in the darkness was a sure invitation to disaster. He had noticed aircars parked behind the luxurious lodge, and in the daylight they could be used to hunt them; and of course the hounds would be on their trail. But they should be able to hide from the air in the thick forest, and the dogs they could outwit.

After setting his mental alarm clock, Allan snuggled up to Gilia for some needed sleep. She uncurled to accommodate her body to his, and he held her close and dozed off.

The faintest touch of gray could be seen through the east window when Allan awakened. He carefully awoke Gilia, and then pondered the problem of doing the same for Bigfoot. He finally decided the direct approach was best, and shook the unwounded arm. The giant stirred instantly, coming erect without a sound, obviously fully awake and ready for trouble.

Hoping some sign language was universal, Allan quickly but gently moved his hand to press lightly against the hair-covered lips. He felt the head turn toward him, the body beneath it stiffening into readiness for combat.

One thing Allan had learned during his years of dealing with animals at all intelligence levels was that stillness was seldom threatening. He stood quietly, not even removing the hand, deliberately forcing his body into a relaxed posture; Bigfoot would know how he was standing. And after a moment, very slowly, he felt the tense form he was touching relax. A huge hand came out of the darkness and plucked Allan's off the wide mouth.

There had been no doubt in Allan's mind about Bigfoot's intelligence since the hominid had stopped trying to escape when threatened with laser fire. The degree, though, was still unknown. Now Allan felt that even the latter was coming through. They might never equal *Homo sapiens,* but on the scales used by P.P.s, the species Bigfoot represented would rate quite highly.

Allan peeped through the window and located their guard. He was sitting, leaning against a stack of firewood a few meters to one side of the storeroom, wrapped in a blanket and sound asleep.

The area outside the little building was suffused with a pale gray glow. Allan estimated the distance to the guard, and then pulled Bigfoot after him to the opposite side of the building. They had to clear away some crates to reach the wall near the center, and Bigfoot helped. When they could touch the base timber, Allan hunted for and found a good grip in the woodwork just above it. He guided a pair of broad hands to a hold just opposite his, braced himself, and heaved. He finally lost his giant helper. Allan removed one hand and pulled on Bigfoot's arm, while lifting himself. His message was understood, and the big hominid set himself, grunted with effort, and heaved with Allan. The wall cleared the concrete, rose, and the entire building tilted up and flipped over behind them.

27

The instant the wall he was holding started moving upward of its own accord, Allan turned and ran around the side of the falling building. This was the most dangerous part of his plan; he had to reach that guard before the man awoke enough to realize what had happened.

The thick timbers had creaked and groaned as Bigfoot and Allan heaved, but the noise was minor. The crash when the structure landed on its side would have awakened a hibernating bear. It smashed into the ground just two meters short of the guard's booted feet; he could almost have touched the sharply pointed roof. When Allan rounded the corner the man was just struggling erect, still partially asleep but already pulling his laser from its holster. Allan launched himself in a hard dive at the guard's knees, and realized he was clasping buckskin when he brought him down; this was one of the Amerindian guides.

For once luck was on Allan's side. The guard's head hit one of the small fireplace logs stacked behind him when he fell. He sat up immediately, but then was motionless, obviously dazed. Allan sent him on into unconsciousness with a hard right over the ear. He recognized the guide as the coolly self-possessed one who had been with Doughtery and had captured Bigfoot.

Neither of the two windows in the storehouse faced the main lodge, and Allan saw that he had made a serious miscalculation. The people there were awake, and bright lights blazed from several windows. As he bent over the guard, searching for the laser, a door opened and a handlight swept their way. As the beam caught him Allan realized that the gun was gone; the Amerindian had lost it when his head hit the log.

"Allan! Come on!" Gilia called from where she and Bigfoot stood at the edge of the woods. To reinforce her words, there were shouts from the lodge. Allan took a last look in the dim light, hoping to spot the red glint of the laser's jewel; they would need that weapon. It was not in sight.

Allan straightened and ran after Gilia, momentarily placing the overturned storehouse between himself and the large house. Another light caught them as they entered the trees, but it was a long way behind. A yell indicated they had been spotted, but no shots followed. And then they were out of sight from the lodge, running through the deep forest shadows.

Allan slowed to a safer speed. They were heading due west,

and he wanted to maintain that direction until they reached a stream that ran north and south. The nearest habitations of which he knew were on Baker Lake, about twenty kilometers to the southwest. Doughtery and his Amerindians would probably realize they had headed that way, but it was still their best course.

The area abounded in small streams, and they reached one within minutes. The clear water was cold in the extreme, being fed from snow on the peaks around them, but neither Gilia nor Bigfoot demurred when Allan motioned for them to walk south down its sand and gravel center. He went on across and emerged on the west bank, took several steps into the woods, and then walked backward in his tracks into the water again. He hurried after his companions, catching them just around the first bend. The false trail he had made might at least delay the dogs a few minutes.

Their pace was determined by the best speed Gilia could make, and she moved rather slowly in the water. Bigfoot kept constantly getting ahead of them and then slowing; it was obvious he wanted to go faster, but would not abandon his new companions.

Bigfoot had thoroughly proven his intelligence. It was becoming equally clear to Allan that the hairy man possessed qualities of loyalty and thoughtfulness as well. The savagery and rapacity Blankenship and Doughtery had automatically ascribed to him because of his physical appearance did not exist.

"Sweetheart, we've got to step it up," Allan called to Gilia after a few minutes. She lifted a white, despairing face, already strained with effort. Allan could almost read her thoughts as she started to tell him to leave her behind, then realized she would only be wasting breath, and that Allan must have something else in mind.

He did. All three stopped, and Allan scooped Gilia up in his arms. Although a small woman she was solidly built, and

223

probably weighed more than fifty kilograms. "Allan!" she protested, knowing he could not possibly carry her very far . . . and Allan walked to Bigfoot and held Gilia out toward him.

The hominid took her instantly, but instead of the tiring arms-forward carry, he laid Gilia on her stomach across the massive right shoulder, her face to the rear. He raised the right arm, placed a hair-covered hand across her buttocks, and set off down the stream at a trot. Allan followed at his own best pace, and their speed almost doubled.

After an hour of hard travel Allan started to lose touch with his lower limbs. His boots were waterproof, but the stream bottom was uneven and he had long ago got into water too deep for them and wet his legs and feet. Now they felt like mushy pillows attached to his lower body, hardly a part of him.

The stomach-down position in which Gilia rode must have been acutely uncomfortable for her, but she had not said a word. Her face was still white and she looked ill, probably from the pressure of the jouncing shoulder against her lower abdomen. But she gave Allan a game smile when she saw him looking at her.

The small stream had widened and deepened. It was time to leave the water. Allan started looking for a suitable place . . . just as they rounded a sharp bend and found themselves standing on the shore of a small lake.

Allan looked both ways. The sun was hidden behind clouds at the moment, but there was plenty of light. To their left the trees ended directly at the water's edge. Forty meters away on the right there was a large rock outcropping that extended well into the lake. It looked easy to climb, and the bare rock would leave no footprints and a minimum of scent. Allan took the lead, moving ahead of Bigfoot through the shallow water near the shore. It was still early morning, and the woods were quiet. The small round lake was barely three-hundred meters in diameter, and Allan felt exposed as they splashed along the edge; anyone in the woods almost anywhere along its shoreline could see them. But they reached the rock he had selected without incident, and Allan started to climb. The top was only four meters above the lake bottom, and he made it without difficulty.

Allan turned around, lying on his stomach, and reached for Gilia. Bigfoot boosted her high enough that Allan could pull her up beside him. And then he backed away from the edge, and the white-haired giant effortlessly swarmed up to join them.

The small ridge sloped downward and sank below the floor of the forest only a few meters into the woods. But at least their trail would not start at the water's edge, the area most likely to be searched. Allan, with Gilia on her feet and Bigfoot bringing up the rear, headed for the concealing trees . . . and as they reached the level ground a controlled voice said, *"Hold it! Hands up, all three of you!"*

A man emerged from behind thick brush to their left, a laser pistol in his hand. Allan recognized him as the second of the two guides who had captured them the day before, the one who had been with Blankenship. And then the party chairman himself followed, this time carrying an automatic shotgun.

Allan felt a black rush of despair. After having got so far it seemed a malignant twist of fate to be captured by a politician who had got up early to hunt ducks. Blankenship had been drunk enough the day before that Allan would not have credited him with the fortitude to arise before dawn. But these early morning ambushes were a part of the hunting "mystique," and Blankenship had conformed with custom. Allan had seen unexpected crudities of both thought and behavior the day before, but there was no denying this man the strength of will that had driven him up the ladder of power.

Now that it was too late, Allan saw the camouflaged blind in which the hunters had been hiding, at the water's edge on the farther side of the rock ridge. They had probably heard them splashing along the shore and set up the ambush.

"By God I guess it does pay to get up early around here," Blankenship said as he reached them. "How the hell did you three get out of the storehouse?"

Allan shrugged, but did not answer. The Amerindian with the laser was keeping his gaze almost entirely on Bigfoot, whom he obviously feared far more than the smaller humans. But the peaceful herbivore, as seemed his way when confronted by superior power, was standing quietly, arms at his sides. *No one had raised their hands as ordered by the guide.*

Allan mentally pushed away the feeling of hopelessness, and his mind started functioning again. As always with hand lasers, the guide had only one beam available before someone could reach him. Blankenship's shotgun almost had to be loaded with medium-weight birdshot. If he could force the Amerindian to fire uselessly . . . as unobtrusively as possible, Allan slipped a hand into his jacket pocket. All tools and weapons had been taken from them the day before, but he had used his pack's small medical kit not long before being captured, and they had let him keep it.

"By God, Odegaard, you're quite a fellow," Blankenship went on. "No wonder so many of our people on the dirty work details want to get rid of you. And here I am, for once, getting my hands into the real action. I've done what all the tough boys at the lower levels haven't managed; I've got Conscience Odegaard."

"That you have," said Allan, drawing the medical kit out of his jacket. *"I'll get the guide!"* he yelled at Bigfoot, and took a short step forward, drawing his arm back. The startled Amerindian turned toward him, laser barrel swinging, and Allan let fly. His throw was good, the kit deflecting the barrel just as the trigger was pressed. The beam burned through underbrush two meters to the side.

Allan took two running steps and reached for the weapon.

226

The guide tried to draw back and keep the laser out of Allan's grasp, but he was too late. With his right hand locked around the barrel, Allan made a roundhouse swing with his left fist. He connected high on the Amerindian's skull. The impact almost broke his hand, but the guide's head snapped back. Allan tried to pull the weapon free, but failed when the man grabbed it with his other hand and tried to swing the barrel toward Allan. The two swayed back and forth, each trying to wrest the pistol away.

The roar of a shotgun shattered the morning stillness behind the struggling men, close and deafeningly loud. As he and the guide twisted and turned in their battle, Blankenship came into Allan's view. He saw the politician fire again, directly into the breast of Bigfoot, whose long arm had almost reached the barrel. And still a third time the rapidfire gun sent a load of birdshot crashing into the primitive man's broad chest; and then one big hand reached the weapon and yanked it away.

Bigfoot's upper body was covered by a swelling flow of blood. Even the "sportsman's" birdshot was deadly at such close range. But none had penetrated to the heart, and the giant was still on his feet. For the first time since Allan had seen him Bigfoot was grunting with anger, his usually impassive features twisted with hate. He probably recognized Blankenship as the same man who had shot him the day before. The politician squalled with fear and turned to run, but it was useless. One long arm grasped him by the shoulder and spun him around. The descendant of *robustus* raised the screaming man above his head and held him there, kicking and yelling like a frightened baby.

As if gripped equally strongly by the drama before them, the Amerindian stopped trying to pull the laser away. He and Allan froze in a breathless truce, and time seemed to hang suspended there on the shore of the small hidden lake. Very abruptly, as if a giant hand had swept the intervening clouds

227

away, sunlight poured across the lake from the east and penetrated beneath the trees, outlining the hairy giant hominid and the writhing leader of the New Romans in golden splendor. A rush of impressions engulfed Allan, so strongly he momentarily forgot he was in the middle of a fight for his life.

A primitive, uncivilized being, not even a true man, held in his hairy hands one of the most powerful men in the known galaxy. The self-assigned task of that man-of-power was the spread of Mankind, regardless of the cost to creatures such as the one holding him. Allan knew, without consciously analyzing it, that he was seeing a symbolic enactment of the eternal struggle. There were billions of other semi-intelligent beings on thousands of worlds, and there were millions of exploiters like Blankenship who wanted the planets on which the less-able creatures lived. After this small battle the struggle would go on, endlessly. But for the moment it had been reduced to these two figures, on this isolated lakeshore, and the end might forecast the larger end to come.

A short distance beyond Bigfoot, just under the first trees, the slanting sunbeams reflected a tinge of dull red. Allan saw a bank of clay as high as himself, the side toward them free of plants. And the suspicion that the symbolism here was almost *too* perfect flashed through his mind. The sudden burst of sunlight, the presence of clay, the peaceful ancient survivor of a species that preceded man, holding aloft an omnivore far more savage than himself . . . the scene might almost have been contrived to illustrate a point dramatically.

Allan's gaze locked on the clay. He saw nothing but the common red earth.

Bigfoot took two steps toward the lake, raising his arms until he seemed to reach the sky, and brought the screaming body of Blankenship smashing down on the low rocks of the ridge. There was a sickening thud, followed by an abrupt and unnatural silence.

The giant hominid turned toward them. Allan saw blood

gushing from the three wounds in the barrel chest, covering his hairy form with a coating of bright red. And then slowly, very slowly, like a great tree yielding to the ax, he swayed, tilted forward, and fell on his face.

The guide let go of the laser, stood for a moment staring at Blankenship and the hairy early man, and then turned and walked into the woods. He did not look back.

The Amerindian's intuitive understanding of the changed situation was correct. Allan was not going to shoot or attempt to detain him. Instead he hurried to Bigfoot, knelt by the great form, and heaved it over on the broad back. Gilia tossed away the branch she had picked up but not had a chance to use in the fight, and followed him.

Allan placed a hand on the rounded chest. Beneath the bloody fur and protective layer of fat he felt the huge ribs, but no heartbeat. Blood was still oozing from the wounds, but with no pressure behind it. Bigfoot was dead.

Allan walked to Blankenship and examined him, though certain it was useless. And he was right. The political leader had died instantly, his skull cracked and the chest caved in by the terrific impact.

There was a gentle humming sound from across the lake, followed by human voices. Allan raised his gaze and saw two small electric powerboats entering the open water from the lake's outlet. The first was painted the deep green of the Forestry Corps. The second was a gaily multicolored boat with the words *Lake Baker Lodge* painted across the bow. The Forest Rangers were peering in their direction, probably looking for the source of the gunshots. When they were spotted, the green boat accelerated and moved toward them.

Even if one of the aircars undoubtedly hunting them stumbled on this scene, they were safe now. Allan ignored the blood and death around them and turned and took Gilia in his arms. He needed human reaffirmation, a new dedication to the course

229

toward which his life had been set. Gilia was crying, a wet rain of tears pouring down her cheeks. She snuggled close to him, and Allan knew she would be there throughout his future. They comforted each other.